SONIC™
THE HEDGEHOG

CHAO RACES
& BADNIK BASES

Facebook: **facebook.com/idwpublishing**
Twitter: **@idwpublishing**
YouTube: **youtube.com/idwpublishing**
Instagram: **@idwpublishing**

Cover Art by
Gigi Dutreix

Cover Colors by
Reggie Graham

Series Assistant Edits by
Riley Farmer

Series Edits by
David Mariotte

Collection Edits by
Alonzo Simon
and **Zac Boone**

Collection Design by
Shawn Lee

ISBN: 978-1-68405-762-7   24 23 22 21   1 2 3 4

Originally published as SONIC THE HEDGEHOG issues #33–36.

Nachie Marsham, Publisher
Blake Kobashigawa, VP of Sales
Tara McCrillis, VP Publishing Operations
John Barber, Editor-in-Chief
Mark Doyle, Editorial Director, Originals
Erika Turner, Executive Editor
Scott Dunbier, Director, Special Projects
Mark Irwin, Editorial Director, Consumer Products Mgr
Joe Hughes, Director, Talent Relations
Anna Morrow, Sr. Marketing Director
Alexandra Hargett, Book & Mass Market Sales Director
Keith Davidsen, Senior Manager, PR
Topher Alford, Sr Digital Marketing Manager
Shauna Monteforte, Sr. Director of Manufacturing Operations
Jamie Miller, Sr. Operations Manager
Nathan Widick, Sr. Art Director, Head of Design
Neil Uyetake, Sr. Art Director Design & Production
Shawn Lee, Art Director Design & Production
Jack Rivera, Art Director, Marketing

Ted Adams and Robbie Robbins, IDW Founders

Special thanks to Mai Kiyotaki, Michael Cisneros, Sandra Jo, Sonic Team,
and everyone at Sega for their invaluable assistance.

STORY **EVAN STANLEY**
ART **EVAN STANLEY** (#33-34, #36)
ADAM BRYCE THOMAS (#35)
COLORS **REGGIE GRAHAM**
LETTERS **SHAWN LEE**

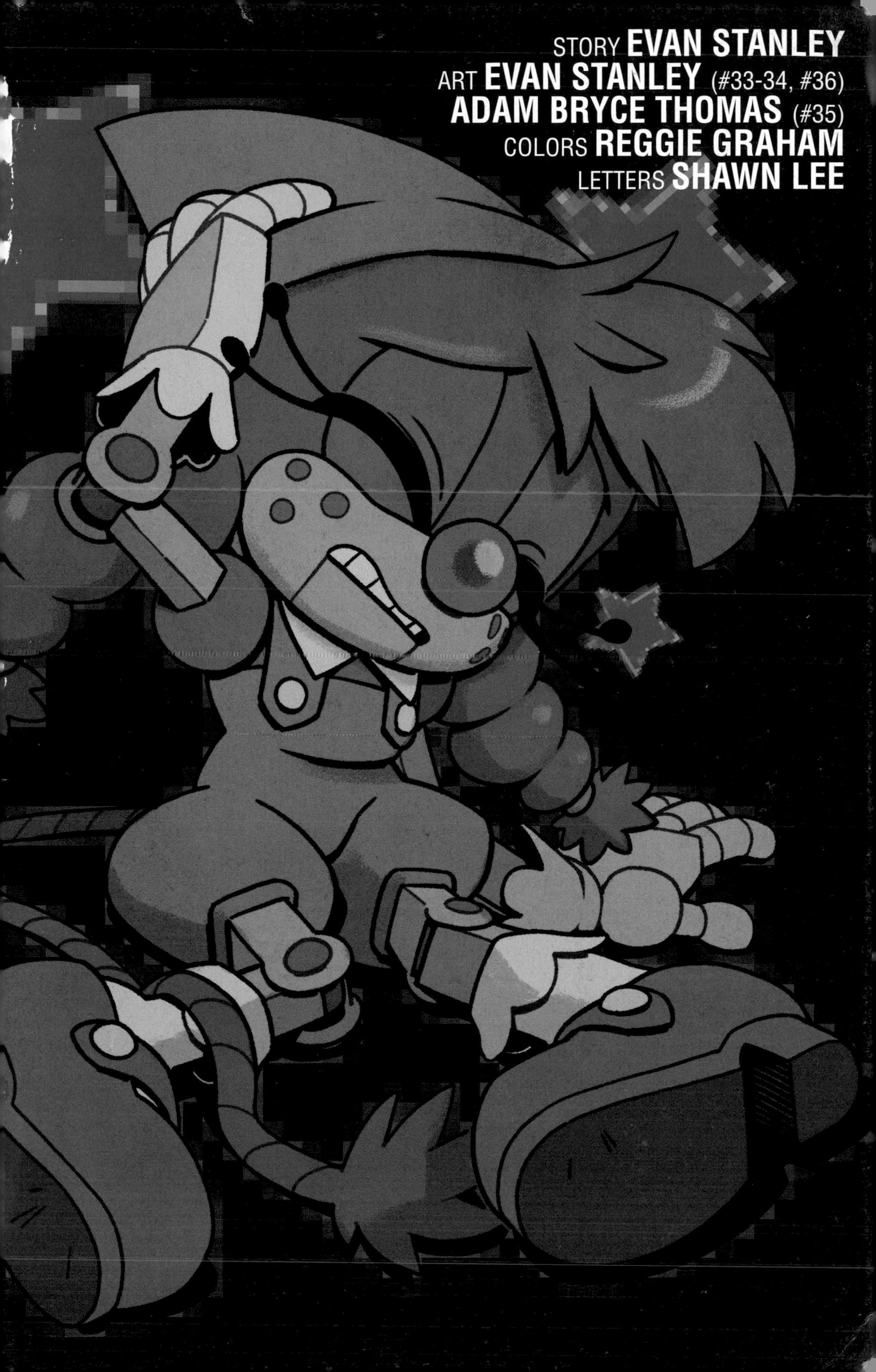

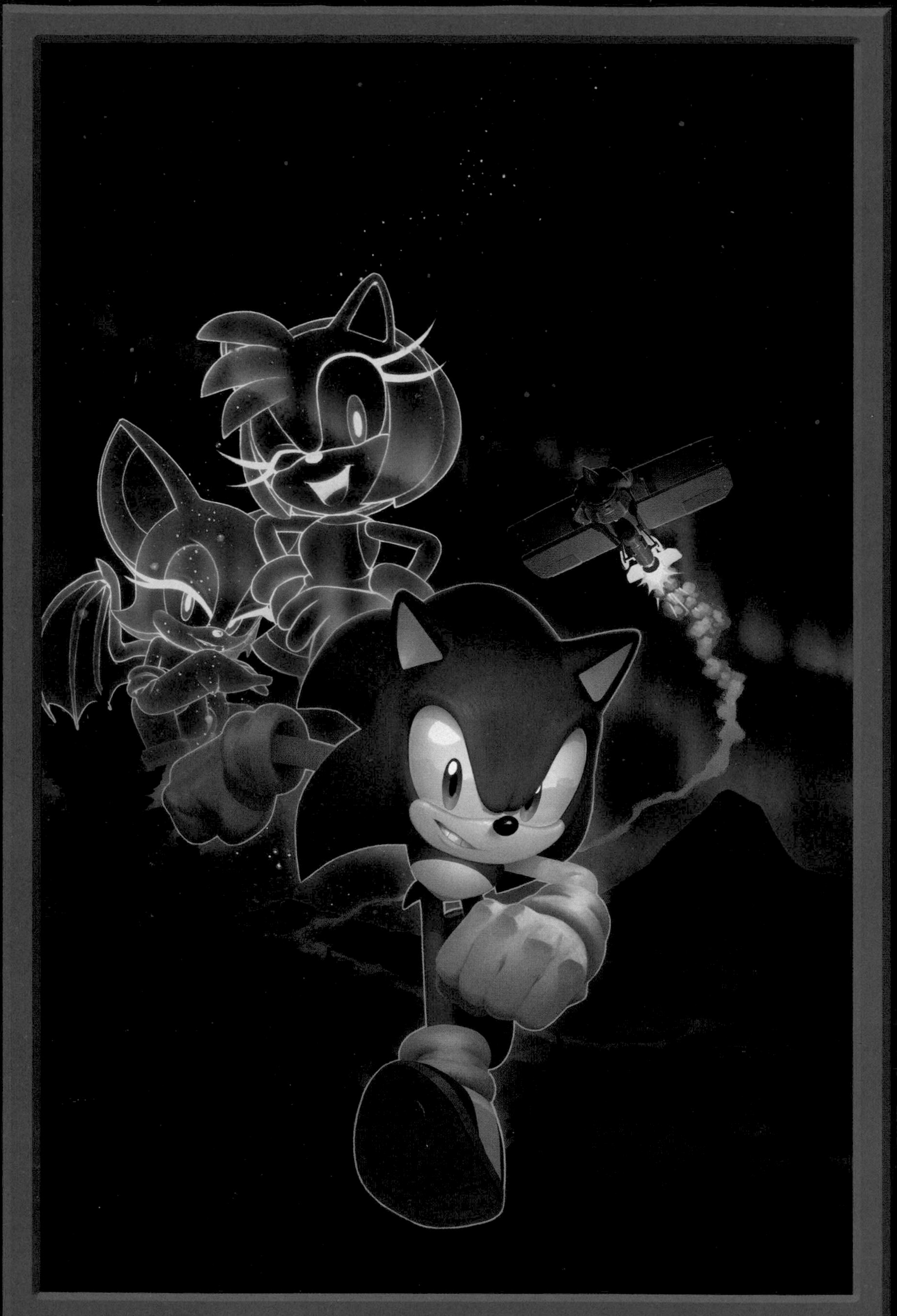

ART BY **EVAN STANLEY**

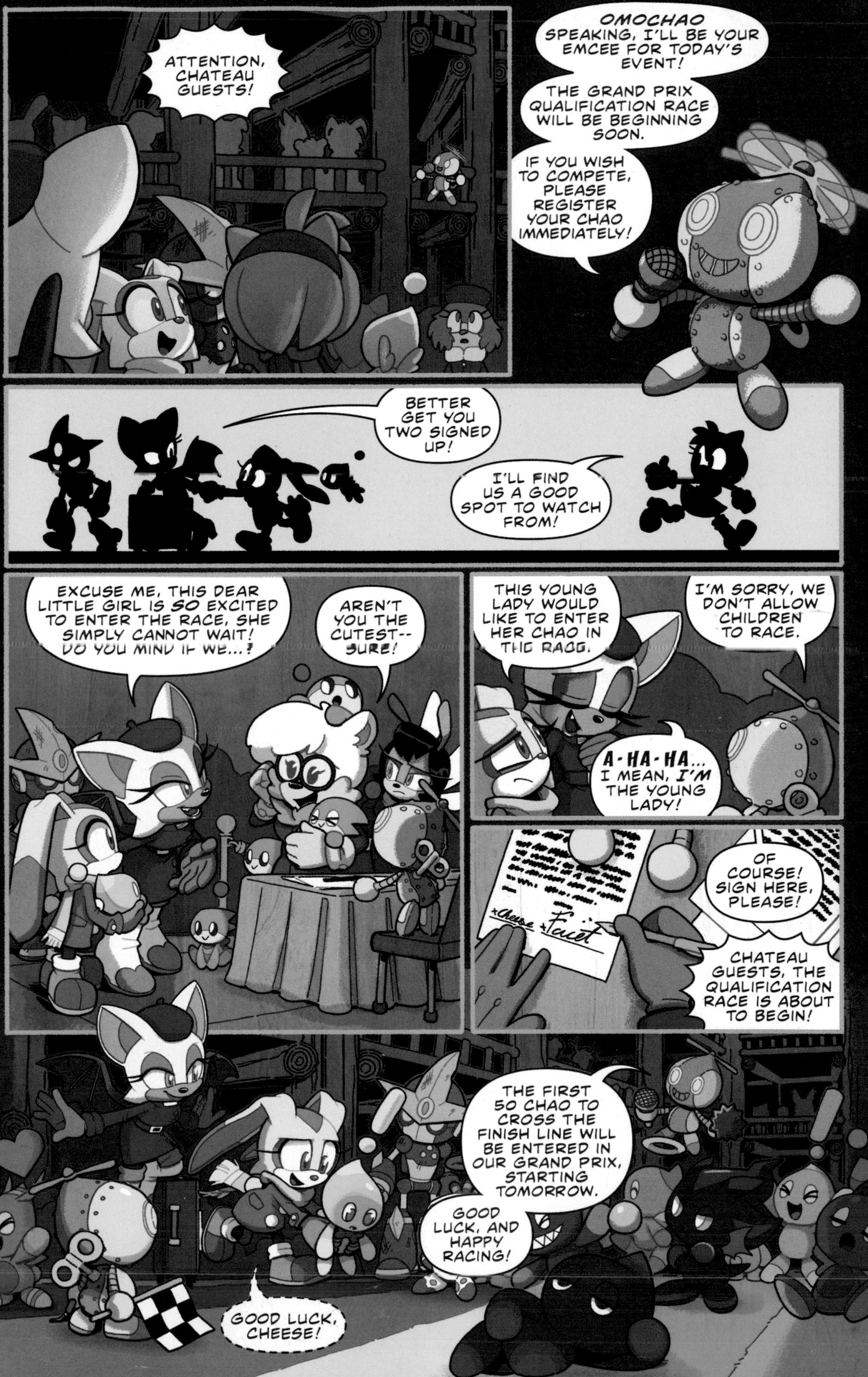
ATTENTION, CHATEAU GUESTS!
OMOCHAO SPEAKING, I'LL BE YOUR EMCEE FOR TODAY'S EVENT!
THE GRAND PRIX QUALIFICATION RACE WILL BE BEGINNING SOON.
IF YOU WISH TO COMPETE, PLEASE REGISTER YOUR CHAO IMMEDIATELY!
BETTER GET YOU TWO SIGNED UP!
I'LL FIND US A GOOD SPOT TO WATCH FROM!
EXCUSE ME, THIS DEAR LITTLE GIRL IS SO EXCITED TO ENTER THE RACE, SHE SIMPLY CANNOT WAIT! DO YOU MIND IF WE...?
AREN'T YOU THE CUTEST-- SURE!
THIS YOUNG LADY WOULD LIKE TO ENTER HER CHAO IN THE RACE.
I'M SORRY, WE DON'T ALLOW CHILDREN TO RACE.
A-HA-HA... I MEAN, I'M THE YOUNG LADY!
OF COURSE! SIGN HERE, PLEASE!
CHATEAU GUESTS, THE QUALIFICATION RACE IS ABOUT TO BEGIN!
THE FIRST 50 CHAO TO CROSS THE FINISH LINE WILL BE ENTERED IN OUR GRAND PRIX, STARTING TOMORROW.
GOOD LUCK, AND HAPPY RACING!
GOOD LUCK, CHEESE!

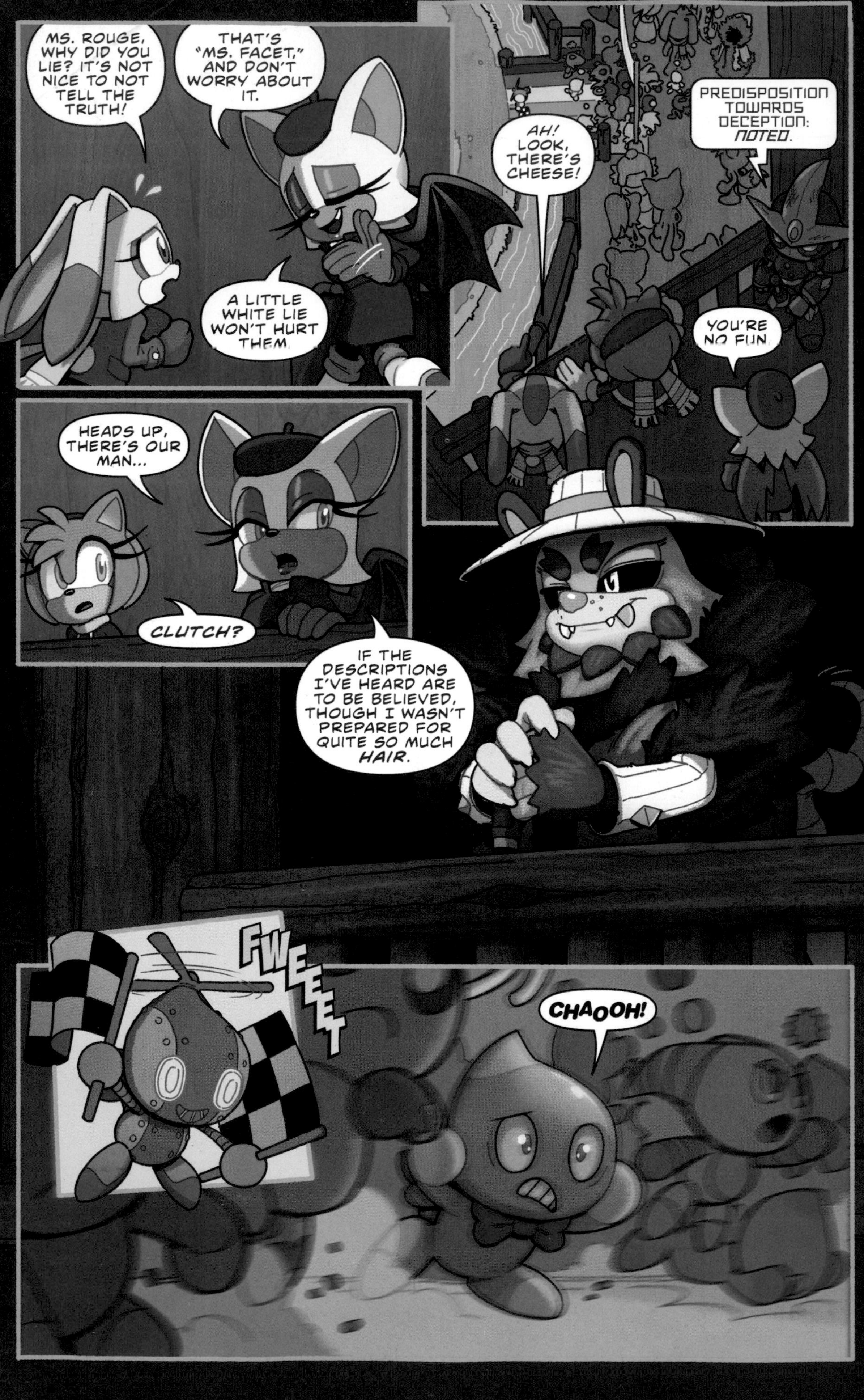

MS. ROUGE, WHY DID YOU LIE? IT'S NOT NICE TO NOT TELL THE TRUTH!
THAT'S "MS. FACET," AND DON'T WORRY ABOUT IT.
A LITTLE WHITE LIE WON'T HURT THEM.
AH! LOOK, THERE'S CHEESE!
PREDISPOSITION TOWARDS DECEPTION: NOTED.
YOU'RE NO FUN.
HEADS UP, THERE'S OUR MAN...
CLUTCH?
IF THE DESCRIPTIONS I'VE HEARD ARE TO BE BELIEVED, THOUGH I WASN'T PREPARED FOR QUITE SO MUCH HAIR.
FWEEET
CHAOOH!

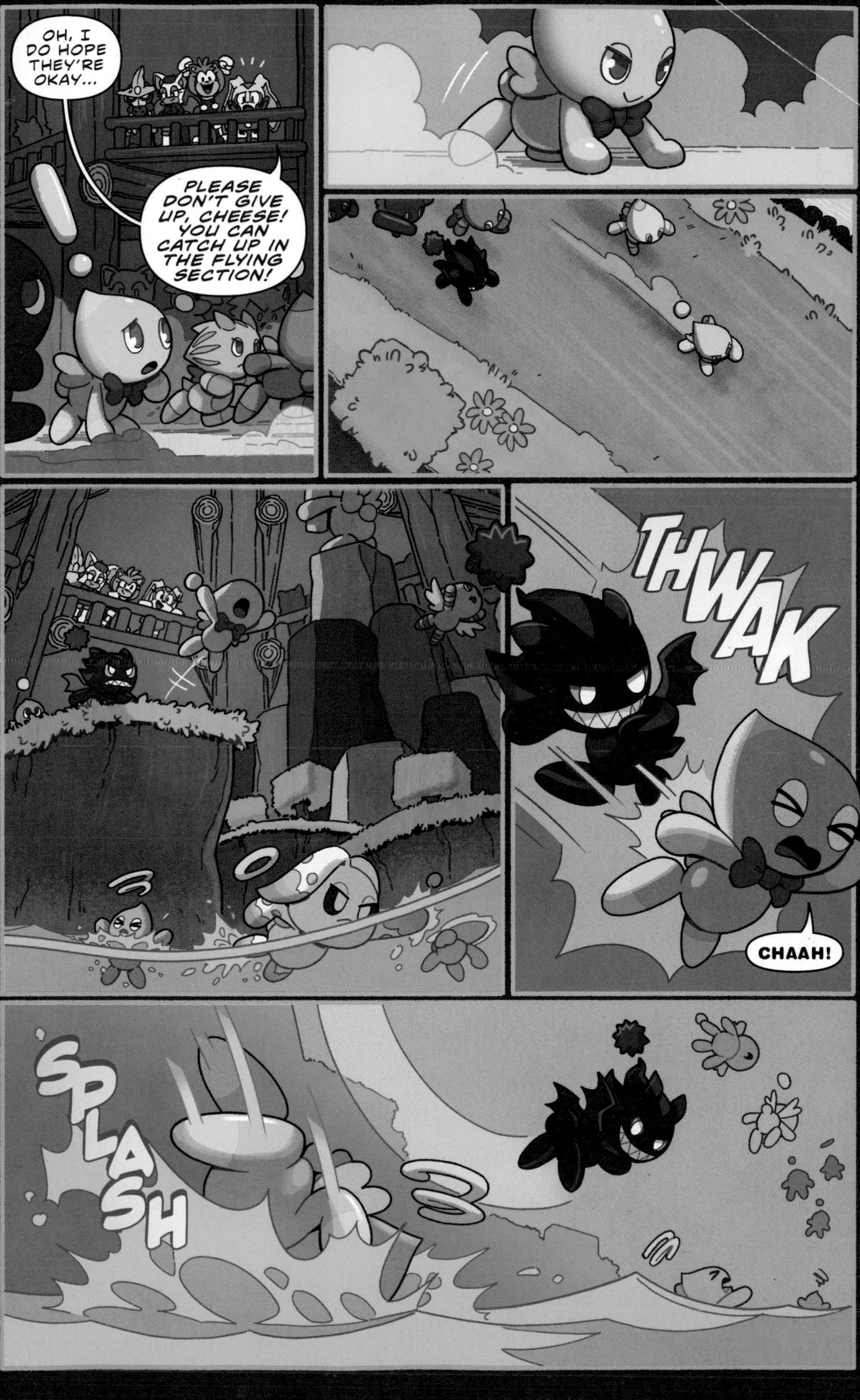

OH, I DO HOPE THEY'RE OKAY...
PLEASE DON'T GIVE UP, CHEESE! YOU CAN CATCH UP IN THE FLYING SECTION!
THWAK
CHAAH!
SPLASH

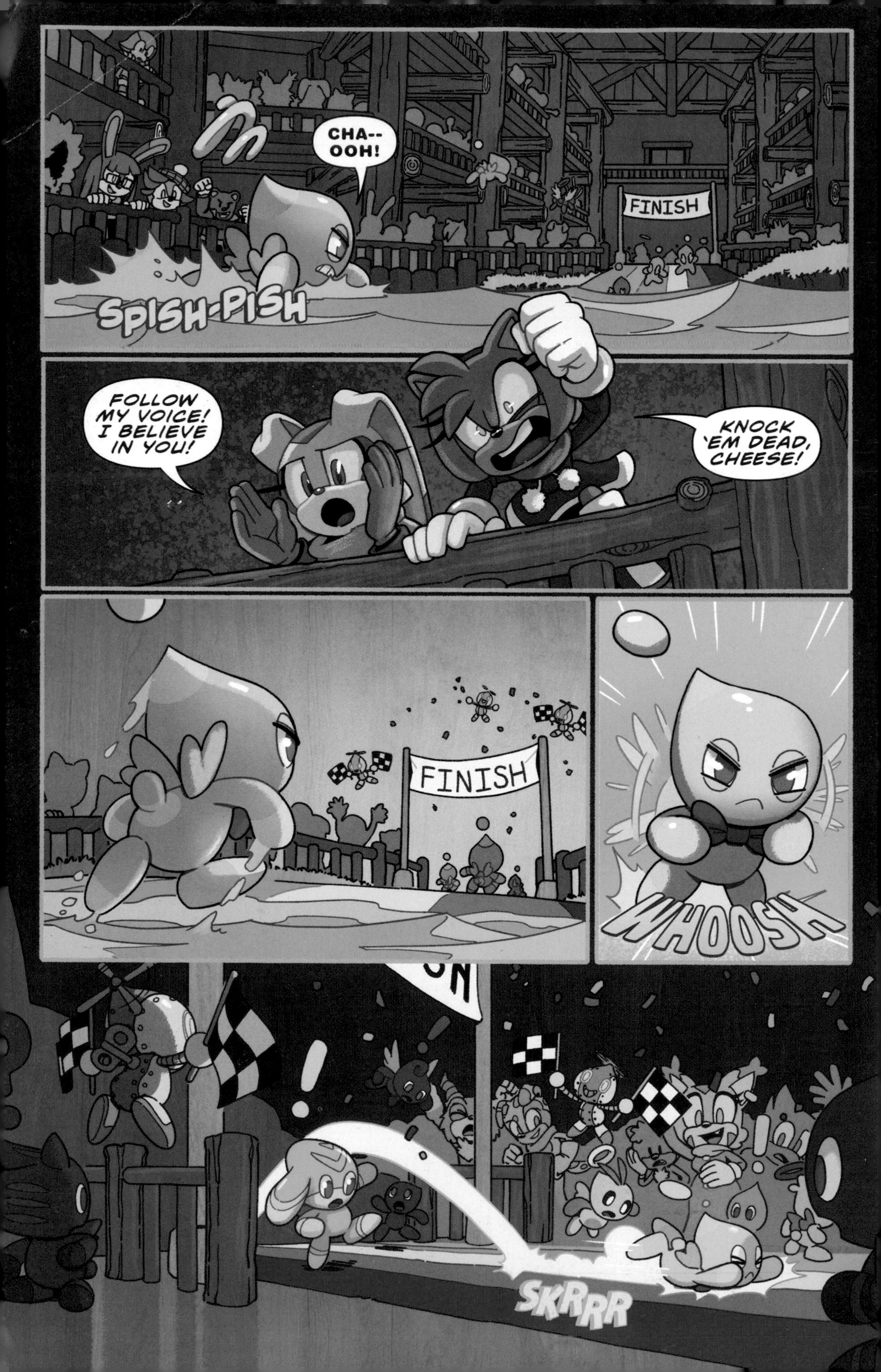

CHA-- OOH!
FINISH
SPISH-PISH
FOLLOW MY VOICE! I BELIEVE IN YOU!
KNOCK 'EM DEAD, CHEESE!
FINISH
WHOOSH
SKRRR

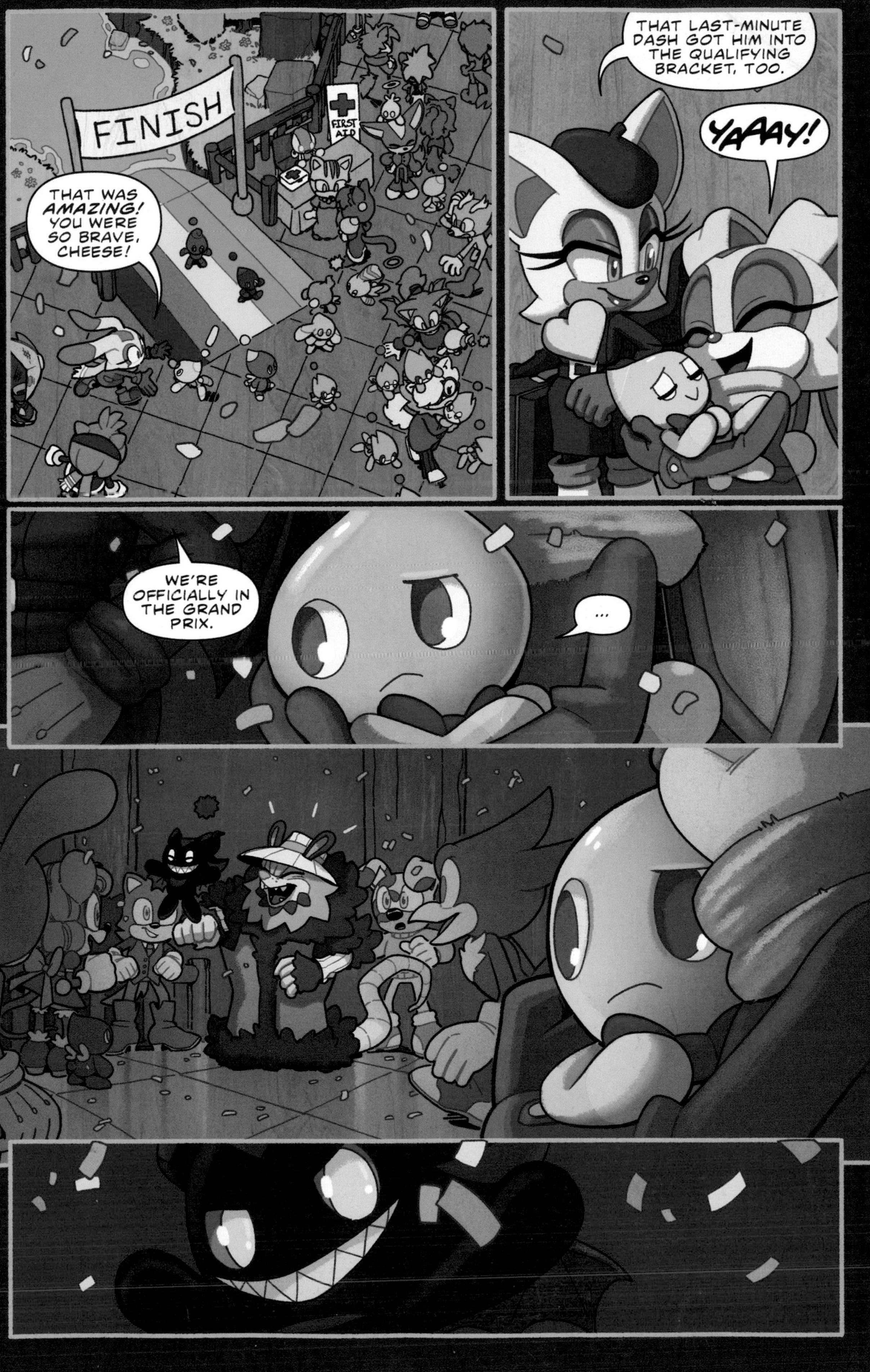

FINISH
FIRST AID
THAT WAS AMAZING! YOU WERE SO BRAVE, CHEESE!
THAT LAST-MINUTE DASH GOT HIM INTO THE QUALIFYING BRACKET, TOO.
YAAAY!
WE'RE OFFICIALLY IN THE GRAND PRIX.
...

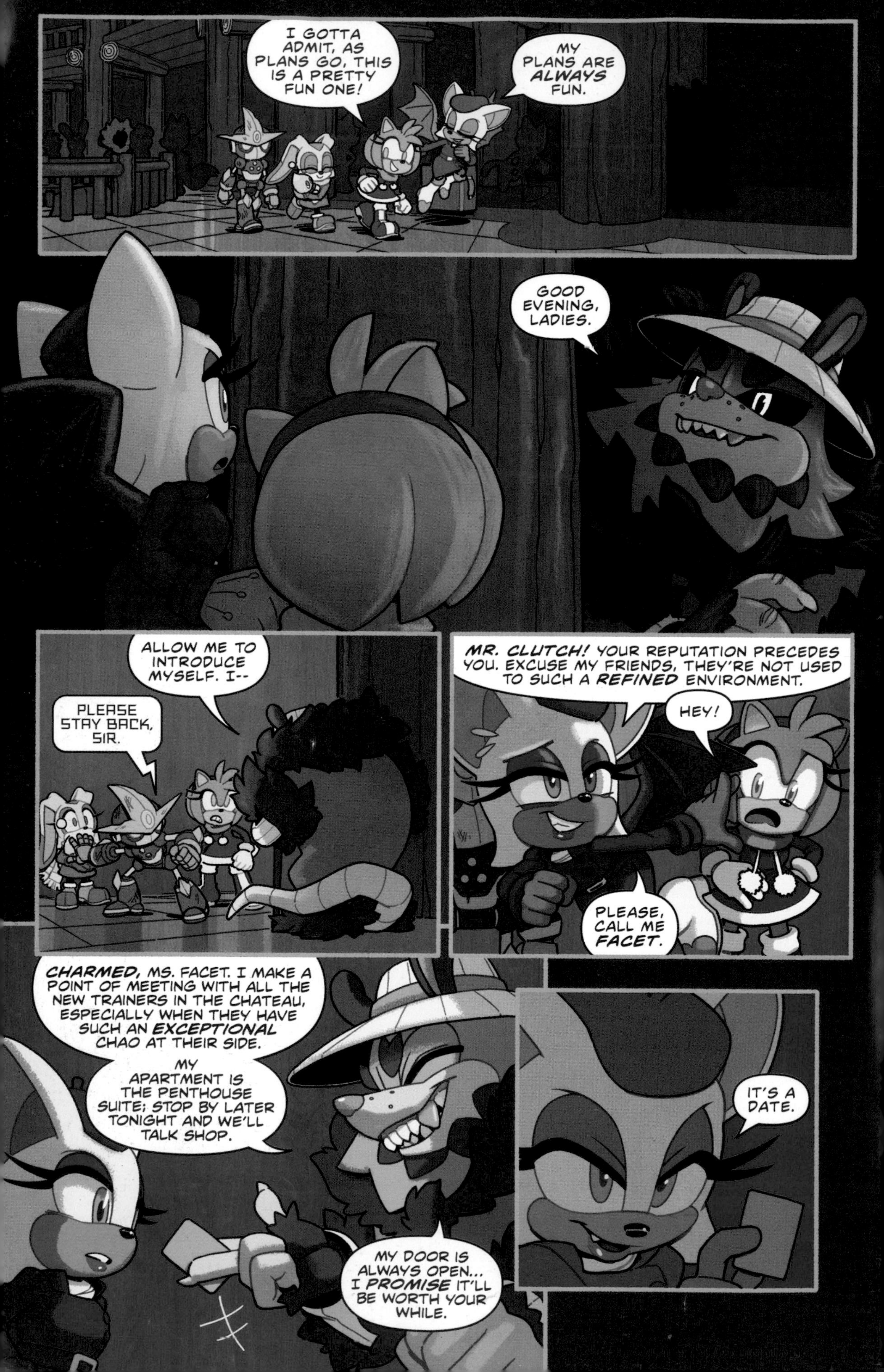

I GOTTA ADMIT, AS PLANS GO, THIS IS A PRETTY FUN ONE!
MY PLANS ARE ALWAYS FUN.
GOOD EVENING, LADIES.
ALLOW ME TO INTRODUCE MYSELF. I--
PLEASE STAY BACK, SIR.
MR. CLUTCH! YOUR REPUTATION PRECEDES YOU. EXCUSE MY FRIENDS, THEY'RE NOT USED TO SUCH A REFINED ENVIRONMENT.
HEY!
PLEASE, CALL ME FACET.
CHARMED, MS. FACET. I MAKE A POINT OF MEETING WITH ALL THE NEW TRAINERS IN THE CHATEAU, ESPECIALLY WHEN THEY HAVE SUCH AN EXCEPTIONAL CHAO AT THEIR SIDE.
MY APARTMENT IS THE PENTHOUSE SUITE; STOP BY LATER TONIGHT AND WE'LL TALK SHOP.
MY DOOR IS ALWAYS OPEN... I PROMISE IT'LL BE WORTH YOUR WHILE.
IT'S A DATE.

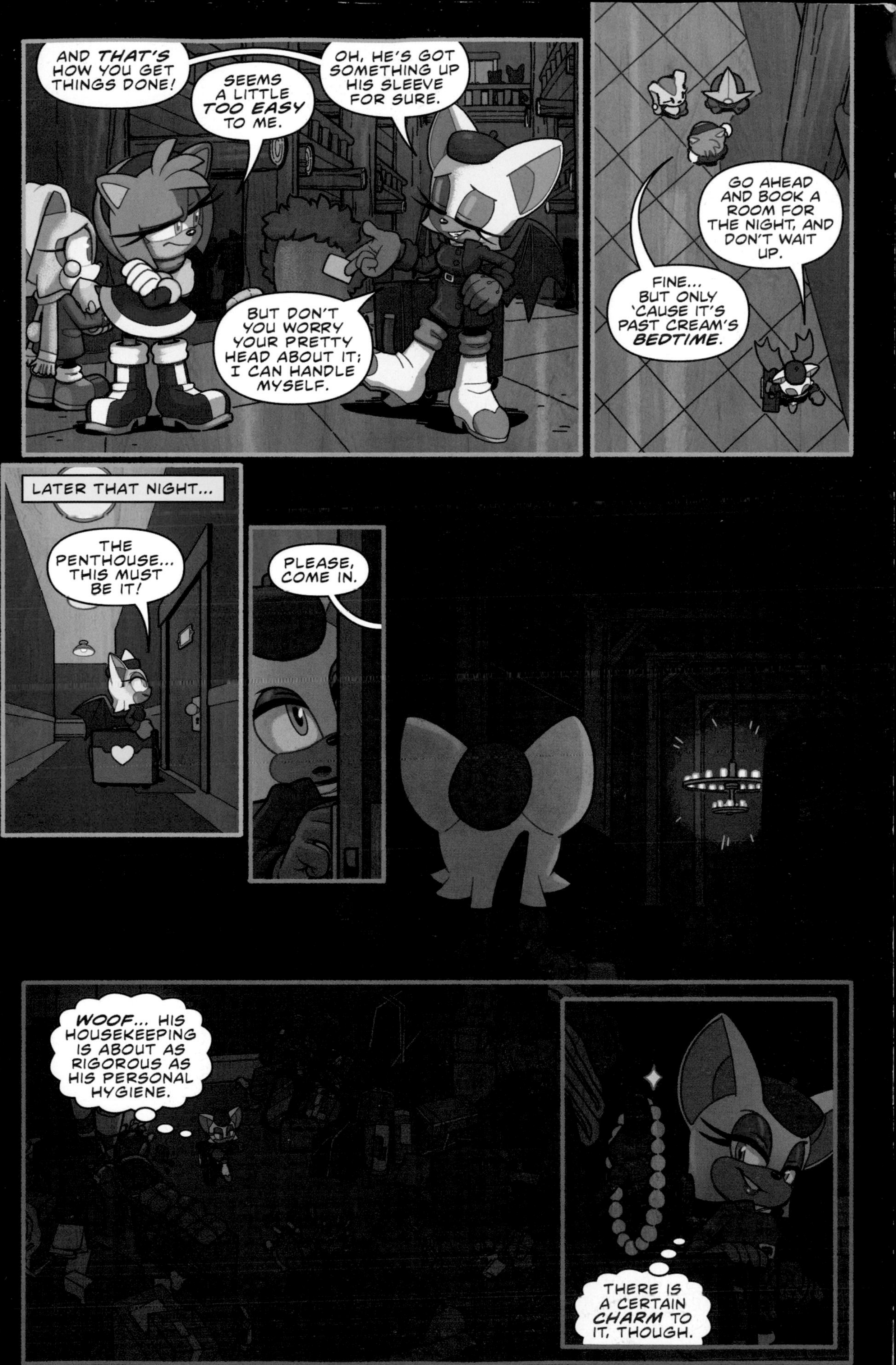
AND *THAT'S* HOW YOU GET THINGS DONE!
SEEMS A LITTLE *TOO EASY* TO ME.
OH, HE'S GOT SOMETHING UP HIS SLEEVE FOR SURE.
BUT DON'T YOU WORRY YOUR PRETTY HEAD ABOUT IT; I CAN HANDLE MYSELF.
GO AHEAD AND BOOK A ROOM FOR THE NIGHT, AND DON'T WAIT UP.
FINE... BUT ONLY 'CAUSE IT'S PAST CREAM'S *BEDTIME*.
LATER THAT NIGHT...
THE PENTHOUSE... THIS MUST BE IT!
PLEASE, COME IN.
WOOF... HIS HOUSEKEEPING IS ABOUT AS RIGOROUS AS HIS PERSONAL HYGIENE.
THERE IS A CERTAIN *CHARM* TO IT, THOUGH.

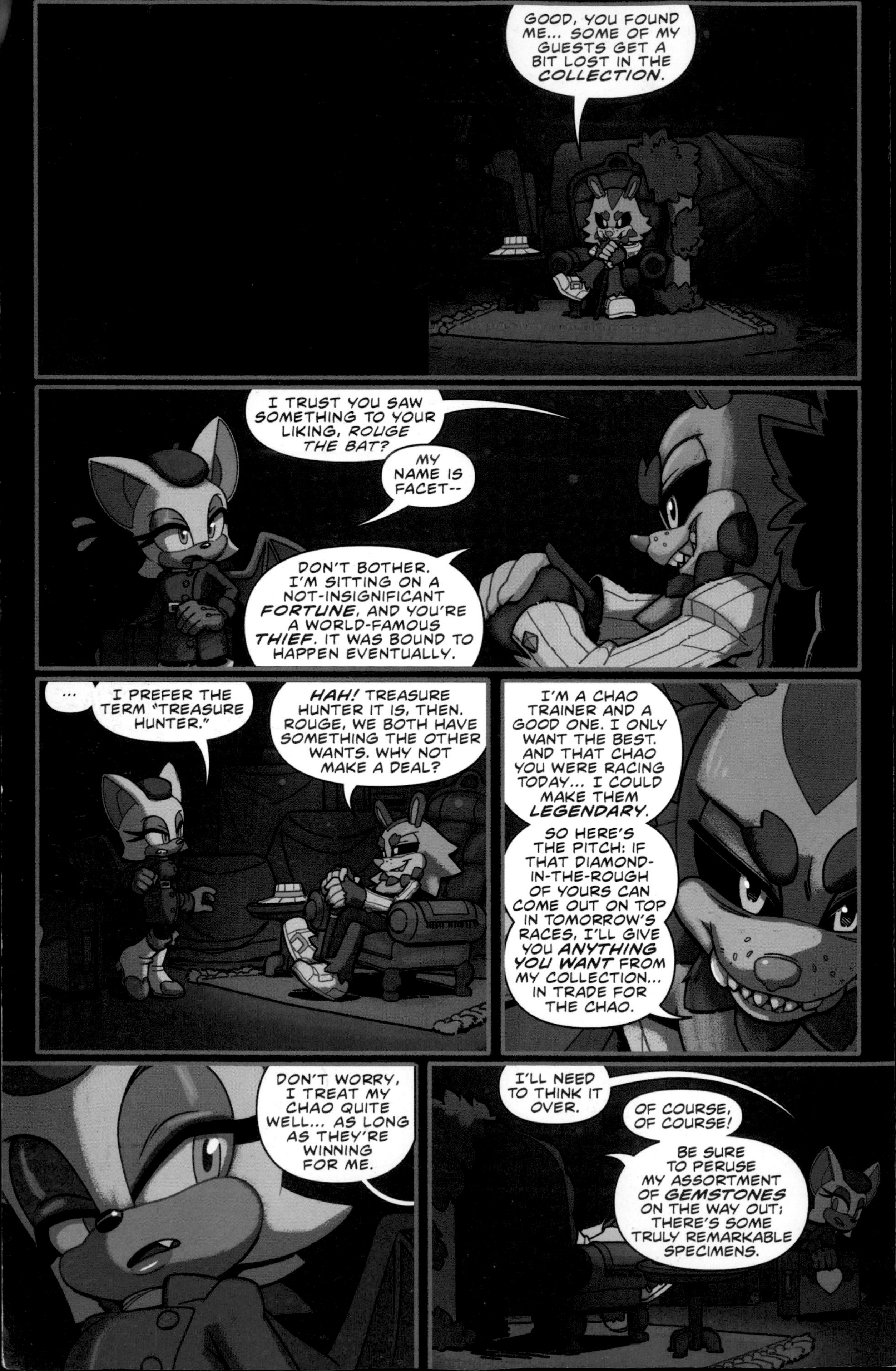
GOOD, YOU FOUND ME... SOME OF MY GUESTS GET A BIT LOST IN THE COLLECTION.
I TRUST YOU SAW SOMETHING TO YOUR LIKING, ROUGE THE BAT?
MY NAME IS FACET--
DON'T BOTHER. I'M SITTING ON A NOT-INSIGNIFICANT FORTUNE, AND YOU'RE A WORLD-FAMOUS THIEF. IT WAS BOUND TO HAPPEN EVENTUALLY.
...
I PREFER THE TERM "TREASURE HUNTER."
HAH! TREASURE HUNTER IT IS, THEN. ROUGE, WE BOTH HAVE SOMETHING THE OTHER WANTS. WHY NOT MAKE A DEAL?
I'M A CHAO TRAINER AND A GOOD ONE. I ONLY WANT THE BEST. AND THAT CHAO YOU WERE RACING TODAY... I COULD MAKE THEM LEGENDARY.
SO HERE'S THE PITCH: IF THAT DIAMOND-IN-THE-ROUGH OF YOURS CAN COME OUT ON TOP IN TOMORROW'S RACES, I'LL GIVE YOU ANYTHING YOU WANT FROM MY COLLECTION... IN TRADE FOR THE CHAO.
DON'T WORRY, I TREAT MY CHAO QUITE WELL... AS LONG AS THEY'RE WINNING FOR ME.
I'LL NEED TO THINK IT OVER.
OF COURSE, OF COURSE!
BE SURE TO PERUSE MY ASSORTMENT OF GEMSTONES ON THE WAY OUT; THERE'S SOME TRULY REMARKABLE SPECIMENS.

DISCREPANCY DETECTED: THE CHAO "CHEESE" IS NOT YOUR PROPERTY. HOW DO YOU INTEND TO OBTAIN HIM? WITH VIOLENCE?

PLEASE. I'M NOT GOING TO GIVE HIM CHEESE.

OF COURSE, CLUTCH DOESN'T NEED TO KNOW THAT.

LISTEN CAREFULLY, OMEGA. I'VE GOT A JOB FOR YOU.

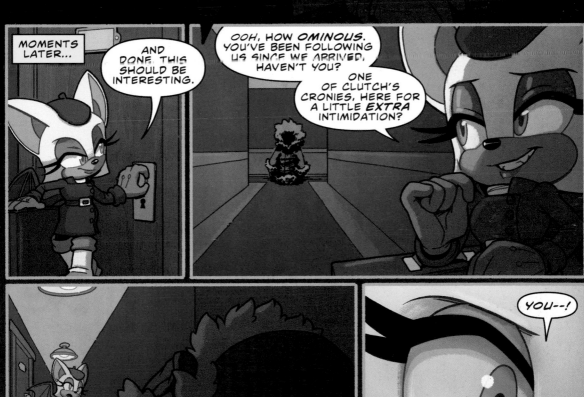

MOMENTS LATER...

AND DONE. THIS SHOULD BE INTERESTING.

OOH, HOW OMINOUS. YOU'VE BEEN FOLLOWING US SINCE WE ARRIVED, HAVEN'T YOU?

ONE OF CLUTCH'S CRONIES, HERE FOR A LITTLE EXTRA INTIMIDATION?

YOU--!

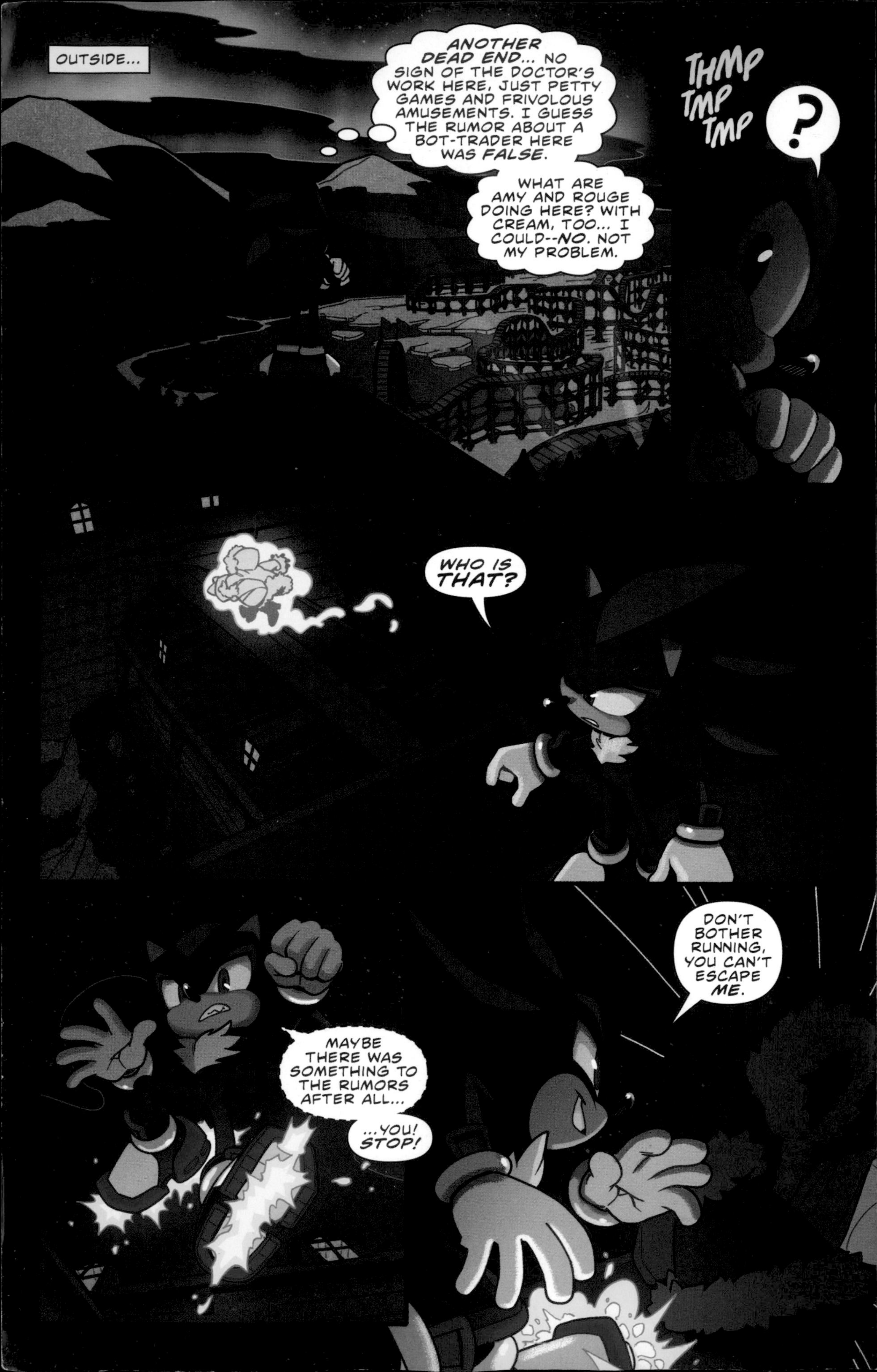
OUTSIDE...
ANOTHER DEAD END... NO SIGN OF THE DOCTOR'S WORK HERE, JUST PETTY GAMES AND FRIVOLOUS AMUSEMENTS. I GUESS THE RUMOR ABOUT A BOT-TRADER HERE WAS FALSE.
WHAT ARE AMY AND ROUGE DOING HERE? WITH CREAM, TOO... I COULD--NO. NOT MY PROBLEM.
THMP TMP TMP
?
WHO IS THAT?
DON'T BOTHER RUNNING, YOU CAN'T ESCAPE ME.
MAYBE THERE WAS SOMETHING TO THE RUMORS AFTER ALL...
...YOU! STOP!

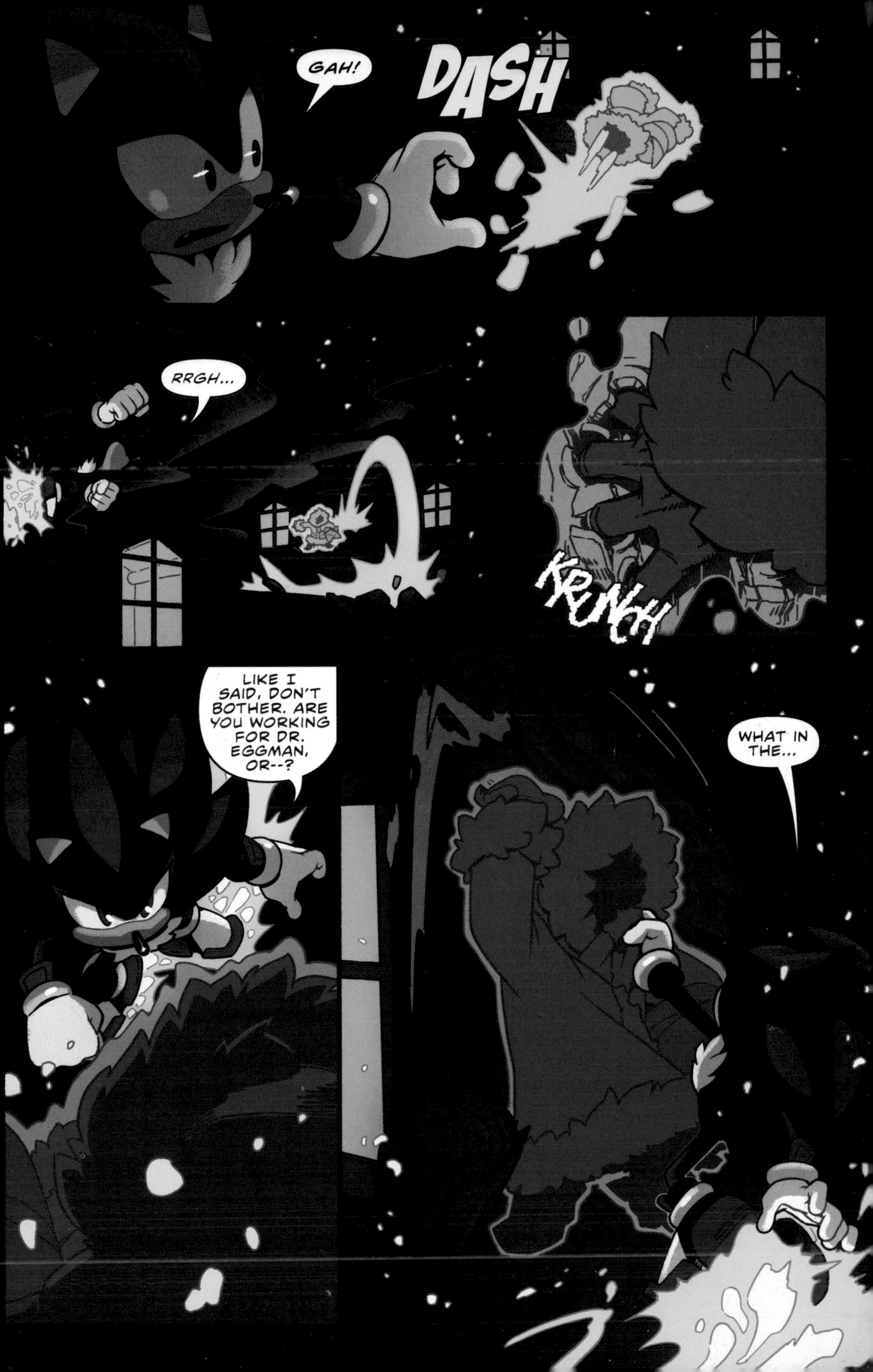
GAH!
DASH
RRGH...
KRUNCH
LIKE I SAID, DON'T BOTHER. ARE YOU WORKING FOR DR. EGGMAN, OR--?
WHAT IN THE...

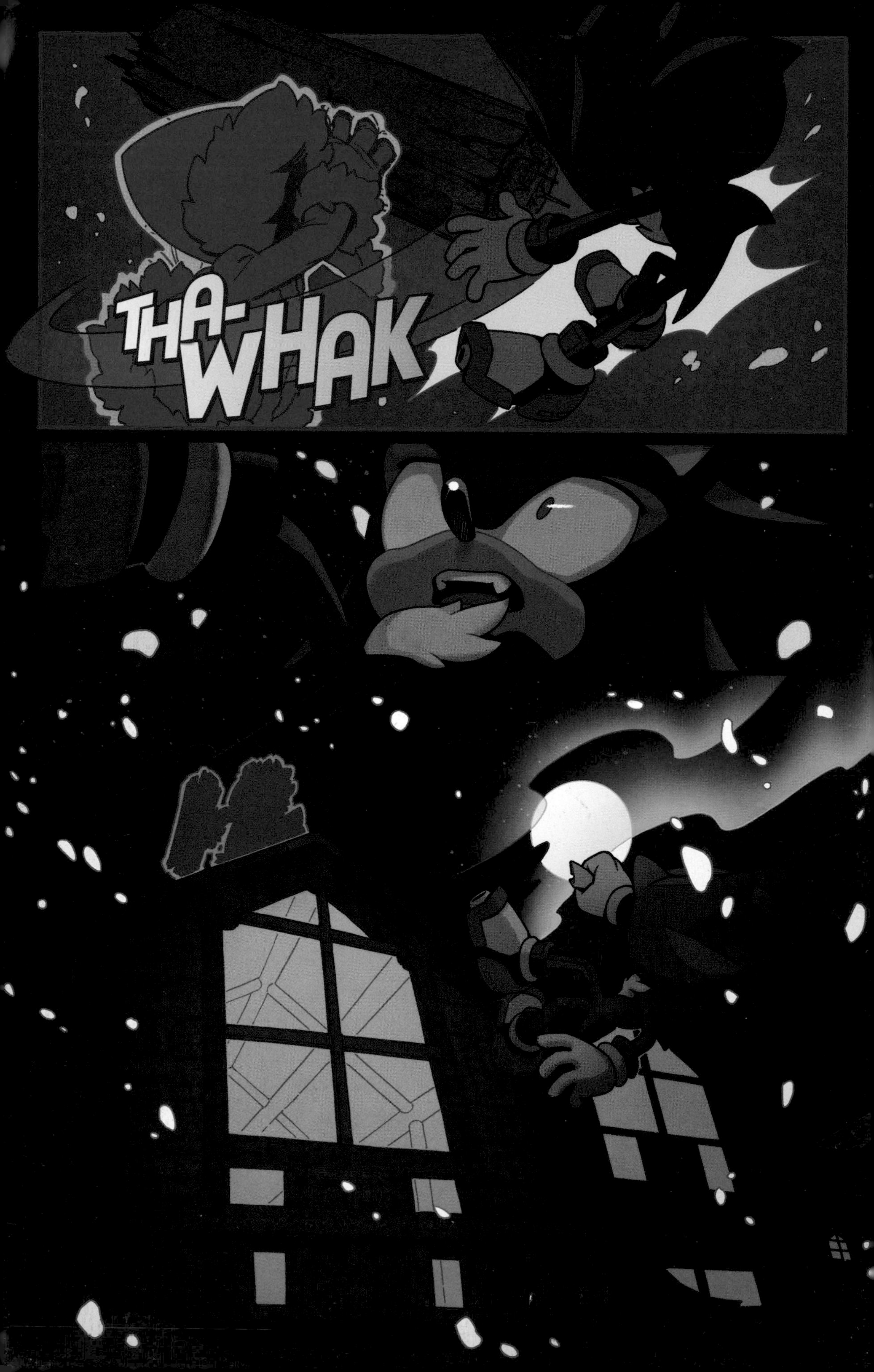
THA-WHAK

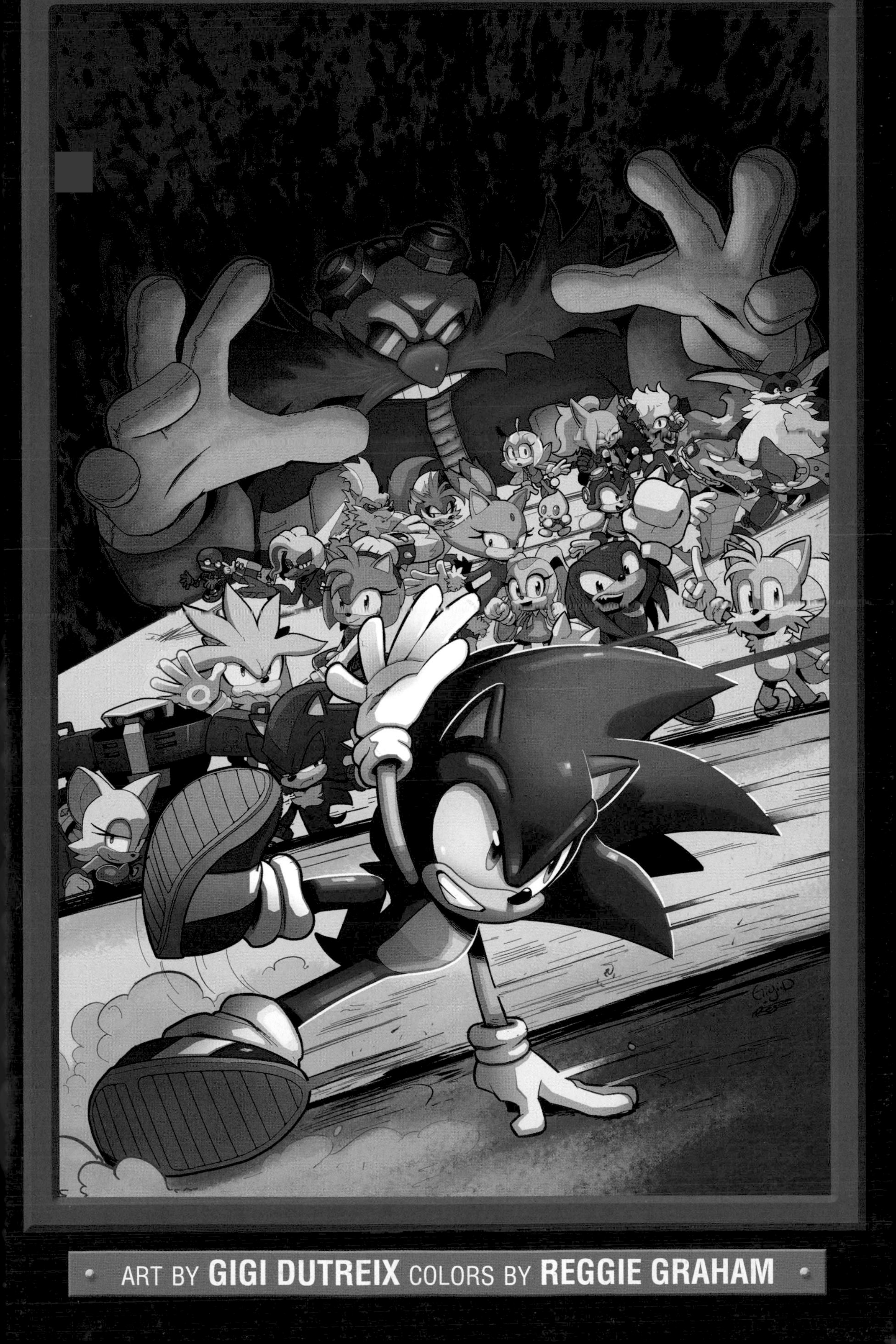
GigiD

ART BY **GIGI DUTREIX** COLORS BY **REGGIE GRAHAM**

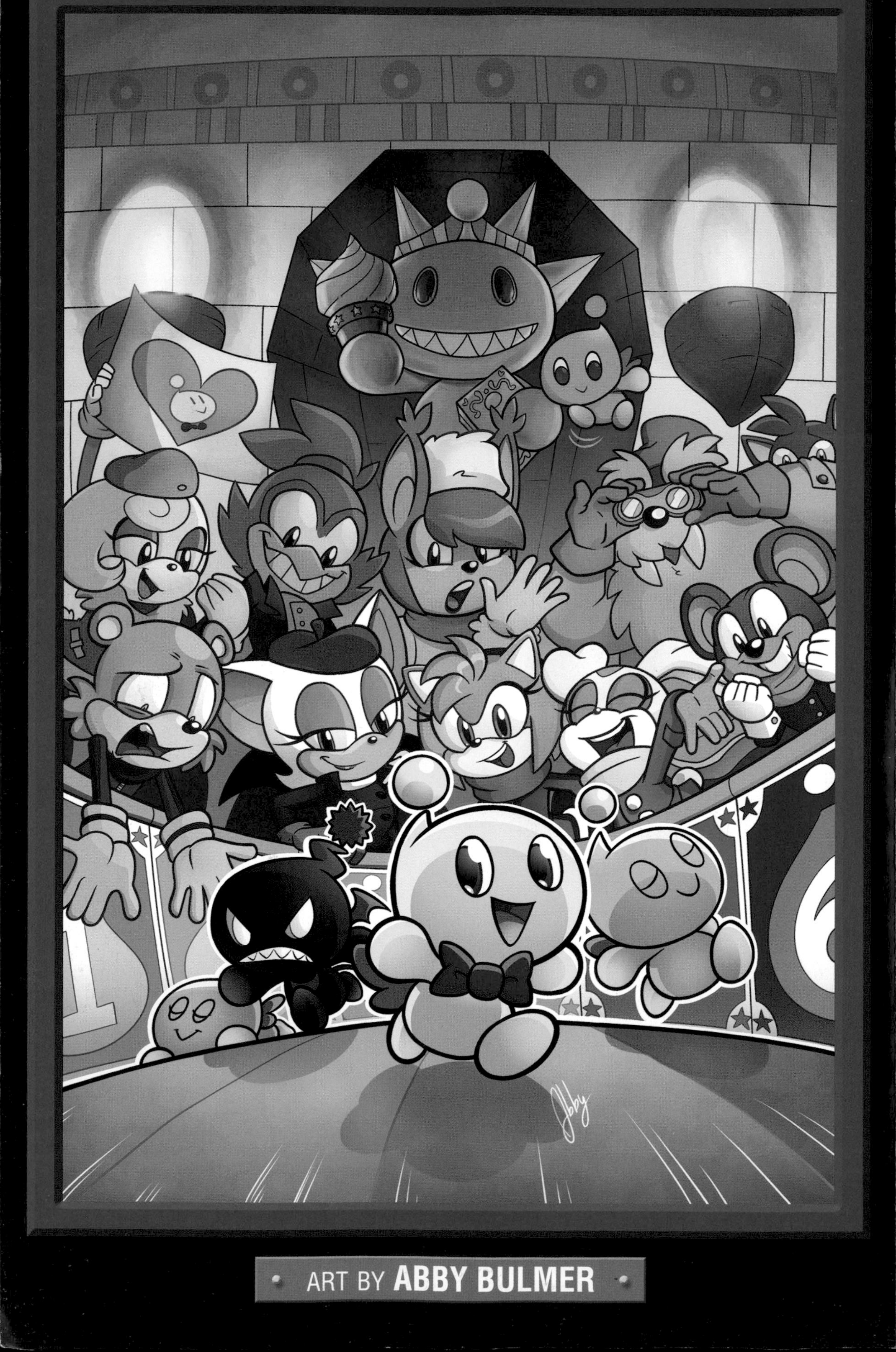

ART BY **ABBY BULMER**

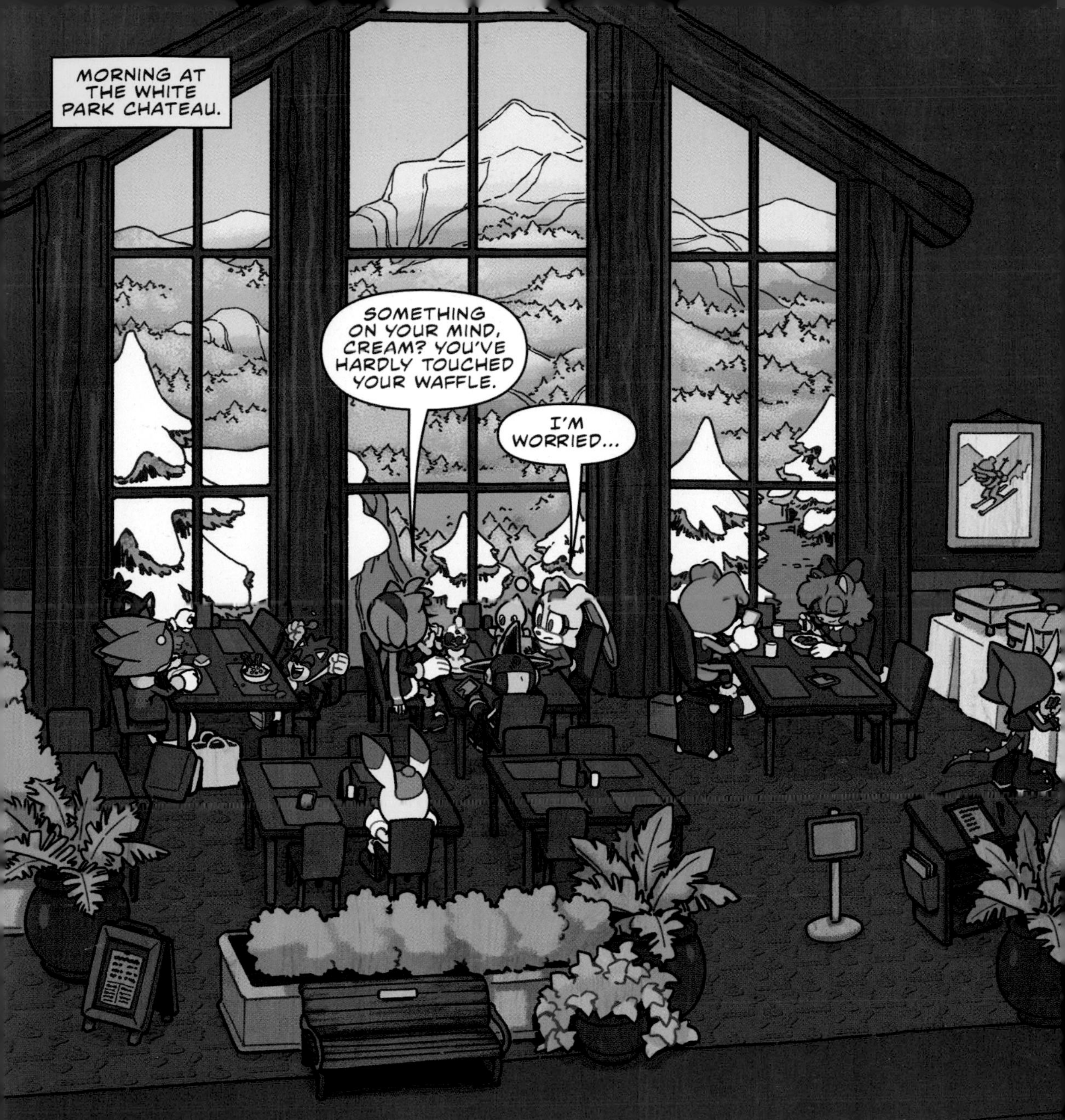
MORNING AT THE WHITE PARK CHATEAU.
SOMETHING ON YOUR MIND, CREAM? YOU'VE HARDLY TOUCHED YOUR WAFFLE.
I'M WORRIED...

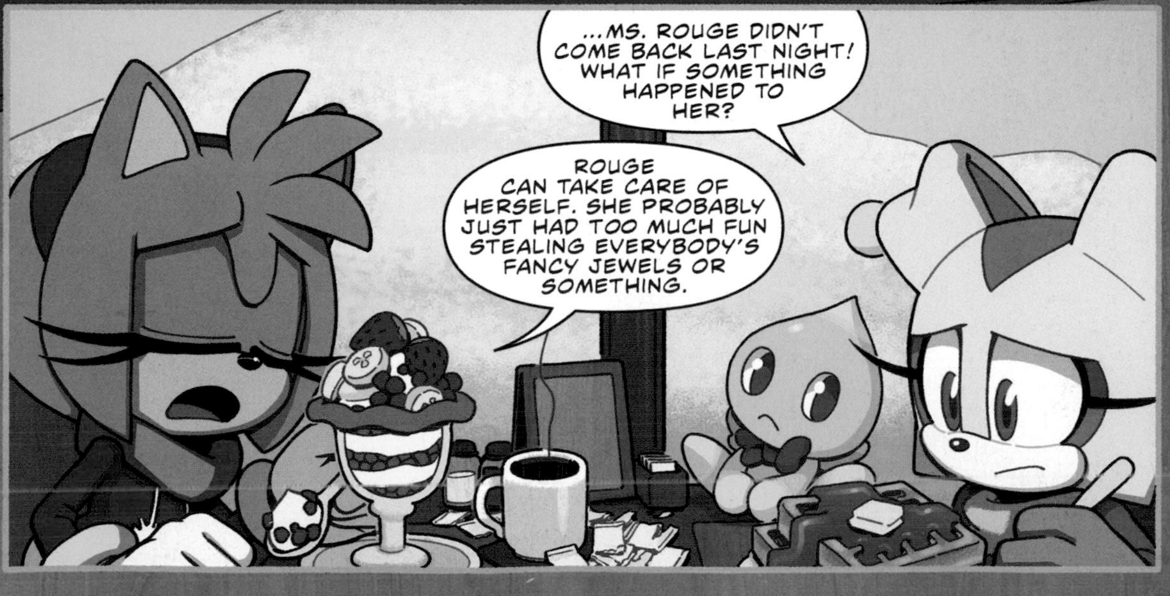
...MS. ROUGE DIDN'T COME BACK LAST NIGHT! WHAT IF SOMETHING HAPPENED TO HER?
ROUGE CAN TAKE CARE OF HERSELF. SHE PROBABLY JUST HAD TOO MUCH FUN STEALING EVERYBODY'S FANCY JEWELS OR SOMETHING.

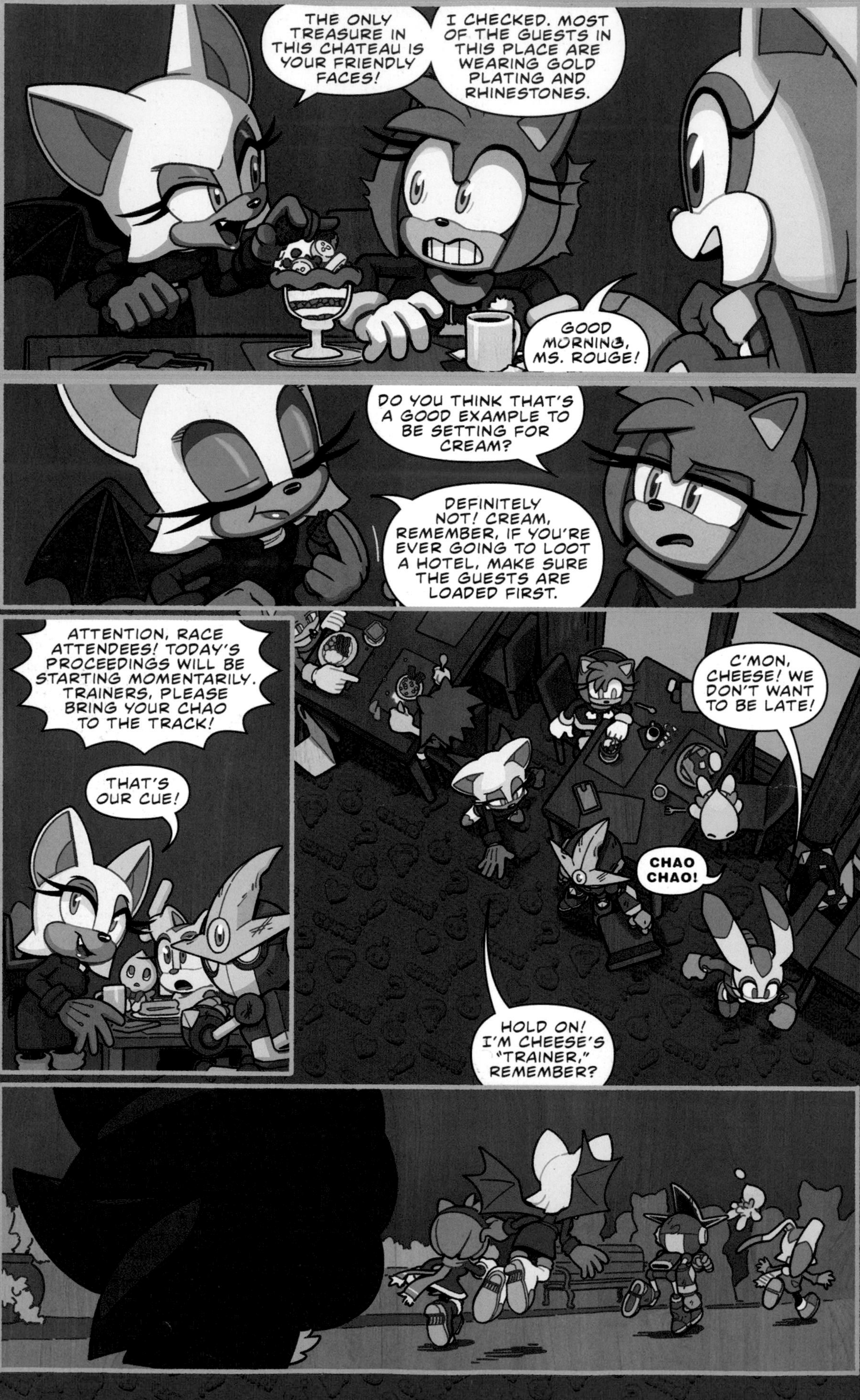
THE ONLY TREASURE IN THIS CHATEAU IS YOUR FRIENDLY FACES!
I CHECKED. MOST OF THE GUESTS IN THIS PLACE ARE WEARING GOLD PLATING AND RHINESTONES.
GOOD MORNING, MS. ROUGE!
DO YOU THINK THAT'S A GOOD EXAMPLE TO BE SETTING FOR CREAM?
DEFINITELY NOT! CREAM, REMEMBER, IF YOU'RE EVER GOING TO LOOT A HOTEL, MAKE SURE THE GUESTS ARE LOADED FIRST.
ATTENTION, RACE ATTENDEES! TODAY'S PROCEEDINGS WILL BE STARTING MOMENTARILY. TRAINERS, PLEASE BRING YOUR CHAO TO THE TRACK!
THAT'S OUR CUE!
C'MON, CHEESE! WE DON'T WANT TO BE LATE!
CHAO CHAO!
HOLD ON! I'M CHEESE'S "TRAINER," REMEMBER?

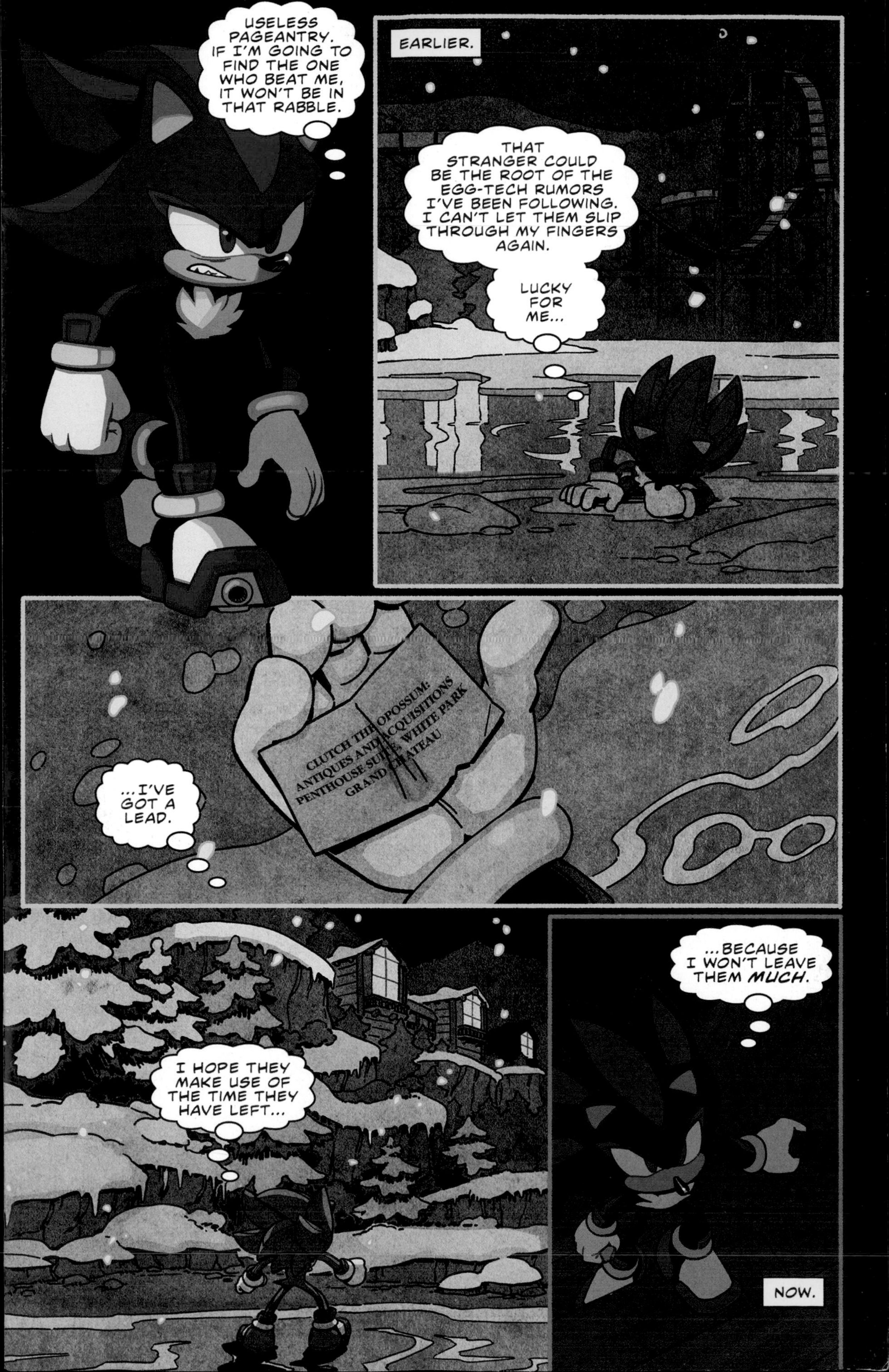
USELESS PAGEANTRY. IF I'M GOING TO FIND THE ONE WHO BEAT ME, IT WON'T BE IN THAT RABBLE.
EARLIER.
THAT STRANGER COULD BE THE ROOT OF THE EGG-TECH RUMORS I'VE BEEN FOLLOWING. I CAN'T LET THEM SLIP THROUGH MY FINGERS AGAIN.
LUCKY FOR ME...
CLUTCH THE OPOSSUM:
ANTIQUES AND ACQUISITIONS
PENTHOUSE SUITE, WHITE PARK
GRAND CHATEAU
...I'VE GOT A LEAD.
I HOPE THEY MAKE USE OF THE TIME THEY HAVE LEFT...
...BECAUSE I WON'T LEAVE THEM MUCH.
NOW.

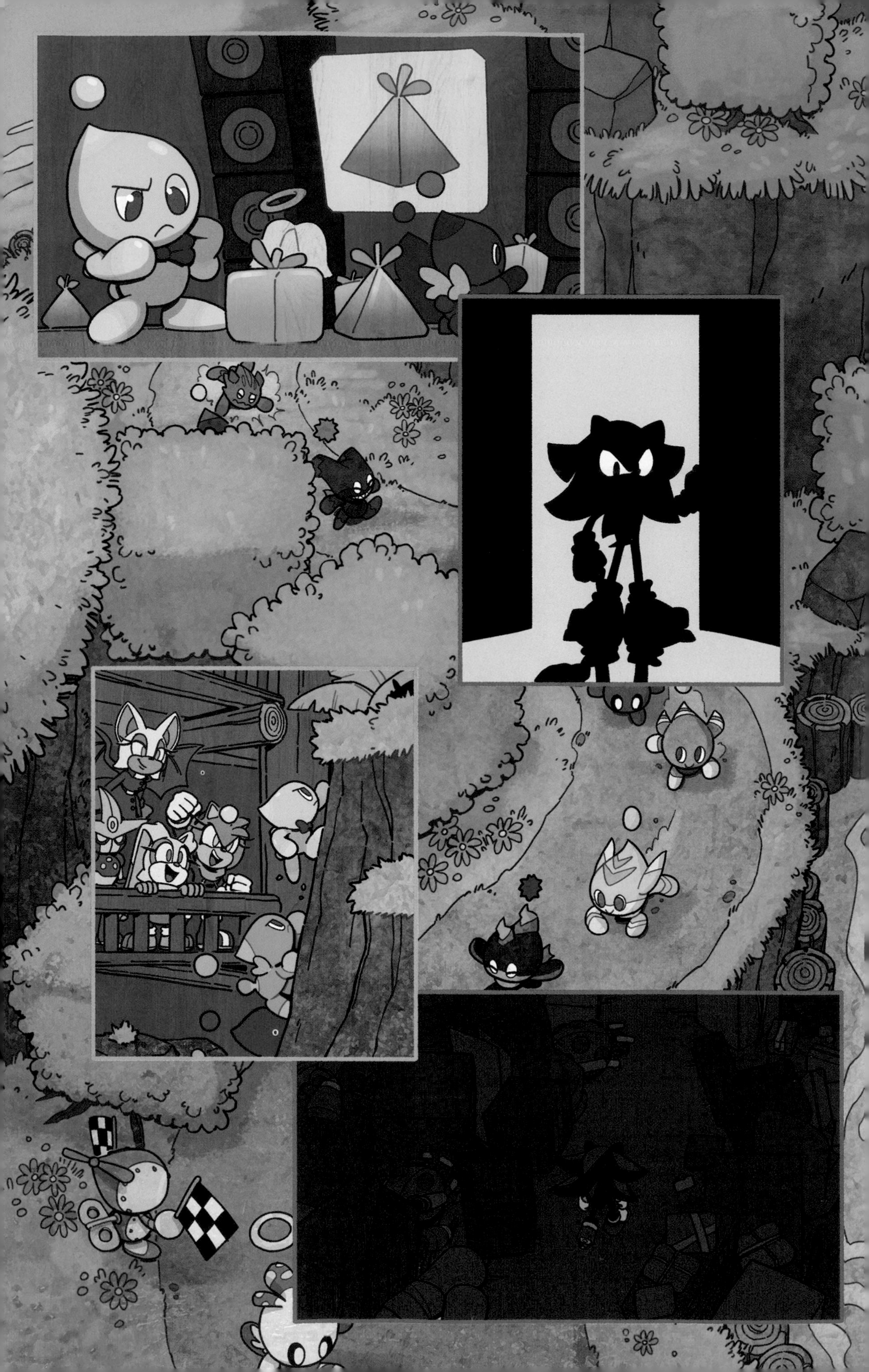

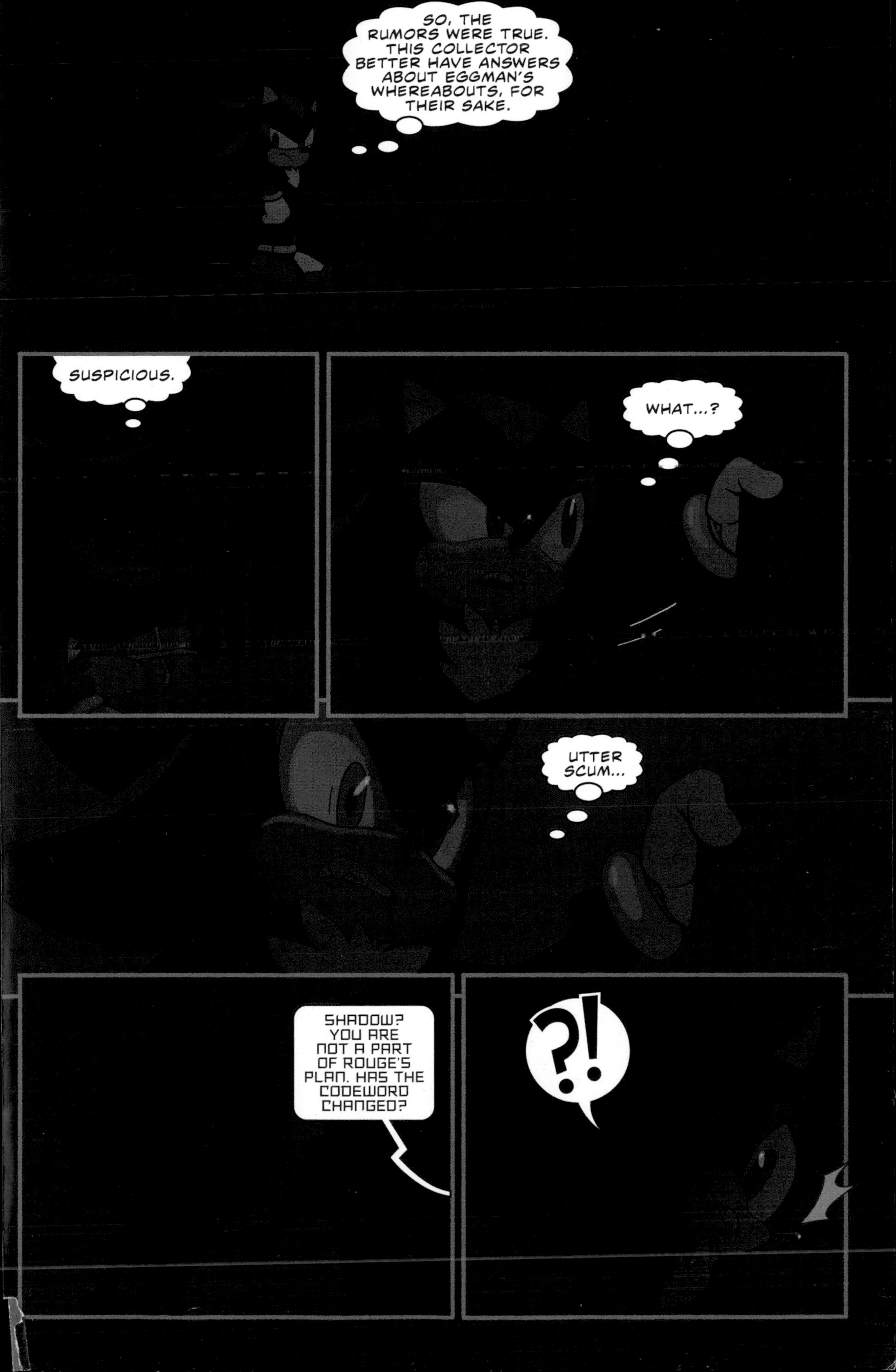
SO, THE RUMORS WERE TRUE. THIS COLLECTOR BETTER HAVE ANSWERS ABOUT EGGMAN'S WHEREABOUTS, FOR THEIR SAKE.
SUSPICIOUS.
WHAT...?
UTTER SCUM...
SHADOW? YOU ARE NOT A PART OF ROUGE'S PLAN. HAS THE CODEWORD CHANGED?
?!

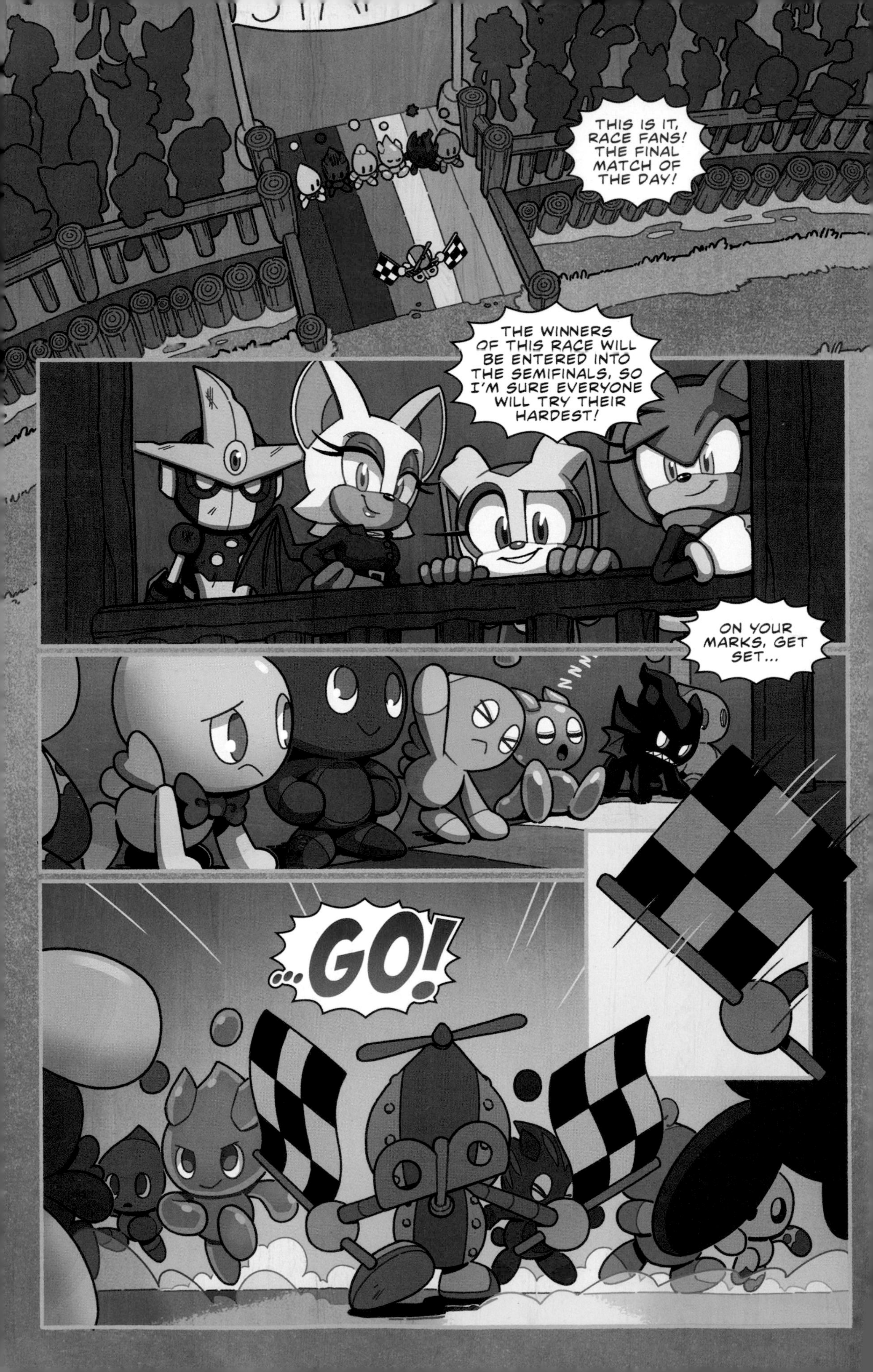
THIS IS IT, RACE FANS! THE FINAL MATCH OF THE DAY!
THE WINNERS OF THIS RACE WILL BE ENTERED INTO THE SEMIFINALS, SO I'M SURE EVERYONE WILL TRY THEIR HARDEST!
ON YOUR MARKS, GET SET...
NNN
...GO!

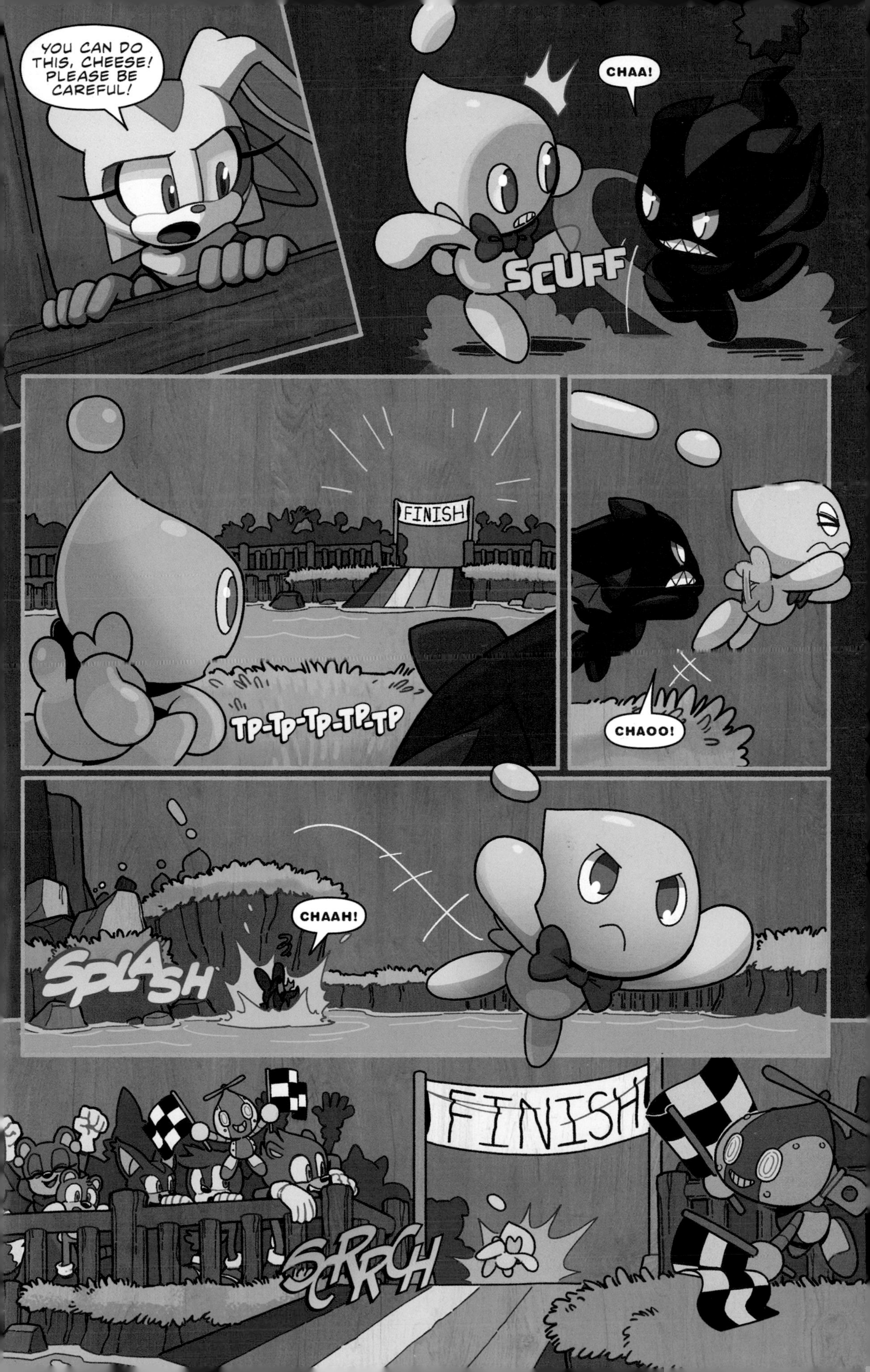
YOU CAN DO THIS, CHEESE! PLEASE BE CAREFUL!
CHAA!
SCUFF
FINISH
TP-TP-TP-TP-TP
CHAOO!
CHAAH!
SPLASH
FINISH
SCRRCH

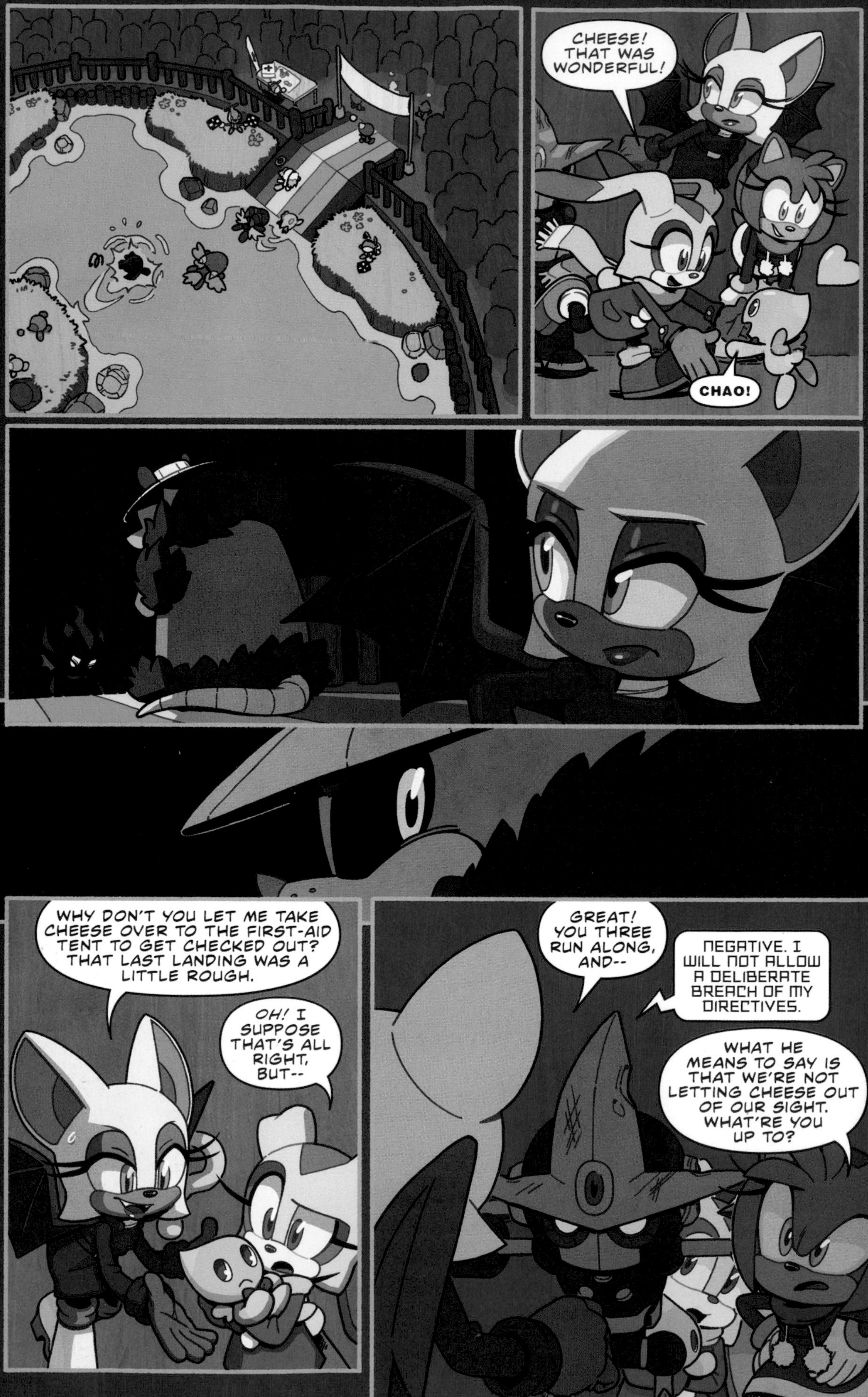
CHEESE! THAT WAS WONDERFUL!
CHAO!
WHY DON'T YOU LET ME TAKE CHEESE OVER TO THE FIRST-AID TENT TO GET CHECKED OUT? THAT LAST LANDING WAS A LITTLE ROUGH.
OH! I SUPPOSE THAT'S ALL RIGHT, BUT--
GREAT! YOU THREE RUN ALONG, AND--
NEGATIVE. I WILL NOT ALLOW A DELIBERATE BREACH OF MY DIRECTIVES.
WHAT HE MEANS TO SAY IS THAT WE'RE NOT LETTING CHEESE OUT OF OUR SIGHT. WHAT'RE YOU UP TO?

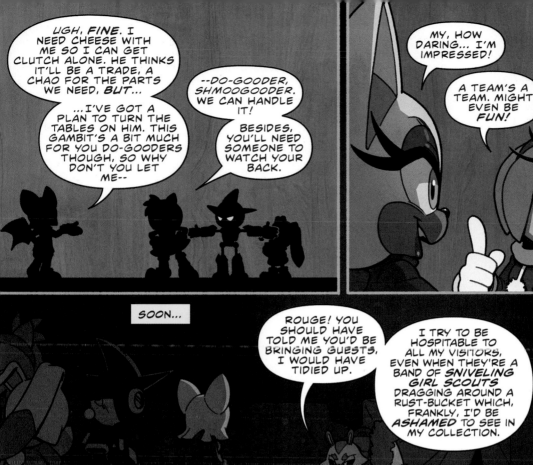

UGH, *FINE*. I NEED CHEESE WITH ME SO I CAN GET CLUTCH ALONE. HE THINKS IT'LL BE A TRADE, A CHAO FOR THE PARTS WE NEED, *BUT*...

...I'VE GOT A PLAN TO TURN THE TABLES ON HIM. THIS GAMBIT'S A BIT MUCH FOR YOU DO-GOODERS THOUGH, SO WHY DON'T YOU LET ME--

--DO-GOODER, SHMOOGOODER. WE CAN HANDLE IT!

BESIDES, YOU'LL NEED SOMEONE TO WATCH YOUR BACK.

MY, HOW DARING... I'M IMPRESSED!

A TEAM'S A TEAM. MIGHT EVEN BE *FUN*!

SOON...

ROUGE! YOU SHOULD HAVE TOLD ME YOU'D BE BRINGING GUESTS, I WOULD HAVE TIDIED UP.

I TRY TO BE HOSPITABLE TO ALL MY VISITORS, EVEN WHEN THEY'RE A BAND OF *SNIVELING GIRL SCOUTS* DRAGGING AROUND A RUST-BUCKET WHICH, FRANKLY, I'D BE *ASHAMED* TO SEE IN MY COLLECTION.

SIMMER DOWN! WE NEED *TACT*, NOT MUSCLE.

YOUR ROBOT'S ENTHUSIASM IS ADMIRABLE...

...BUT YOU SHOULD KNOW THAT WHILE I LIKE TO DO BUSINESS IN A *RELAXED* SETTING, I AM BY *NO* MEANS DEFENSELESS. INTERESTED IN A DEMONSTRATION?

WE'RE HERE FOR THE TRADE, PLAIN AND SIMPLE.

JUST THE WAY I LIKE IT. SHOW ME THE CHAO.

DON'T WORRY. I'VE GOT THIS UNDER CONTROL.

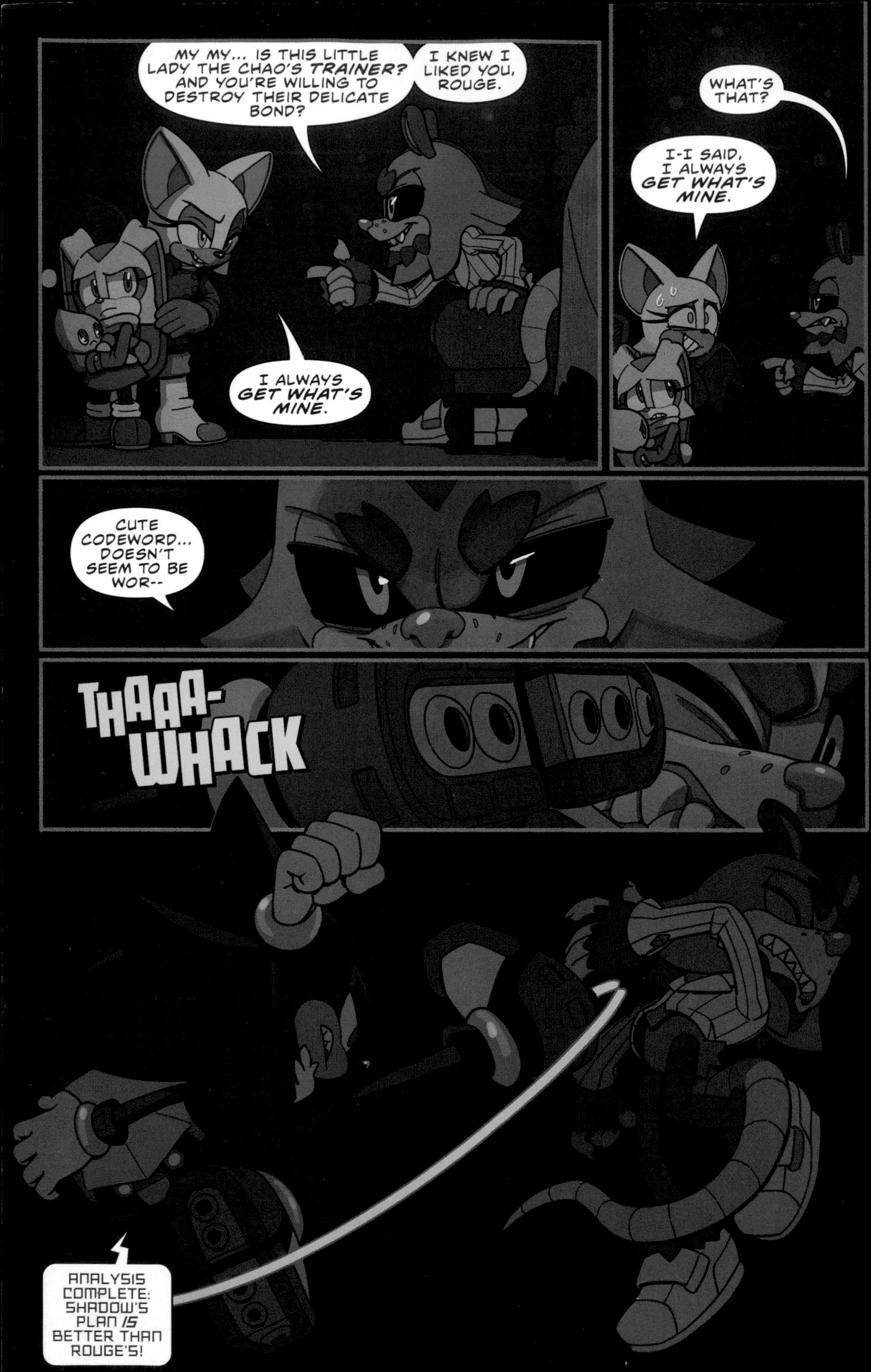
MY MY... IS THIS LITTLE LADY THE CHAO'S TRAINER? AND YOU'RE WILLING TO DESTROY THEIR DELICATE BOND?
I KNEW I LIKED YOU, ROUGE.
I ALWAYS GET WHAT'S MINE.
WHAT'S THAT?
I-I SAID, I ALWAYS GET WHAT'S MINE.
CUTE CODEWORD... DOESN'T SEEM TO BE WOR--
THAAA-WHACK
ANALYSIS COMPLETE: SHADOW'S PLAN IS BETTER THAN ROUGE'S!

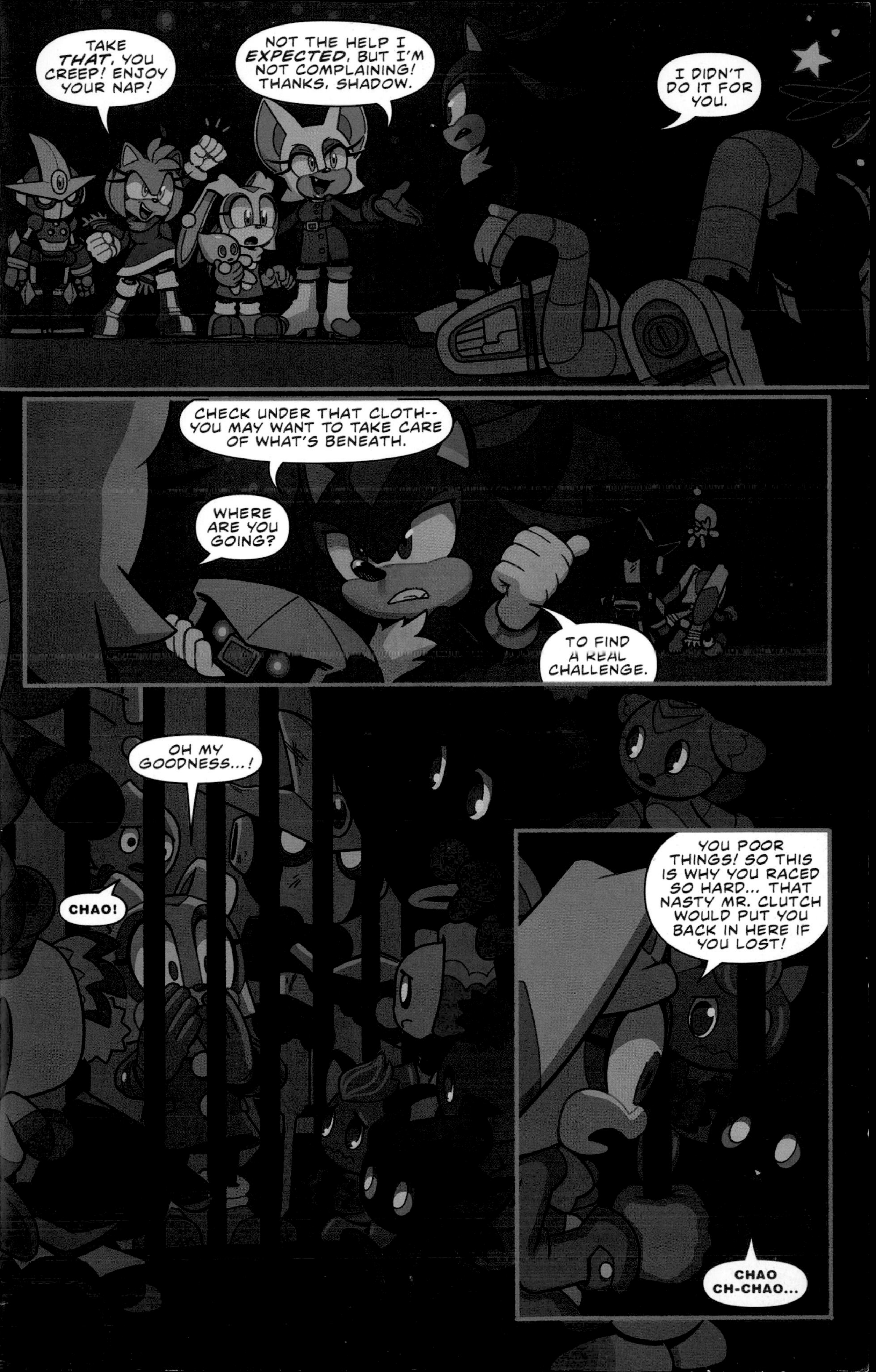
TAKE THAT, YOU CREEP! ENJOY YOUR NAP!
NOT THE HELP I EXPECTED, BUT I'M NOT COMPLAINING! THANKS, SHADOW.
I DIDN'T DO IT FOR YOU.
CHECK UNDER THAT CLOTH-- YOU MAY WANT TO TAKE CARE OF WHAT'S BENEATH.
WHERE ARE YOU GOING?
TO FIND A REAL CHALLENGE.
OH MY GOODNESS...!
CHAO!
YOU POOR THINGS! SO THIS IS WHY YOU RACED SO HARD... THAT NASTY MR. CLUTCH WOULD PUT YOU BACK IN HERE IF YOU LOST!
CHAO CH-CHAO...

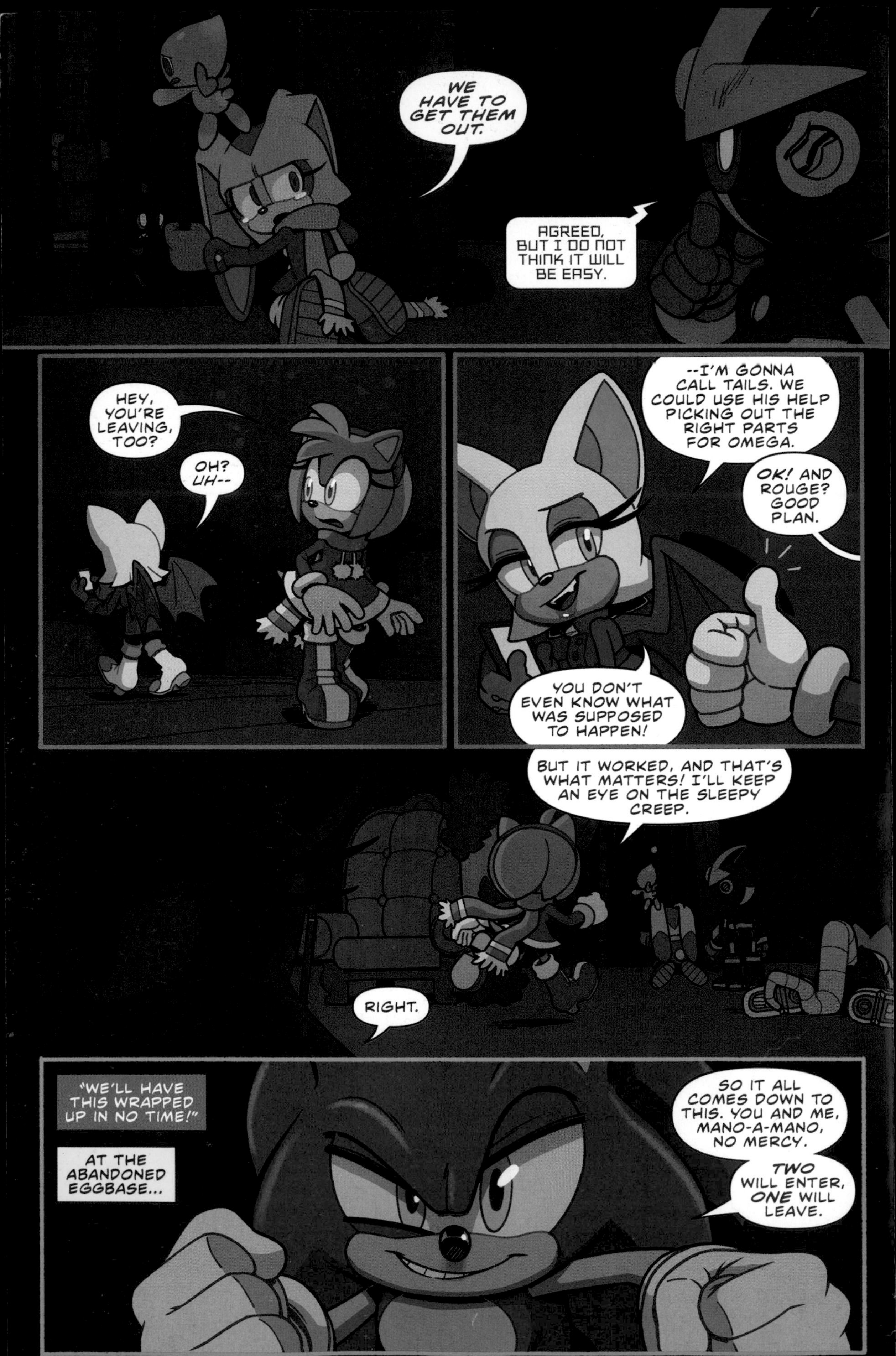
WE HAVE TO GET THEM OUT.
AGREED, BUT I DO NOT THINK IT WILL BE EASY.
HEY, YOU'RE LEAVING, TOO?
OH? UH--
--I'M GONNA CALL TAILS. WE COULD USE HIS HELP PICKING OUT THE RIGHT PARTS FOR OMEGA.
OK! AND ROUGE? GOOD PLAN.
YOU DON'T EVEN KNOW WHAT WAS SUPPOSED TO HAPPEN!
BUT IT WORKED, AND THAT'S WHAT MATTERS! I'LL KEEP AN EYE ON THE SLEEPY CREEP.
RIGHT.
"WE'LL HAVE THIS WRAPPED UP IN NO TIME!"
AT THE ABANDONED EGGBASE...
SO IT ALL COMES DOWN TO THIS. YOU AND ME, MANO-A-MANO, NO MERCY.
TWO WILL ENTER, *ONE* WILL LEAVE.

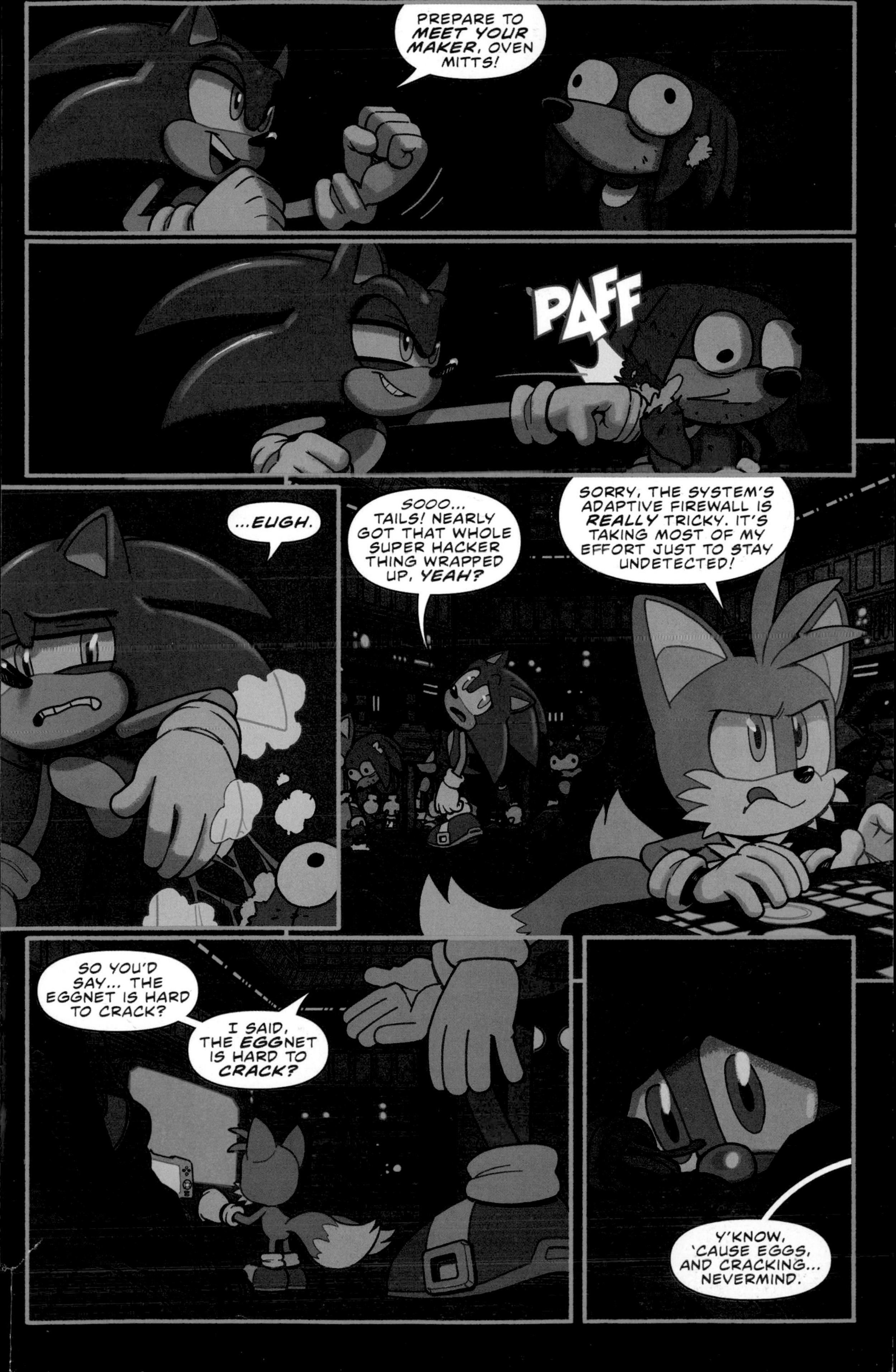
PREPARE TO MEET YOUR MAKER, OVEN MITTS!
PAFF
...EUGH.
SOOO... TAILS! NEARLY GOT THAT WHOLE SUPER HACKER THING WRAPPED UP, YEAH?
SORRY, THE SYSTEM'S ADAPTIVE FIREWALL IS REALLY TRICKY. IT'S TAKING MOST OF MY EFFORT JUST TO STAY UNDETECTED!
SO YOU'D SAY... THE EGGNET IS HARD TO CRACK?
I SAID, THE EGGNET IS HARD TO CRACK?
Y'KNOW, 'CAUSE EGGS, AND CRACKING... NEVERMIND.

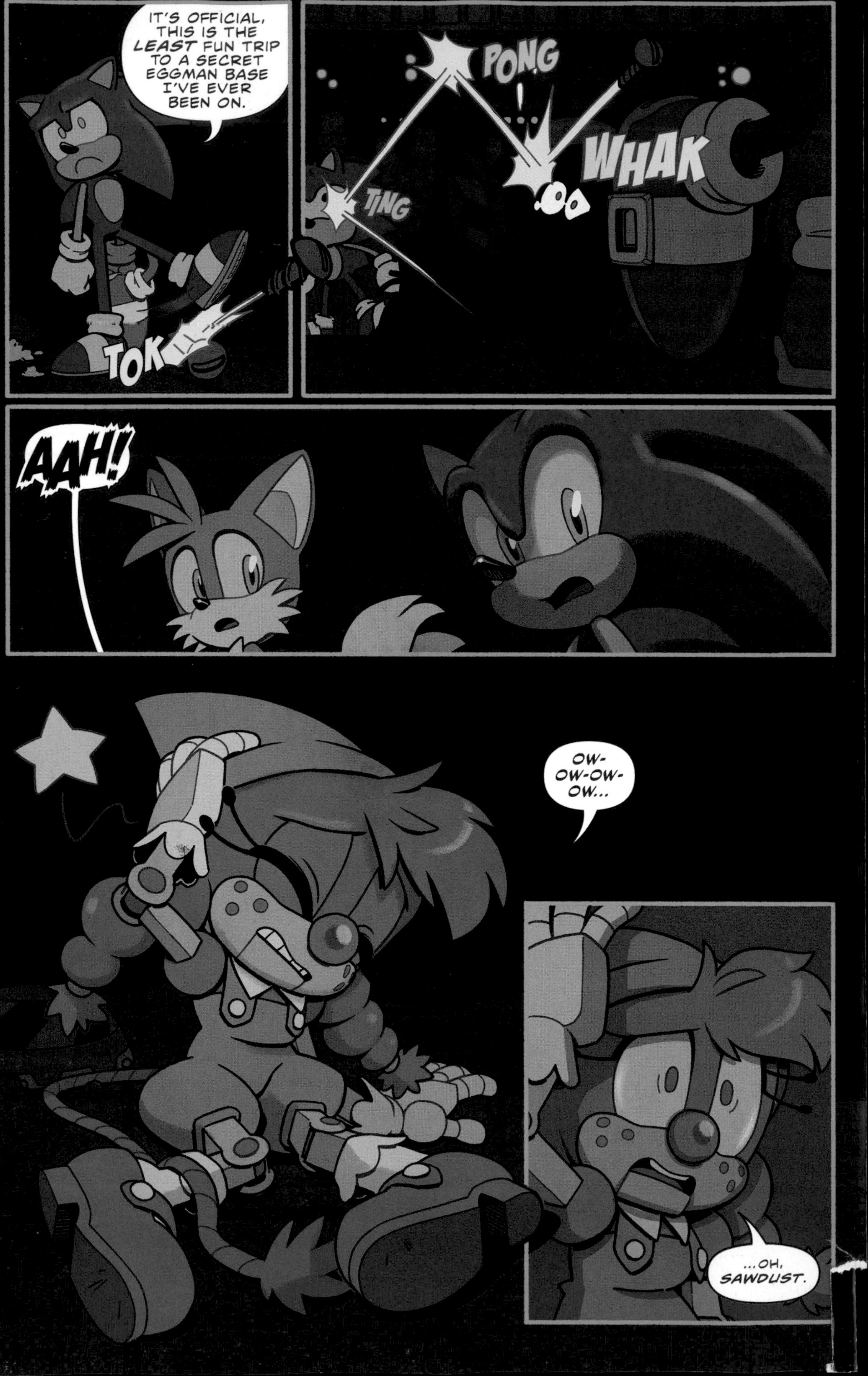
IT'S OFFICIAL, THIS IS THE LEAST FUN TRIP TO A SECRET EGGMAN BASE I'VE EVER BEEN ON.
TOK
TING
PONG
WHAK
AAH!
OW-OW-OW-OW...
...OH, SAWDUST.

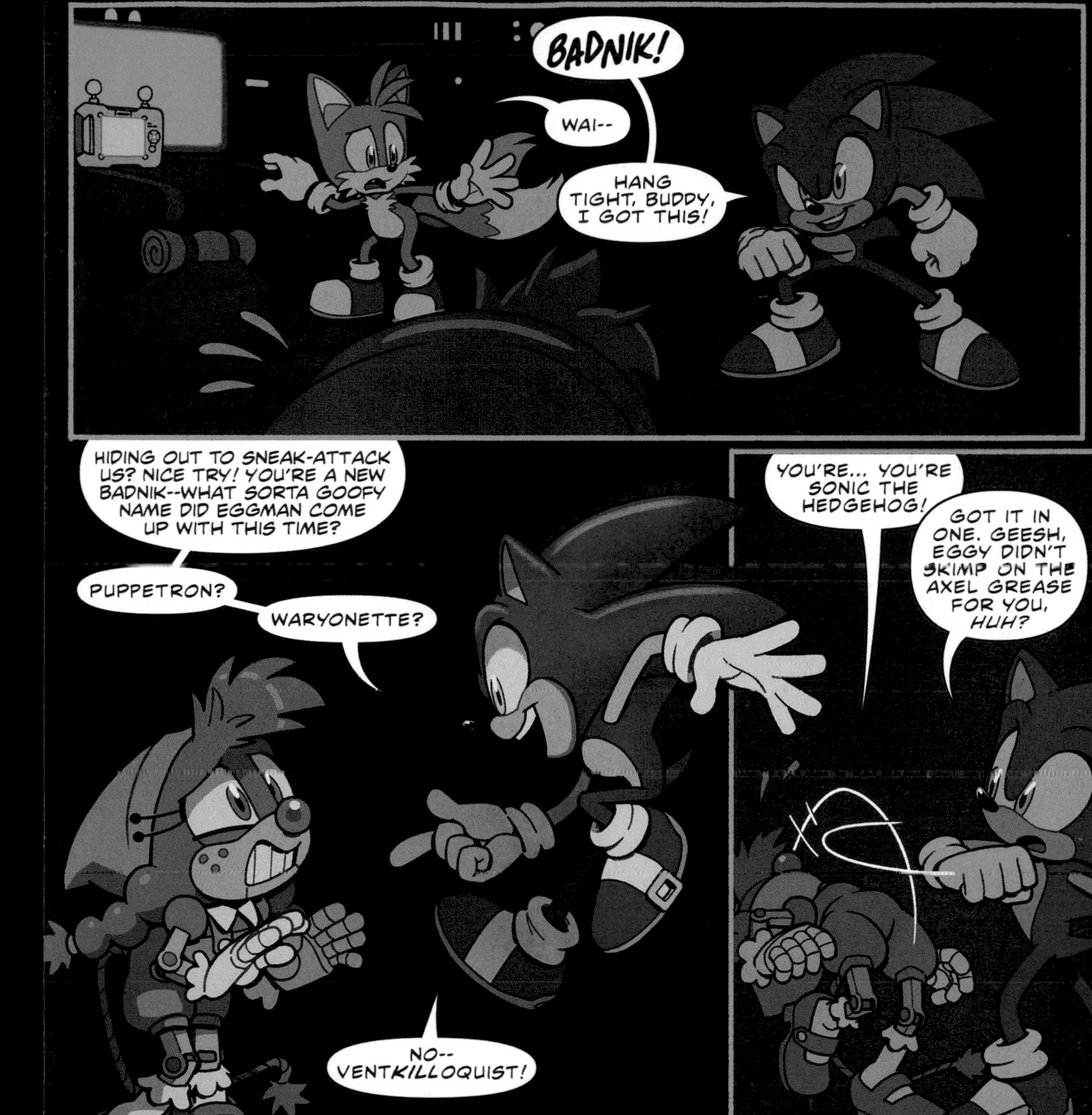

BADNIK!
WAI--
HANG TIGHT, BUDDY, I GOT THIS!
HIDING OUT TO SNEAK-ATTACK US? NICE TRY! YOU'RE A NEW BADNIK--WHAT SORTA GOOFY NAME DID EGGMAN COME UP WITH THIS TIME?
PUPPETRON?
WARYONETTE?
NO-- VENTKILLOQUIST!
YOU'RE... YOU'RE SONIC THE HEDGEHOG!
GOT IT IN ONE. GEESH, EGGY DIDN'T SKIMP ON THE AXEL GREASE FOR YOU, HUH?
I DON'T WANT TO-- YEEK!
SONIC, I DON'T THINK THAT'S A BADNIK!

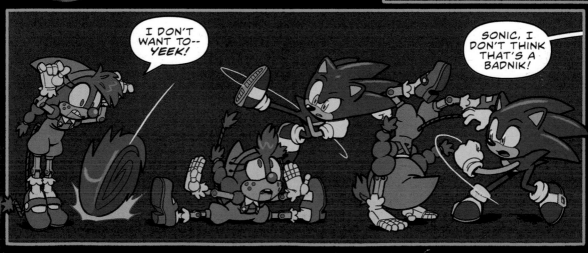

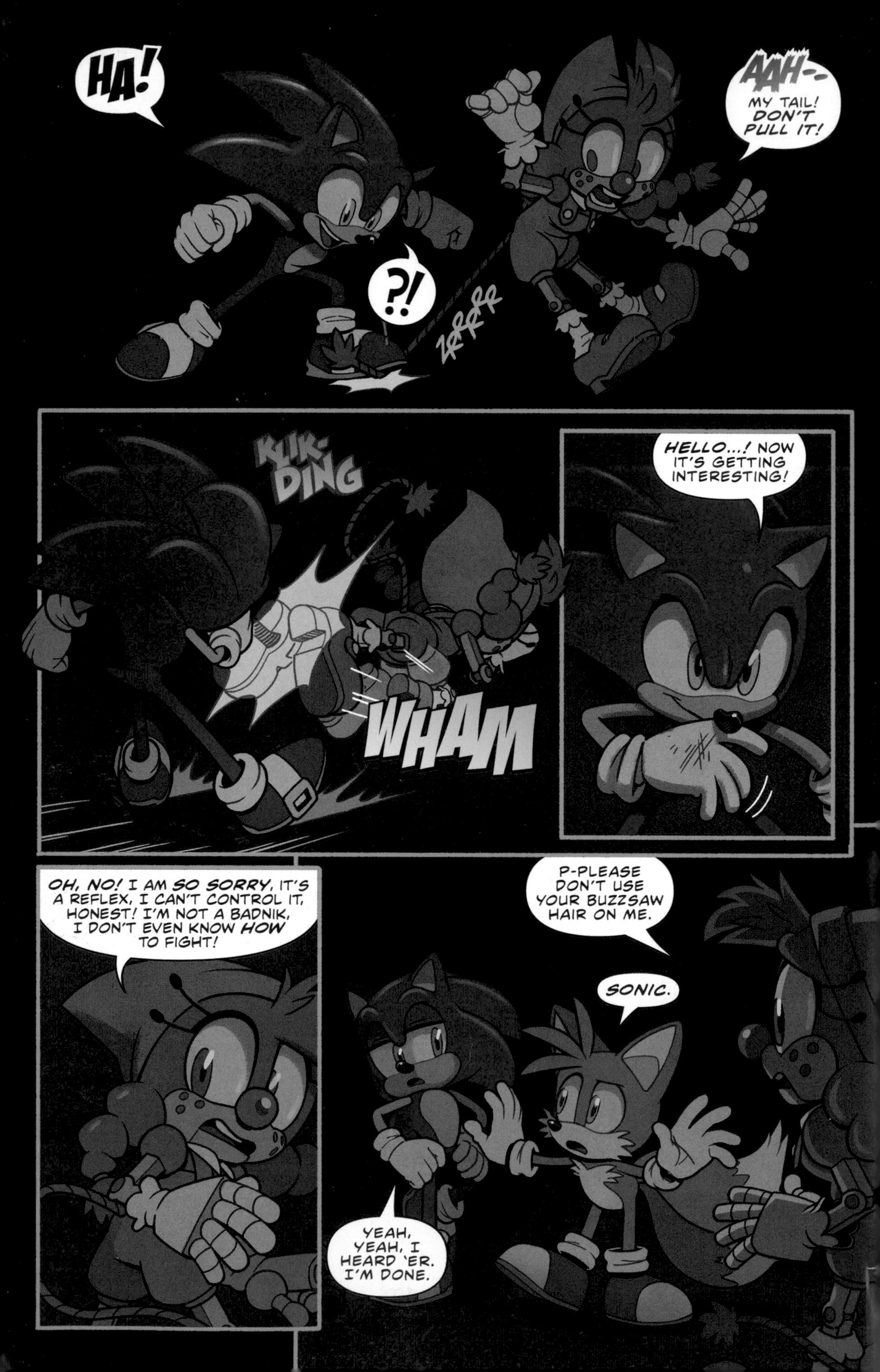
HA!
AAH--
MY TAIL! DON'T PULL IT!
?!
ZRRRR
KLIK-DING
WHAM
HELLO...! NOW IT'S GETTING INTERESTING!
OH, NO! I AM SO SORRY, IT'S A REFLEX, I CAN'T CONTROL IT, HONEST! I'M NOT A BADNIK, I DON'T EVEN KNOW HOW TO FIGHT!
P-PLEASE DON'T USE YOUR BUZZSAW HAIR ON ME.
SONIC.
YEAH, YEAH, I HEARD 'ER. I'M DONE.

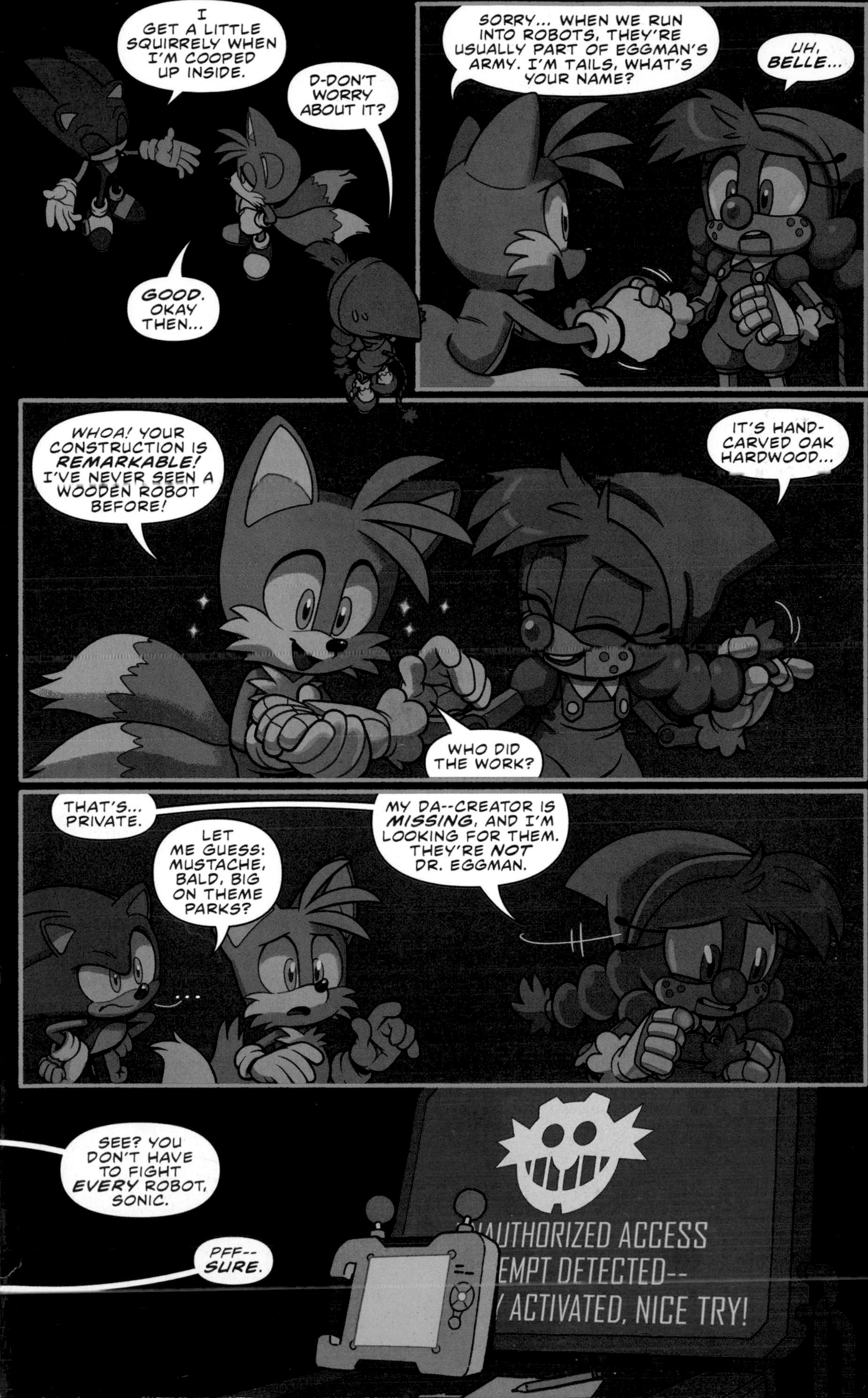
I GET A LITTLE SQUIRRELY WHEN I'M COOPED UP INSIDE.
D-DON'T WORRY ABOUT IT?
GOOD. OKAY THEN...
SORRY... WHEN WE RUN INTO ROBOTS, THEY'RE USUALLY PART OF EGGMAN'S ARMY. I'M TAILS, WHAT'S YOUR NAME?
UH, BELLE...
WHOA! YOUR CONSTRUCTION IS REMARKABLE! I'VE NEVER SEEN A WOODEN ROBOT BEFORE!
IT'S HAND-CARVED OAK HARDWOOD...
WHO DID THE WORK?
THAT'S... PRIVATE.
MY DA--CREATOR IS MISSING, AND I'M LOOKING FOR THEM. THEY'RE NOT DR. EGGMAN.
LET ME GUESS: MUSTACHE, BALD, BIG ON THEME PARKS?
...
SEE? YOU DON'T HAVE TO FIGHT EVERY ROBOT, SONIC.
PFF-- SURE.
UNAUTHORIZED ACCESS
EMPT DETECTED--
ACTIVATED, NICE TRY!

BREEP
BREEP
BREEP

SHOOT! I FORGOT ABOUT THE FIREWALL!

EVERYTHING'S LOCKED...

...HORIZED ACCESS ...PT DETECTED-- ...ACTIVATED, NICE TRY!

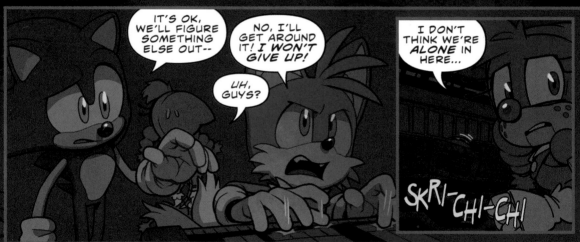
IT'S OK, WE'LL FIGURE SOMETHING ELSE OUT--

NO, I'LL GET AROUND IT! I WON'T GIVE UP!

UH, GUYS?

I DON'T THINK WE'RE ALONE IN HERE...

SKRI-CHI-CHI

CRASH

YEEK!

GEARS AND STARTERS!

YOU CAN SAY THAT AGAIN.

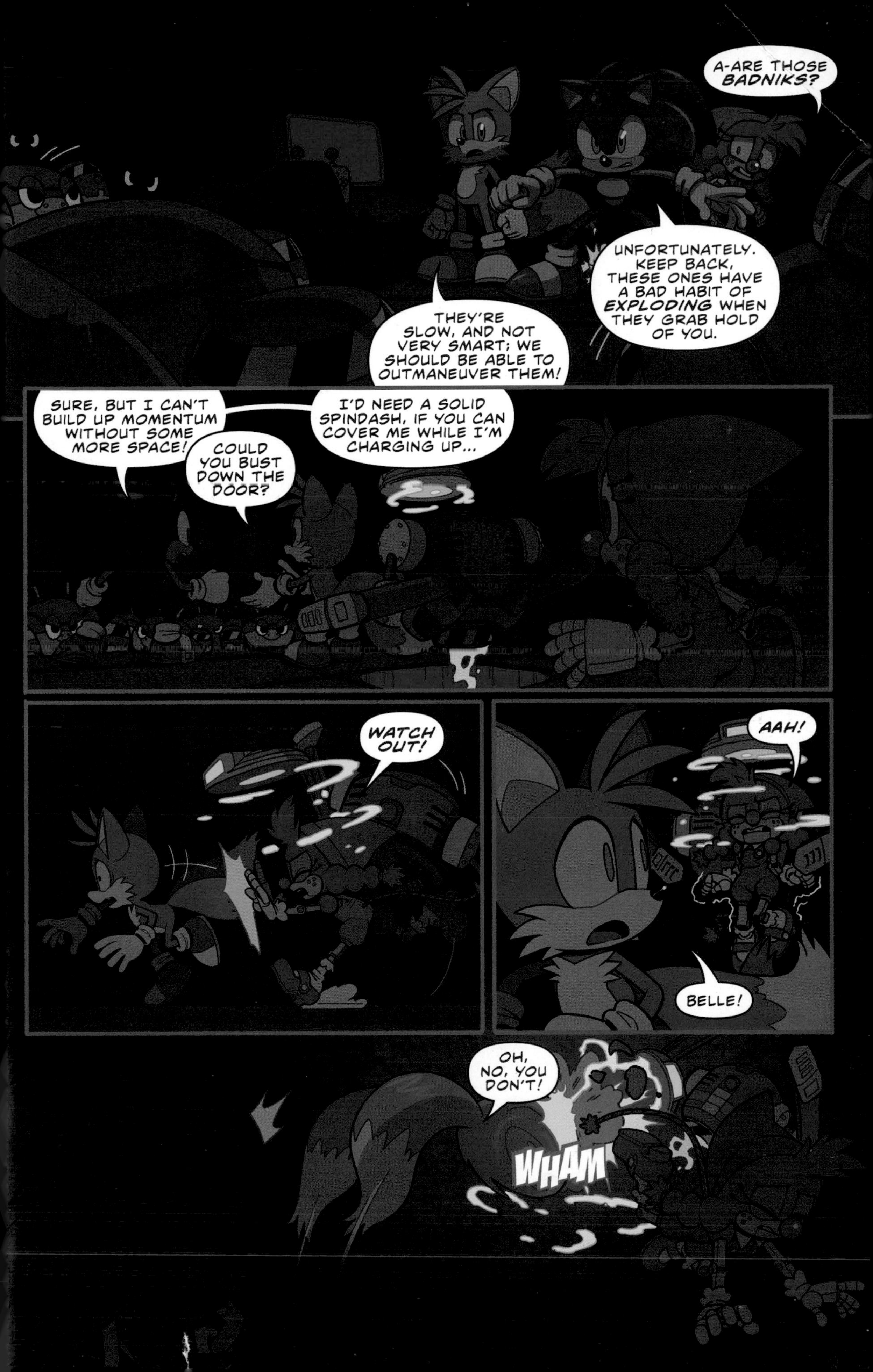
A-ARE THOSE *BADNIKS?*
UNFORTUNATELY. KEEP BACK, THESE ONES HAVE A BAD HABIT OF *EXPLODING* WHEN THEY GRAB HOLD OF YOU.
THEY'RE SLOW, AND NOT VERY SMART; WE SHOULD BE ABLE TO OUTMANEUVER THEM!
SURE, BUT I CAN'T BUILD UP MOMENTUM WITHOUT SOME MORE SPACE!
I'D NEED A SOLID SPINDASH, IF YOU CAN COVER ME WHILE I'M CHARGING UP...
COULD YOU BUST DOWN THE DOOR?
WATCH OUT!
AAH!
BELLE!
OH, NO, YOU DON'T!
WHAM

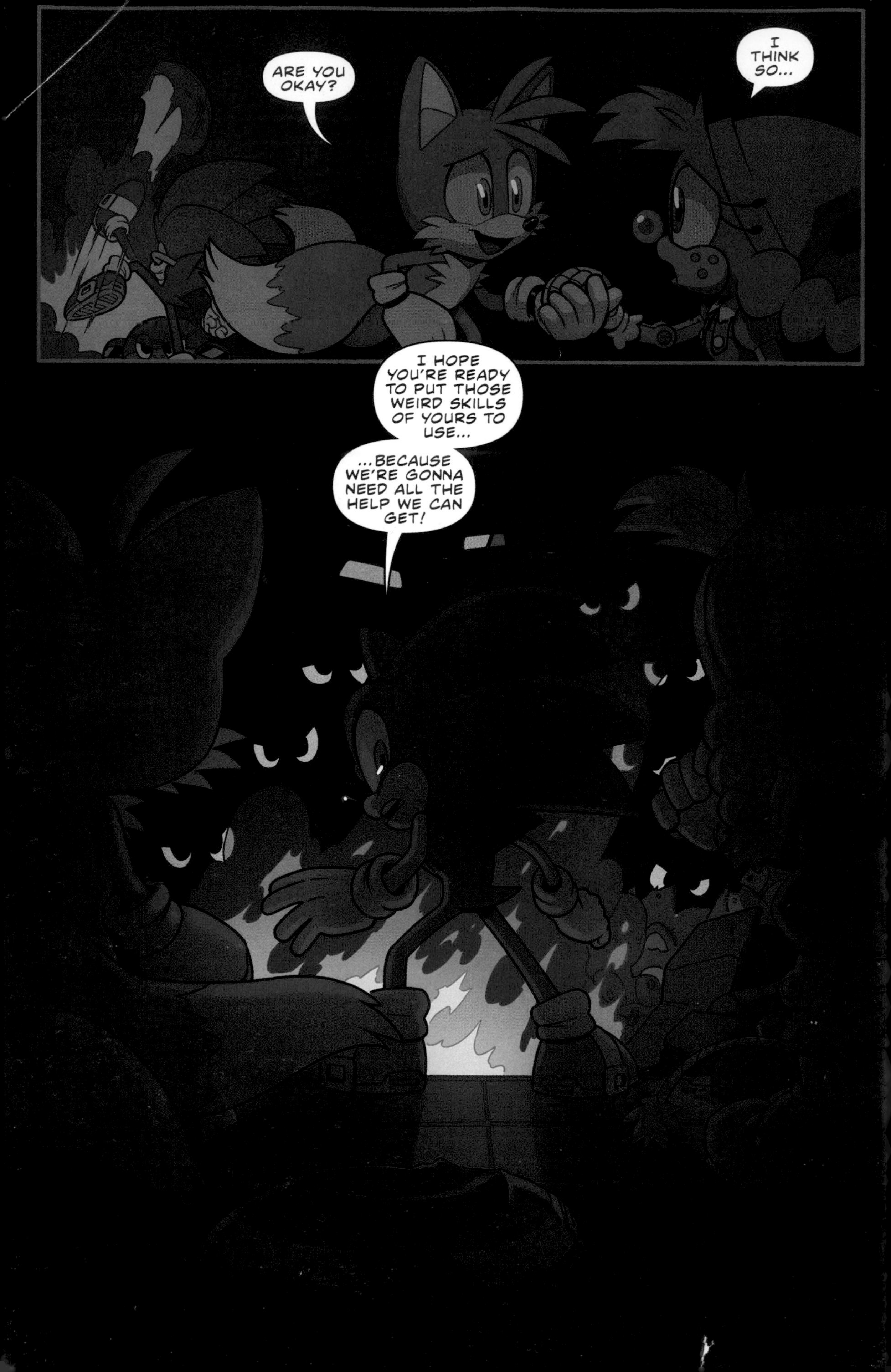
ARE YOU OKAY?
I THINK SO...
I HOPE YOU'RE READY TO PUT THOSE WEIRD SKILLS OF YOURS TO USE...
...BECAUSE WE'RE GONNA NEED ALL THE HELP WE CAN GET!

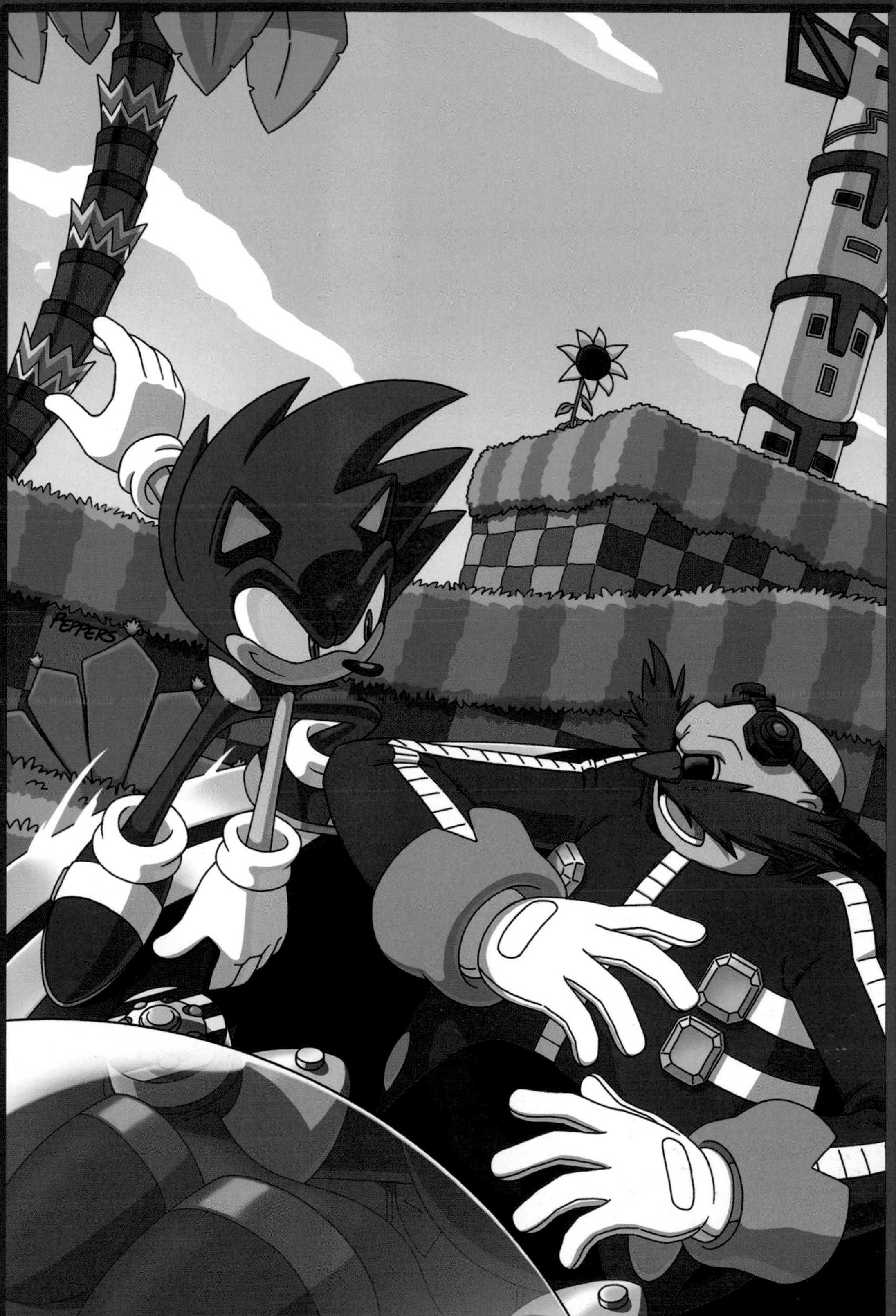
PEPPERS

ART BY **JAMAL PEPPERS**

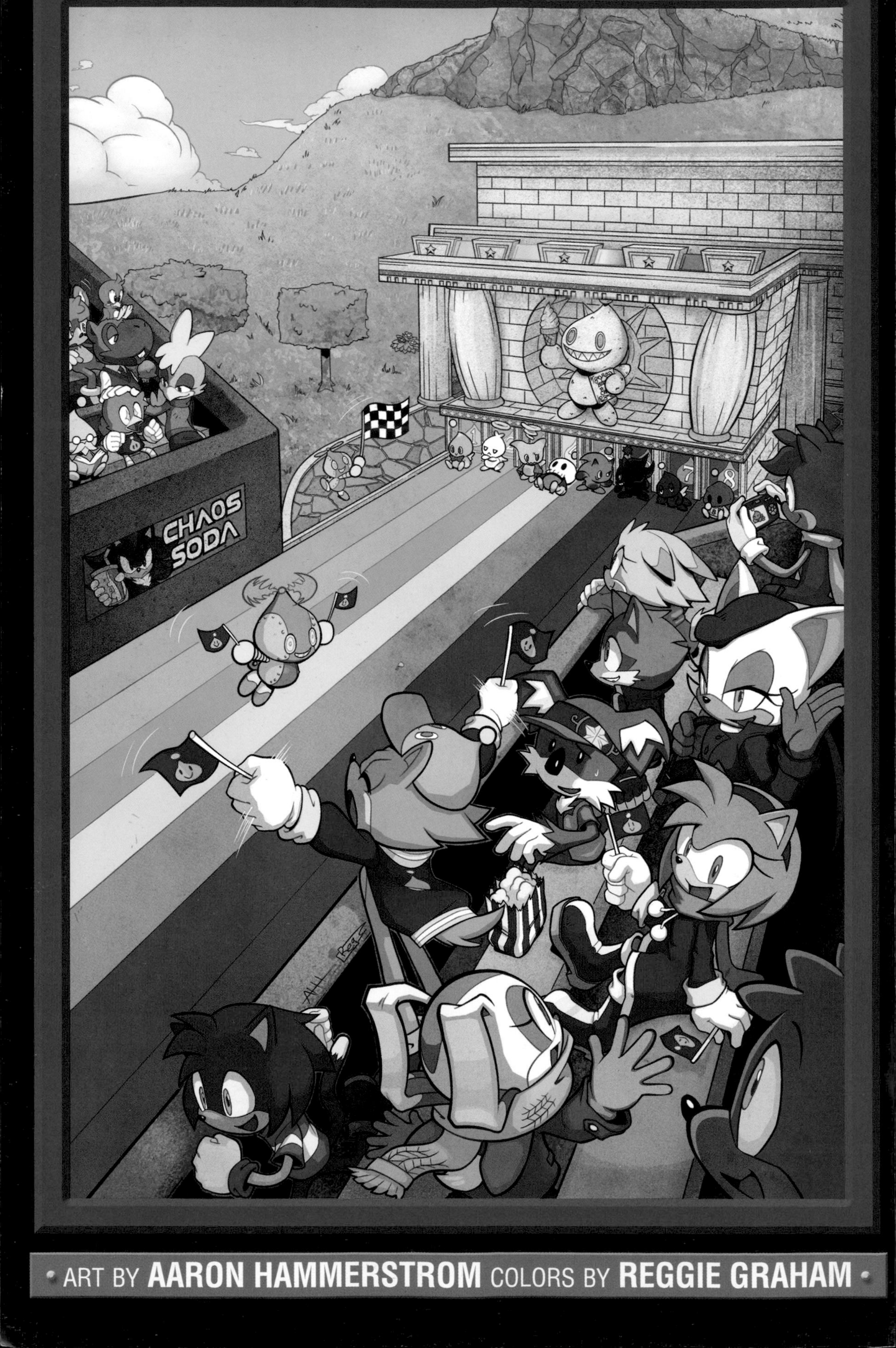
CHAOS
SODA

ART BY **AARON HAMMERSTROM** COLORS BY **REGGIE GRAHAM**

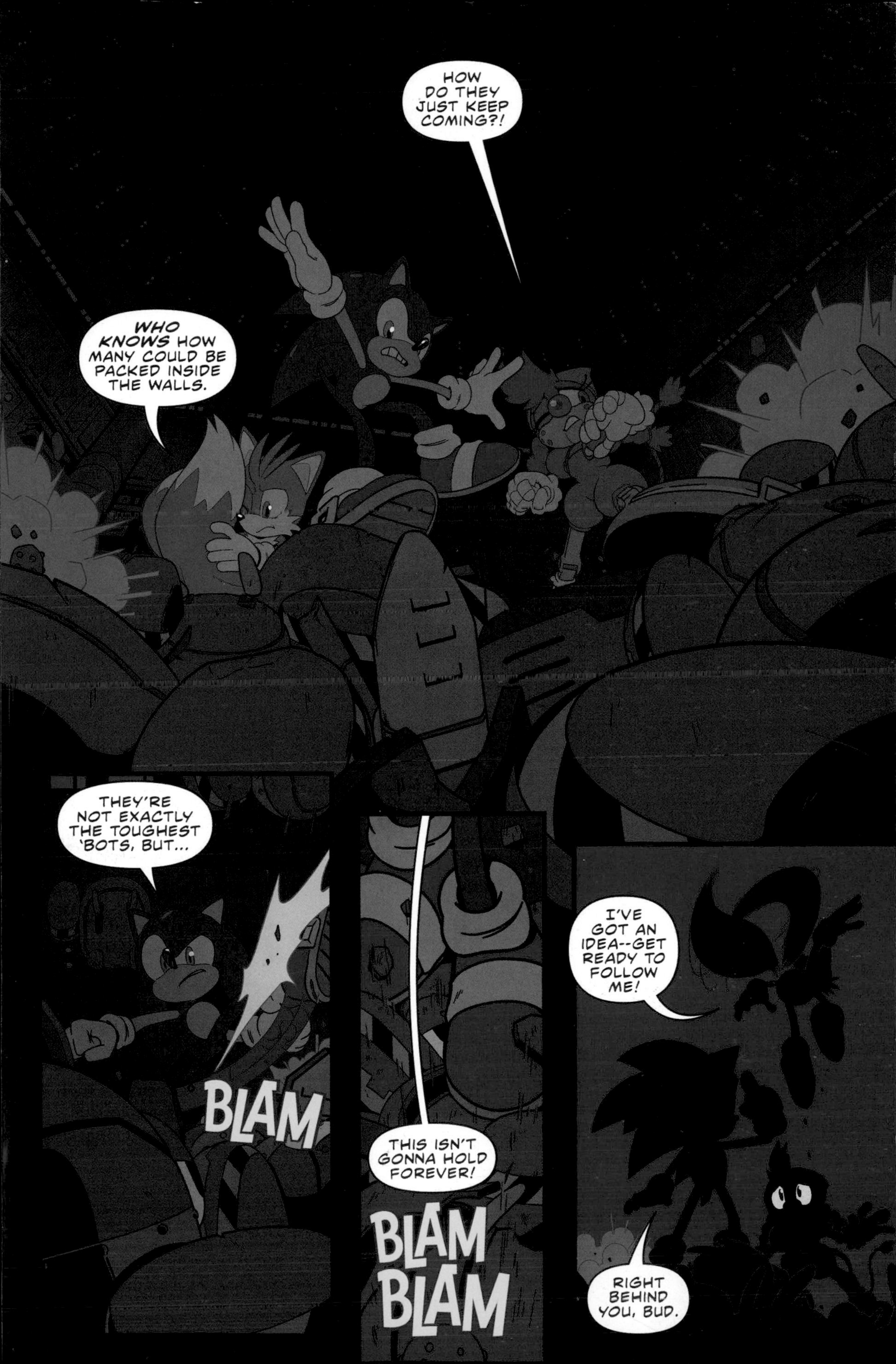
HOW DO THEY JUST KEEP COMING?!
WHO KNOWS HOW MANY COULD BE PACKED INSIDE THE WALLS.
THEY'RE NOT EXACTLY THE TOUGHEST 'BOTS, BUT...
BLAM
THIS ISN'T GONNA HOLD FOREVER!
BLAM
BLAM
I'VE GOT AN IDEA--GET READY TO FOLLOW ME!
RIGHT BEHIND YOU, BUD.

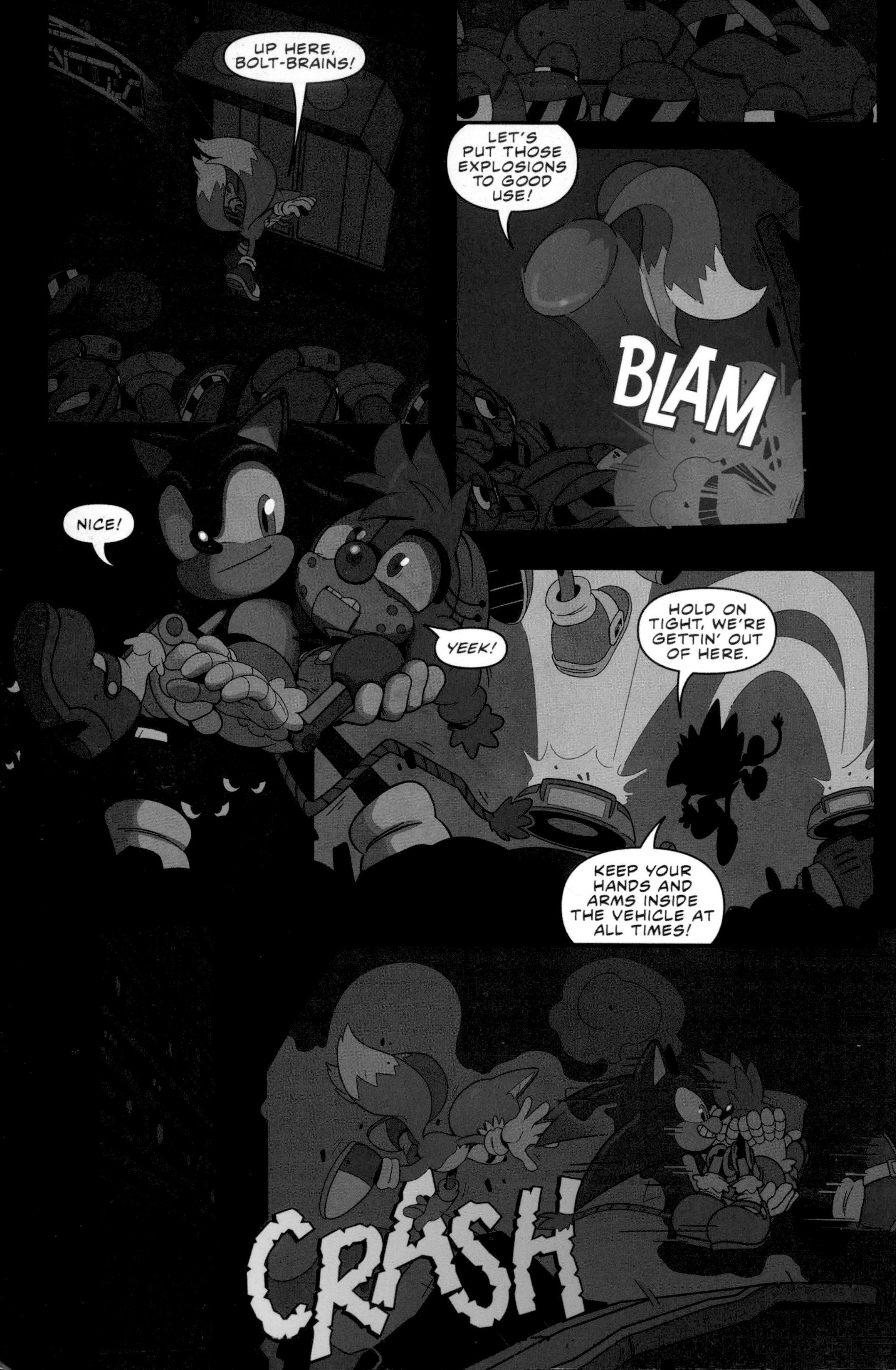
UP HERE, BOLT-BRAINS!
LET'S PUT THOSE EXPLOSIONS TO GOOD USE!
BLAM
NICE!
YEEK!
HOLD ON TIGHT, WE'RE GETTIN' OUT OF HERE.
KEEP YOUR HANDS AND ARMS INSIDE THE VEHICLE AT ALL TIMES!
CRASH

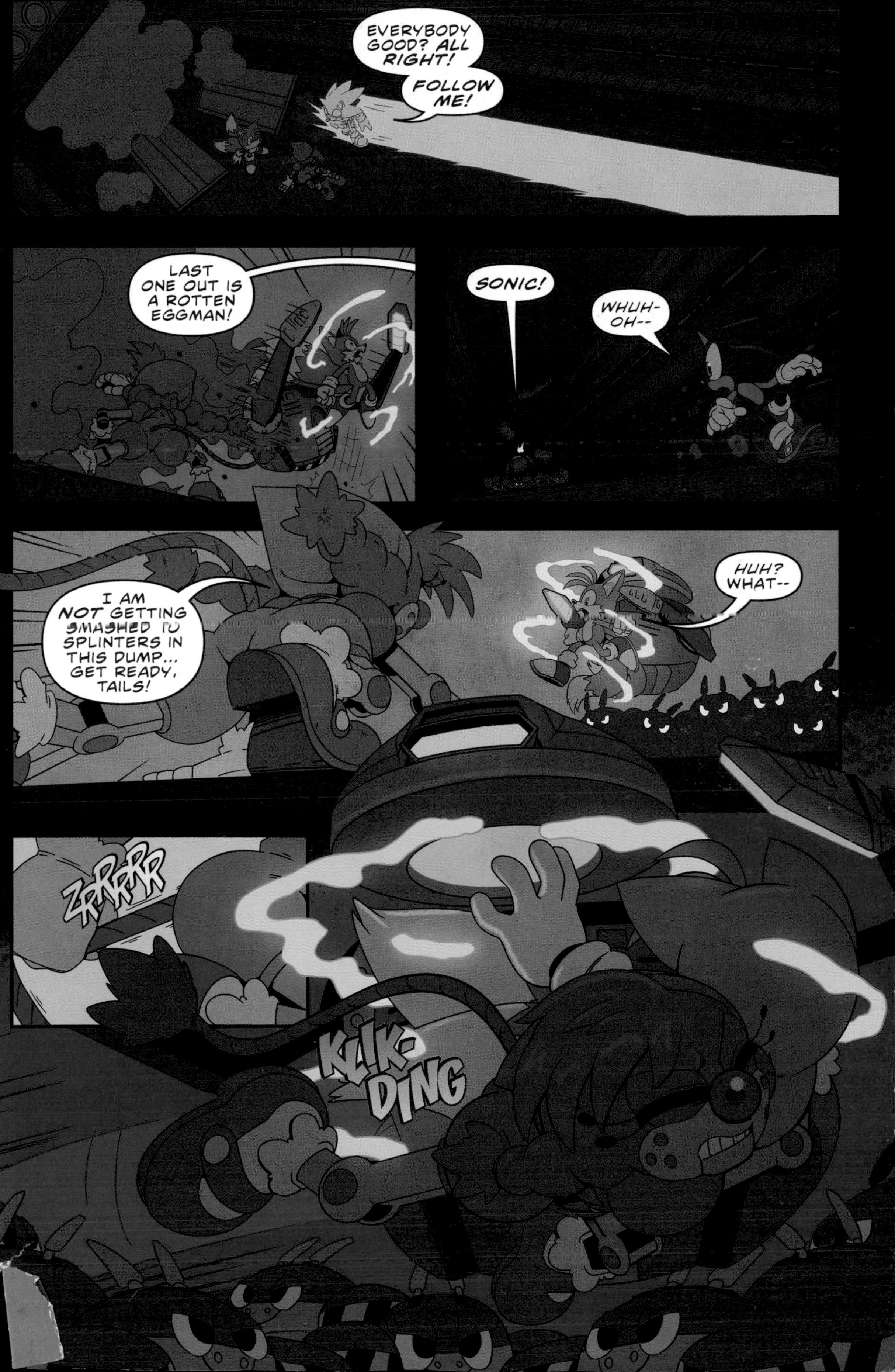
EVERYBODY GOOD? ALL RIGHT!
FOLLOW ME!
LAST ONE OUT IS A ROTTEN EGGMAN!
SONIC!
WHUH-OH--
I AM NOT GETTING SMASHED TO SPLINTERS IN THIS DUMP... GET READY, TAILS!
HUH? WHAT--
ZRRRRR
KLIK-DING

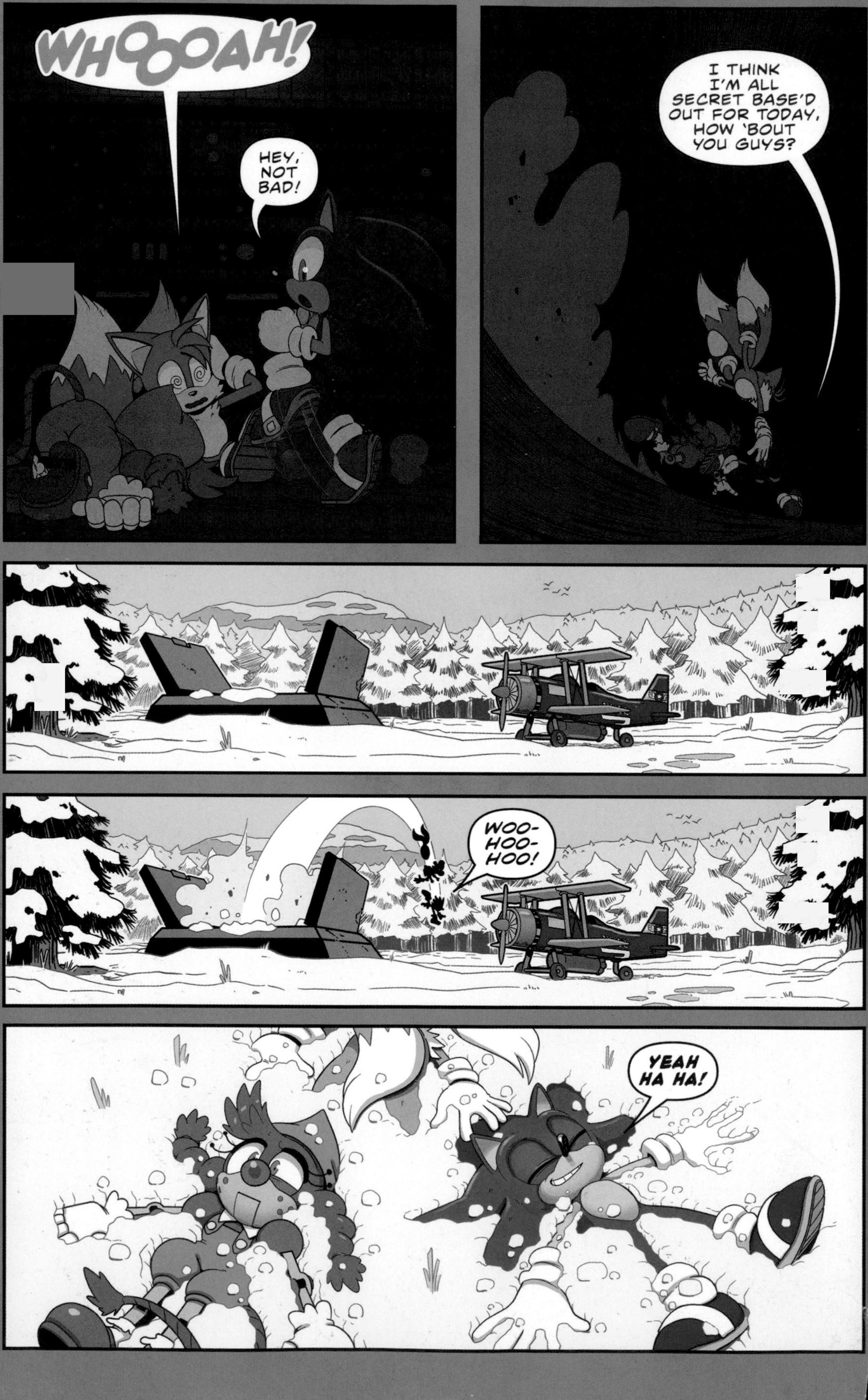
WHOOOOAH!
HEY, NOT BAD!
I THINK I'M ALL SECRET BASE'D OUT FOR TODAY, HOW 'BOUT YOU GUYS?
WOO-HOO-HOO!
YEAH HA HA!

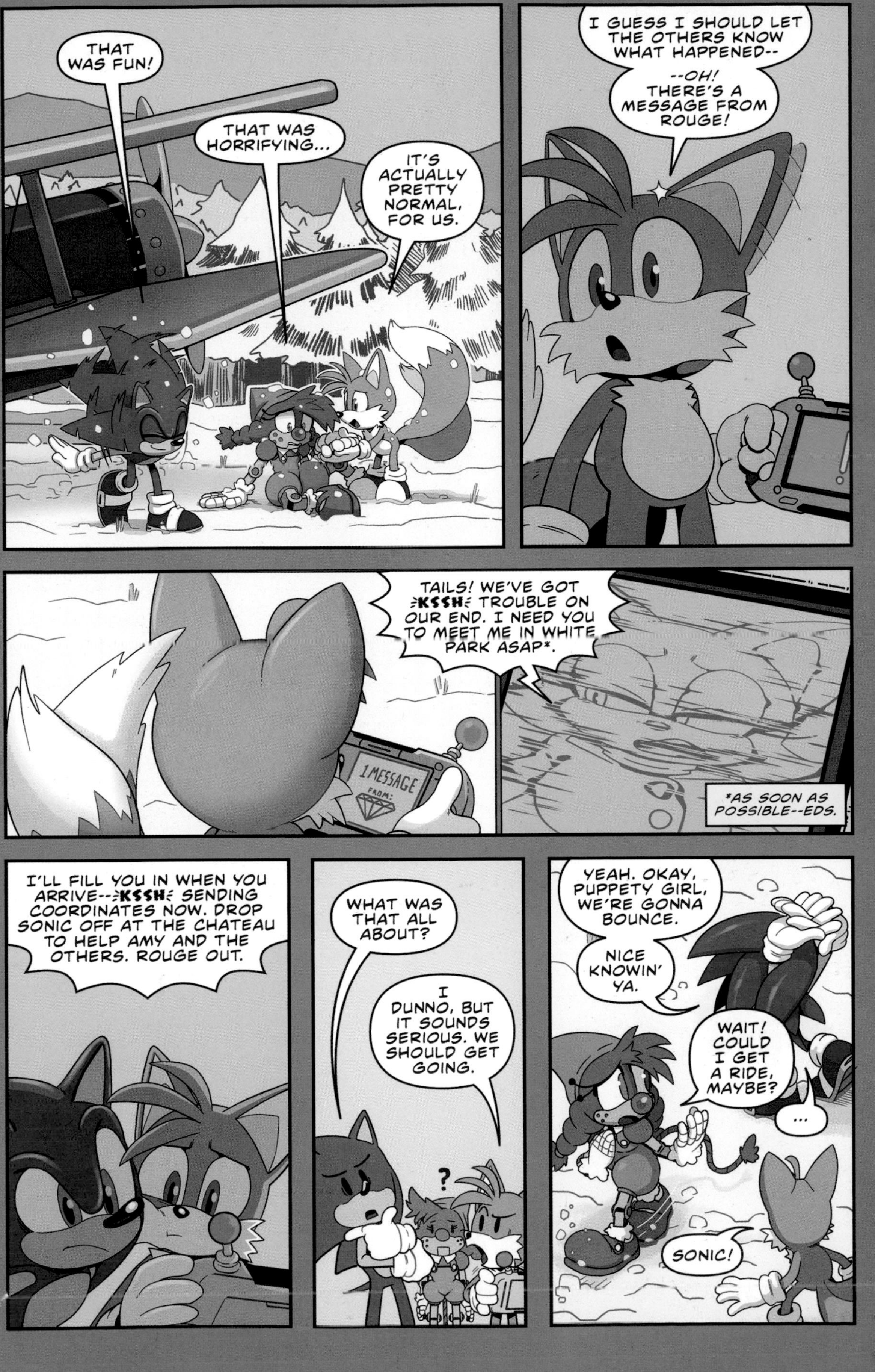
THAT WAS FUN!
THAT WAS HORRIFYING...
IT'S ACTUALLY PRETTY NORMAL, FOR US.
I GUESS I SHOULD LET THE OTHERS KNOW WHAT HAPPENED--
--OH! THERE'S A MESSAGE FROM ROUGE!
TAILS! WE'VE GOT KSSH TROUBLE ON OUR END. I NEED YOU TO MEET ME IN WHITE PARK ASAP*.
1 MESSAGE FROM:
*AS SOON AS POSSIBLE--EDS.
I'LL FILL YOU IN WHEN YOU ARRIVE--KSSH SENDING COORDINATES NOW. DROP SONIC OFF AT THE CHATEAU TO HELP AMY AND THE OTHERS. ROUGE OUT.
WHAT WAS THAT ALL ABOUT?
I DUNNO, BUT IT SOUNDS SERIOUS. WE SHOULD GET GOING.
?
YEAH. OKAY, PUPPETY GIRL, WE'RE GONNA BOUNCE.
NICE KNOWIN' YA.
WAIT! COULD I GET A RIDE, MAYBE?
...
SONIC!

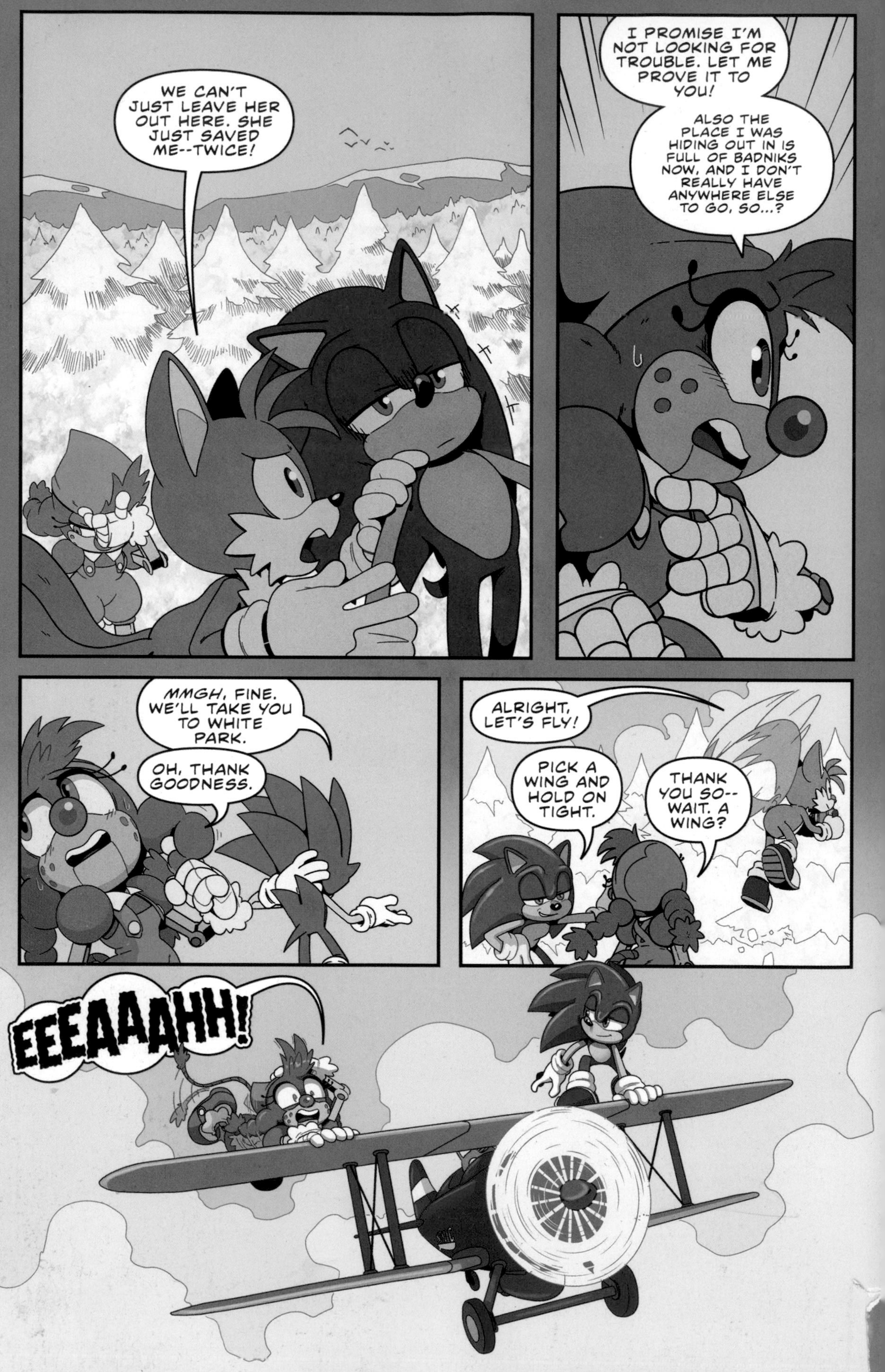
WE CAN'T JUST LEAVE HER OUT HERE. SHE JUST SAVED ME--TWICE!
I PROMISE I'M NOT LOOKING FOR TROUBLE. LET ME PROVE IT TO YOU!
ALSO THE PLACE I WAS HIDING OUT IN IS FULL OF BADNIKS NOW, AND I DON'T REALLY HAVE ANYWHERE ELSE TO GO, SO...?
MMGH, FINE. WE'LL TAKE YOU TO WHITE PARK.
OH, THANK GOODNESS.
ALRIGHT, LET'S FLY!
PICK A WING AND HOLD ON TIGHT.
THANK YOU SO-- WAIT. A WING?
EEEAAAHH!

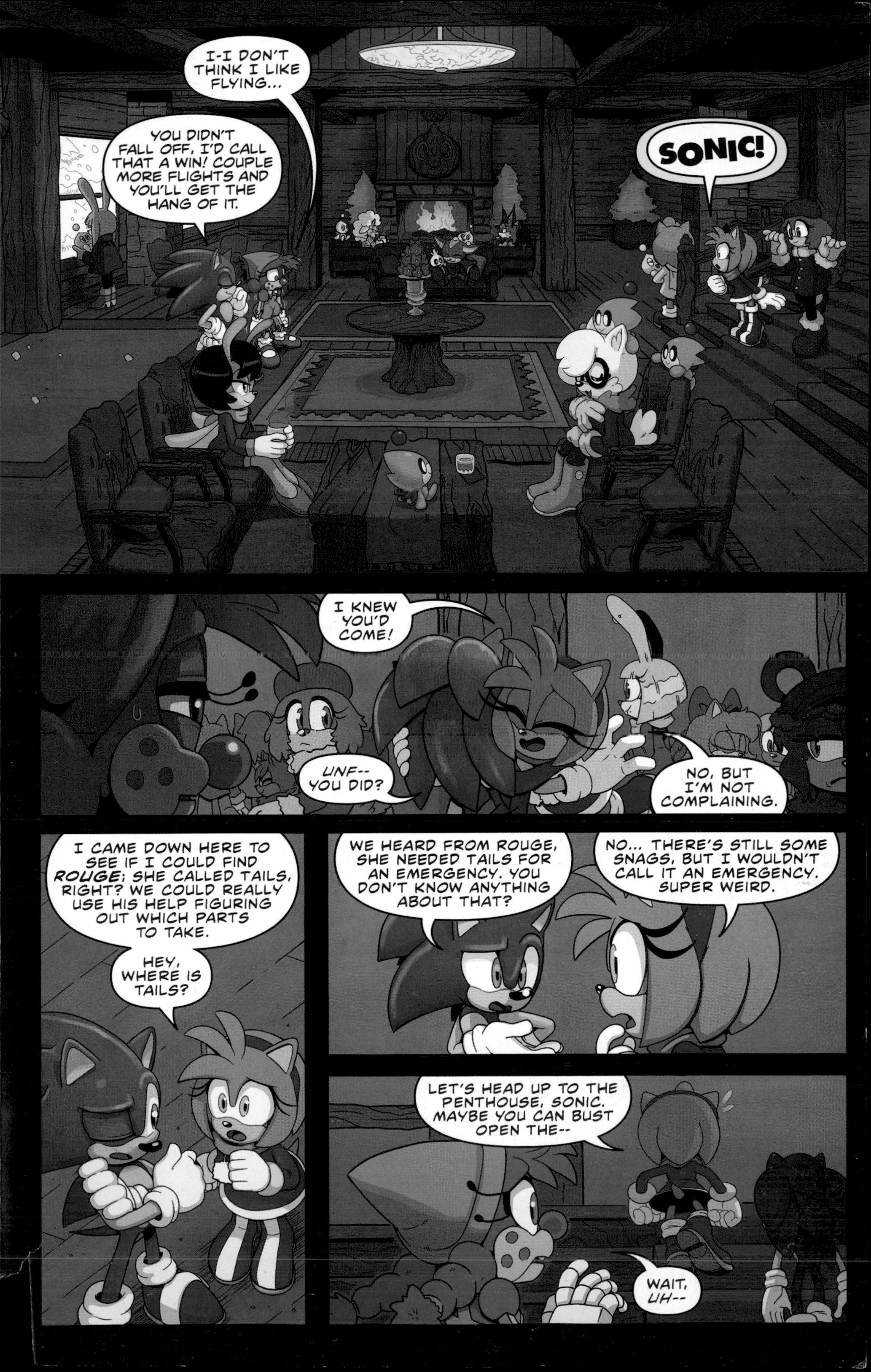
YOU DIDN'T FALL OFF, I'D CALL THAT A WIN! COUPLE MORE FLIGHTS AND YOU'LL GET THE HANG OF IT.
I-I DON'T THINK I LIKE FLYING...
SONIC!
I KNEW YOU'D COME!
UNF-- YOU DID?
NO, BUT I'M NOT COMPLAINING.
I CAME DOWN HERE TO SEE IF I COULD FIND ROUGE; SHE CALLED TAILS, RIGHT? WE COULD REALLY USE HIS HELP FIGURING OUT WHICH PARTS TO TAKE.
HEY, WHERE IS TAILS?
WE HEARD FROM ROUGE, SHE NEEDED TAILS FOR AN EMERGENCY. YOU DON'T KNOW ANYTHING ABOUT THAT?
NO... THERE'S STILL SOME SNAGS, BUT I WOULDN'T CALL IT AN EMERGENCY. SUPER WEIRD.
LET'S HEAD UP TO THE PENTHOUSE, SONIC. MAYBE YOU CAN BUST OPEN THE--
WAIT, UH--

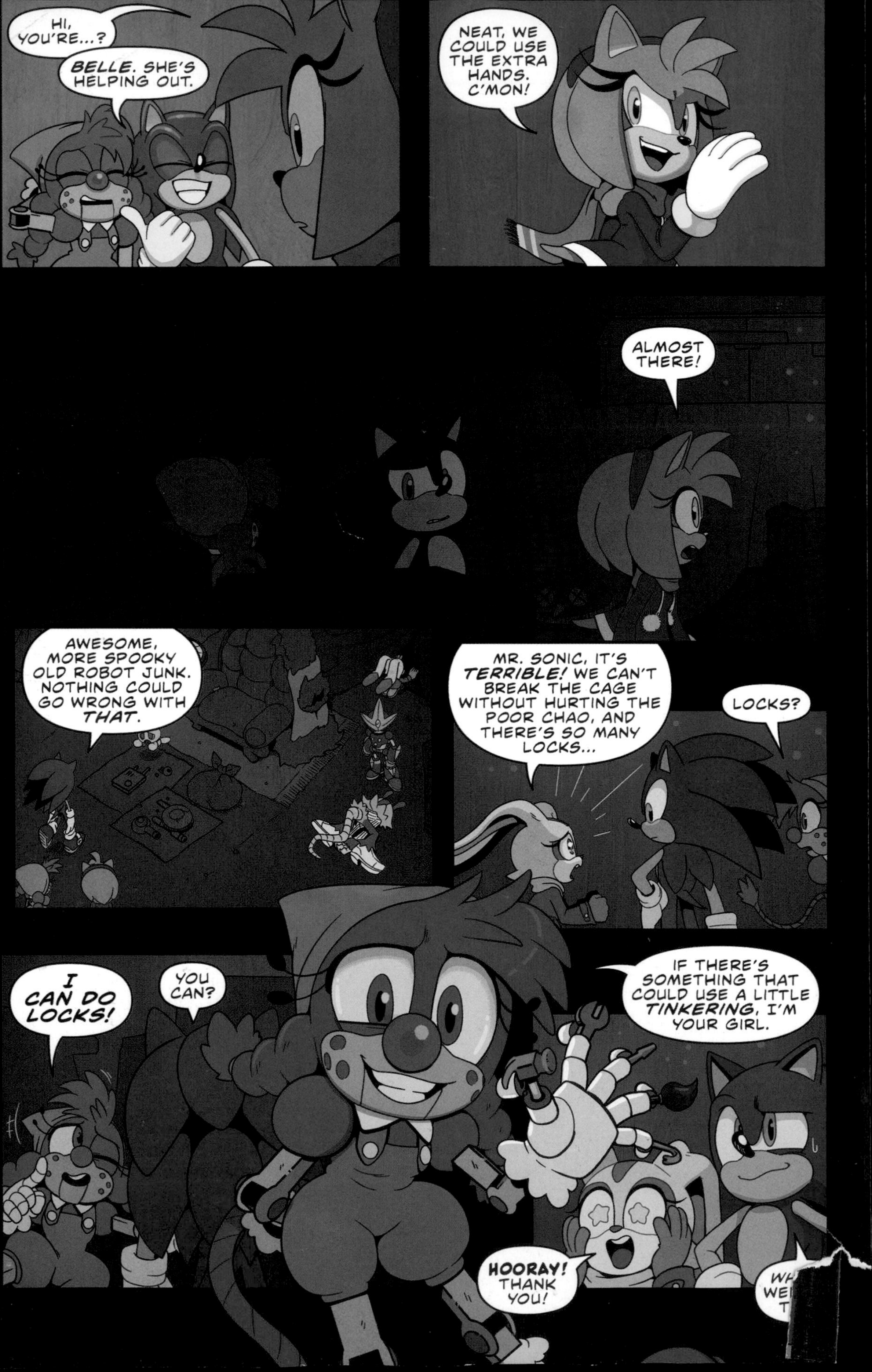
HI, YOU'RE...?
BELLE. SHE'S HELPING OUT.
NEAT, WE COULD USE THE EXTRA HANDS. C'MON!
ALMOST THERE!
AWESOME, MORE SPOOKY OLD ROBOT JUNK. NOTHING COULD GO WRONG WITH *THAT*.
MR. SONIC, IT'S *TERRIBLE!* WE CAN'T BREAK THE CAGE WITHOUT HURTING THE POOR CHAO, AND THERE'S SO MANY LOCKS...
LOCKS?
I CAN DO LOCKS!
YOU CAN?
IF THERE'S SOMETHING THAT COULD USE A LITTLE *TINKERING*, I'M YOUR GIRL.
HOORAY! THANK YOU!

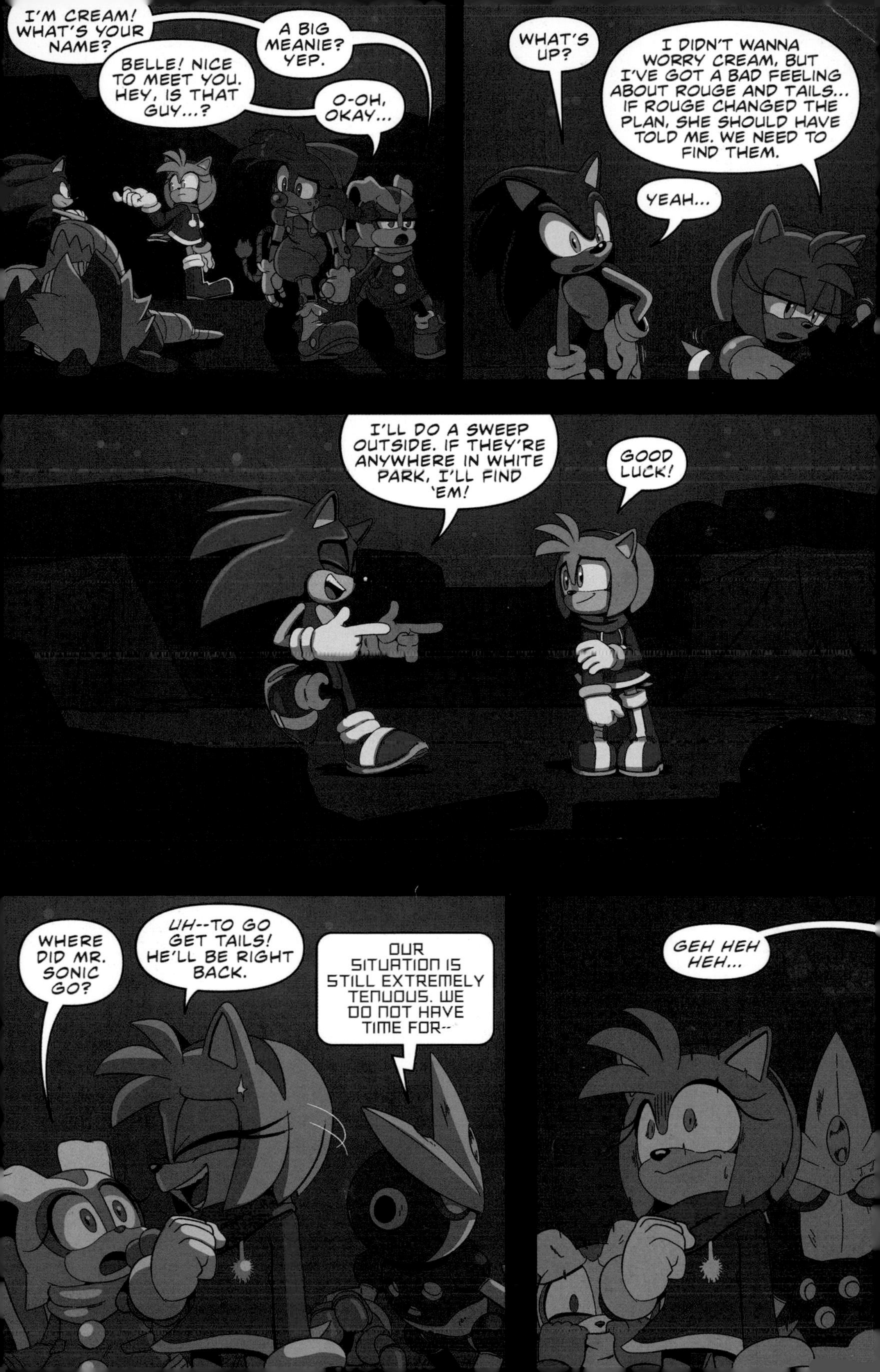
I'M CREAM! WHAT'S YOUR NAME?
BELLE! NICE TO MEET YOU. HEY, IS THAT GUY...?
A BIG MEANIE? YEP.
O-OH, OKAY...
WHAT'S UP?
I DIDN'T WANNA WORRY CREAM, BUT I'VE GOT A BAD FEELING ABOUT ROUGE AND TAILS... IF ROUGE CHANGED THE PLAN, SHE SHOULD HAVE TOLD ME. WE NEED TO FIND THEM.
YEAH...
I'LL DO A SWEEP OUTSIDE. IF THEY'RE ANYWHERE IN WHITE PARK, I'LL FIND 'EM!
GOOD LUCK!
WHERE DID MR. SONIC GO?
UH--TO GO GET TAILS! HE'LL BE RIGHT BACK.
OUR SITUATION IS STILL EXTREMELY TENUOUS. WE DO NOT HAVE TIME FOR--
GEH HEH HEH...

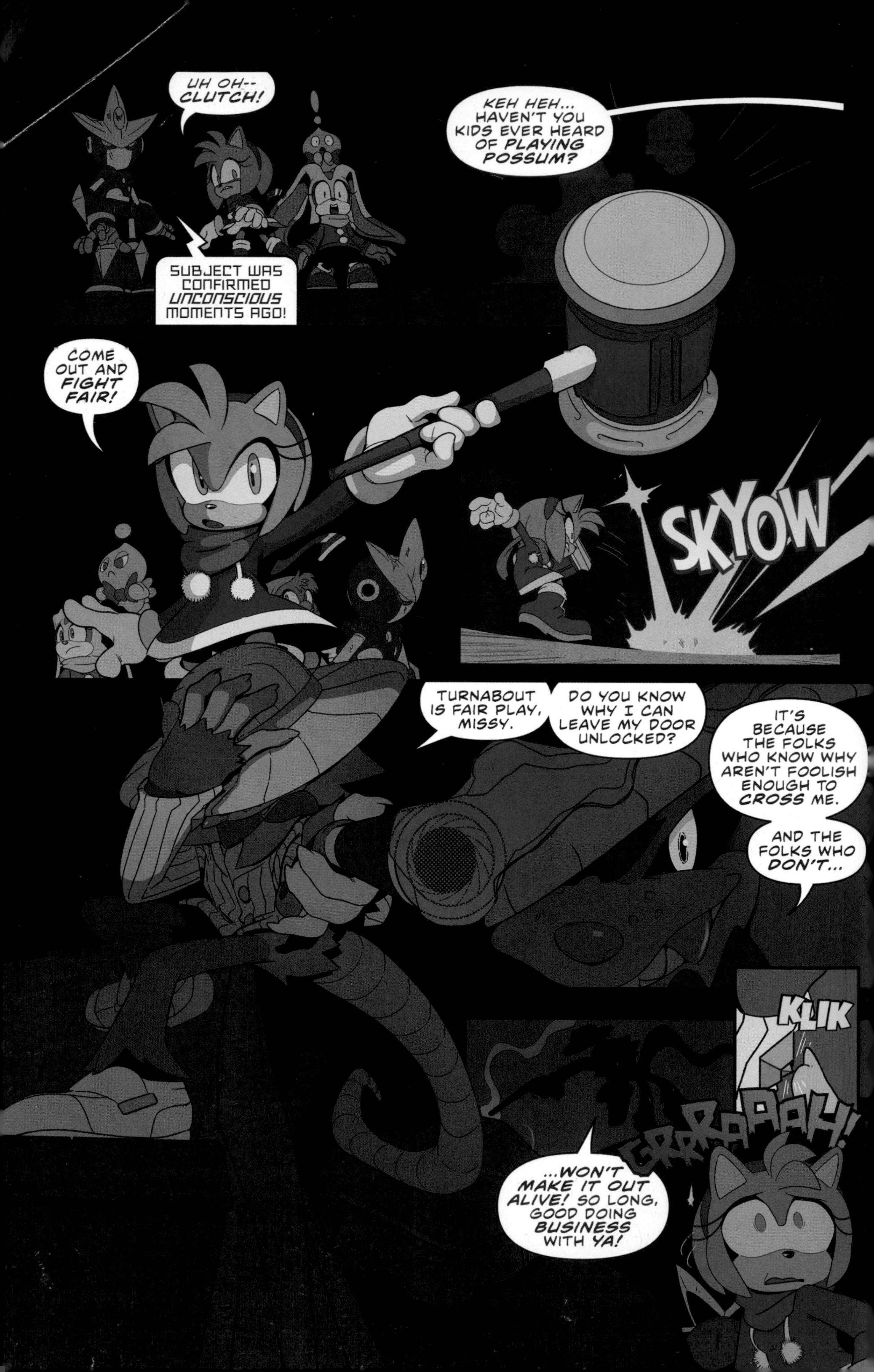
UH OH-- CLUTCH!
SUBJECT WAS CONFIRMED UNCONSCIOUS MOMENTS AGO!
KEH HEH... HAVEN'T YOU KIDS EVER HEARD OF PLAYING POSSUM?
COME OUT AND FIGHT FAIR!
SKYOW
TURNABOUT IS FAIR PLAY, MISSY.
DO YOU KNOW WHY I CAN LEAVE MY DOOR UNLOCKED?
IT'S BECAUSE THE FOLKS WHO KNOW WHY AREN'T FOOLISH ENOUGH TO CROSS ME.
AND THE FOLKS WHO DON'T...
KLIK
GRRRAAAAH!
...WON'T MAKE IT OUT ALIVE! SO LONG, GOOD DOING BUSINESS WITH YA!

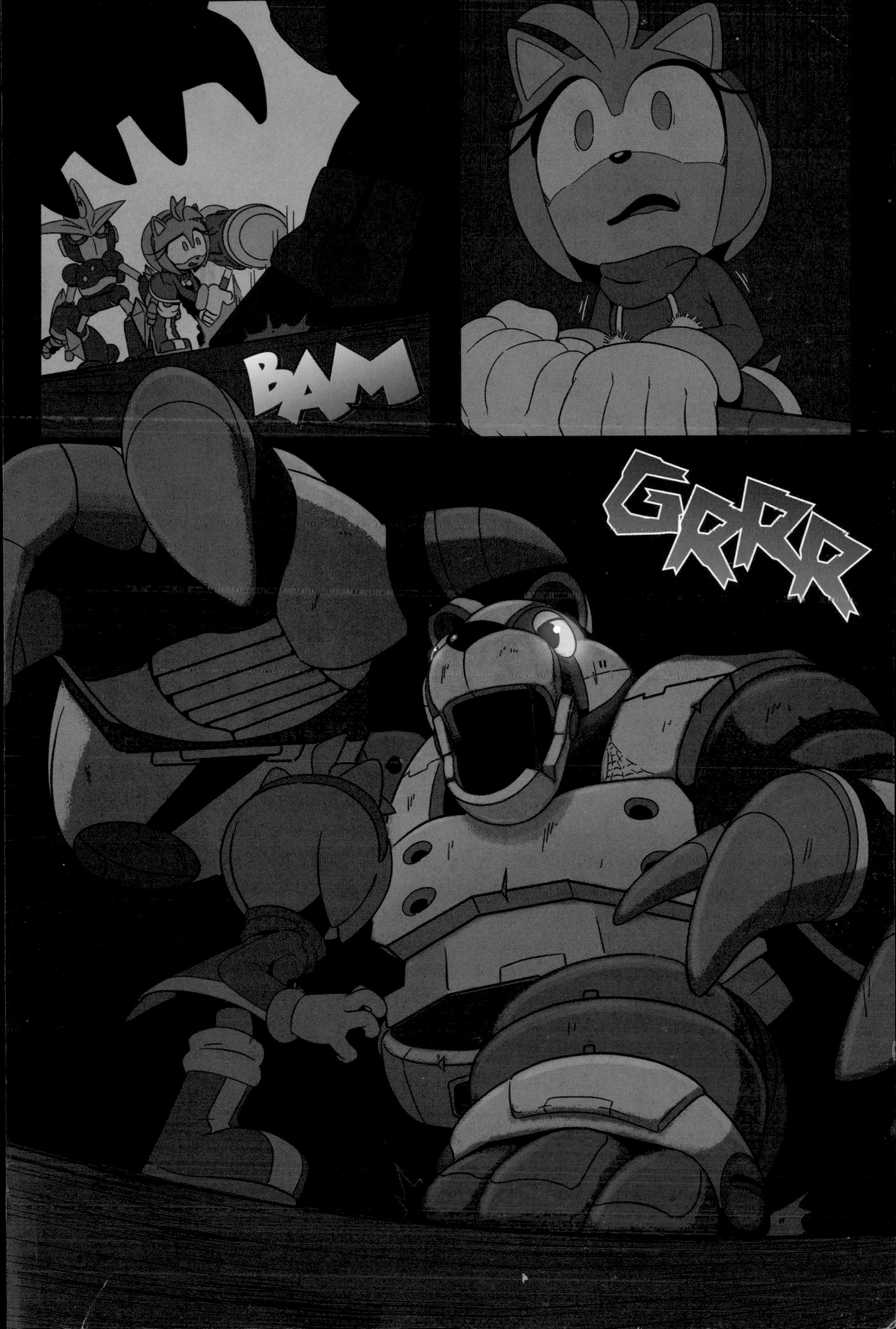
BAM
GRRR

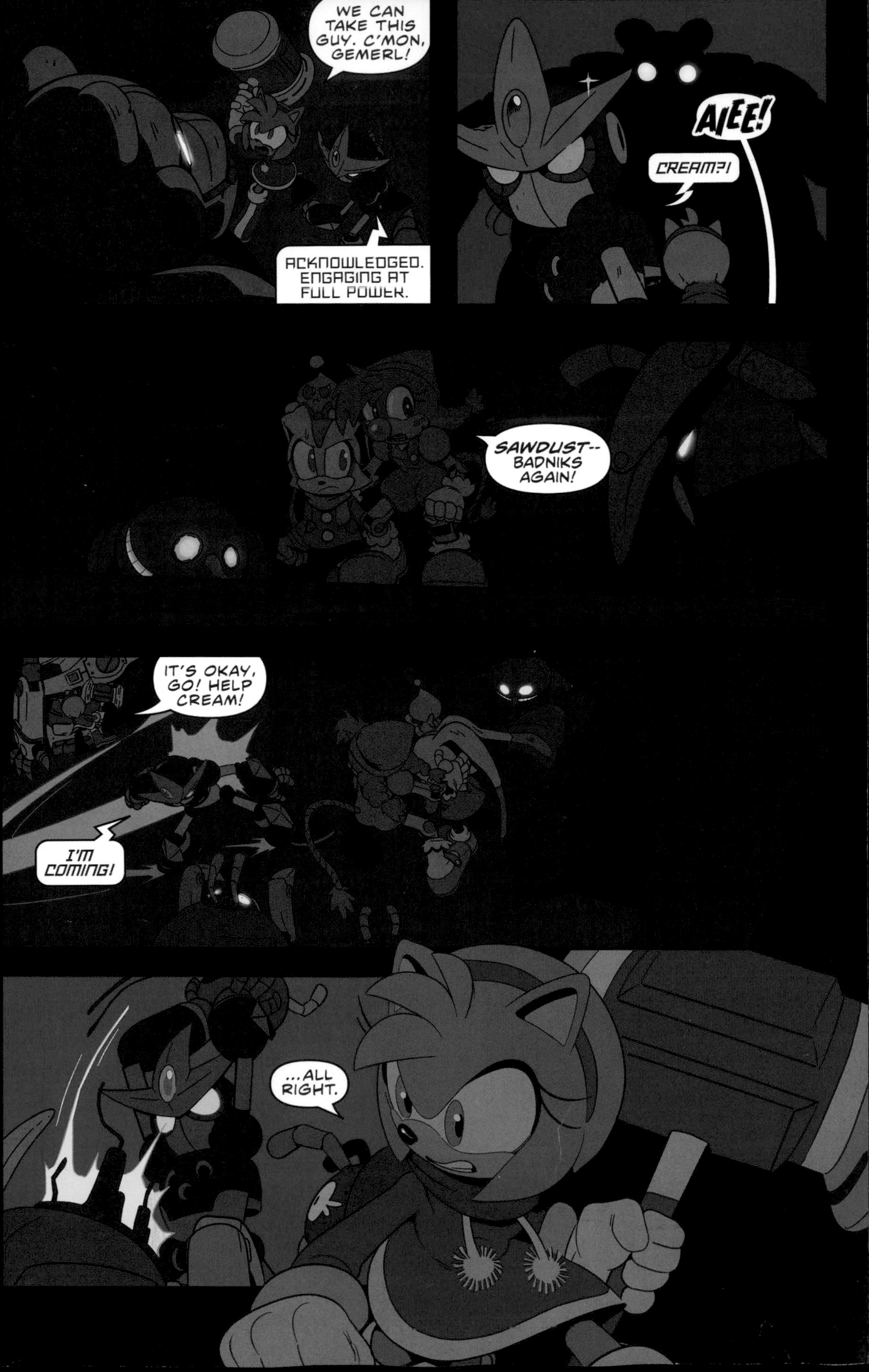
WE CAN TAKE THIS GUY. C'MON, GEMERL!
ACKNOWLEDGED. ENGAGING AT FULL POWER.
AIEE!
CREAM?!
SAWDUST-- BADNIKS AGAIN!
IT'S OKAY, GO! HELP CREAM!
I'M COMING!
...ALL RIGHT.

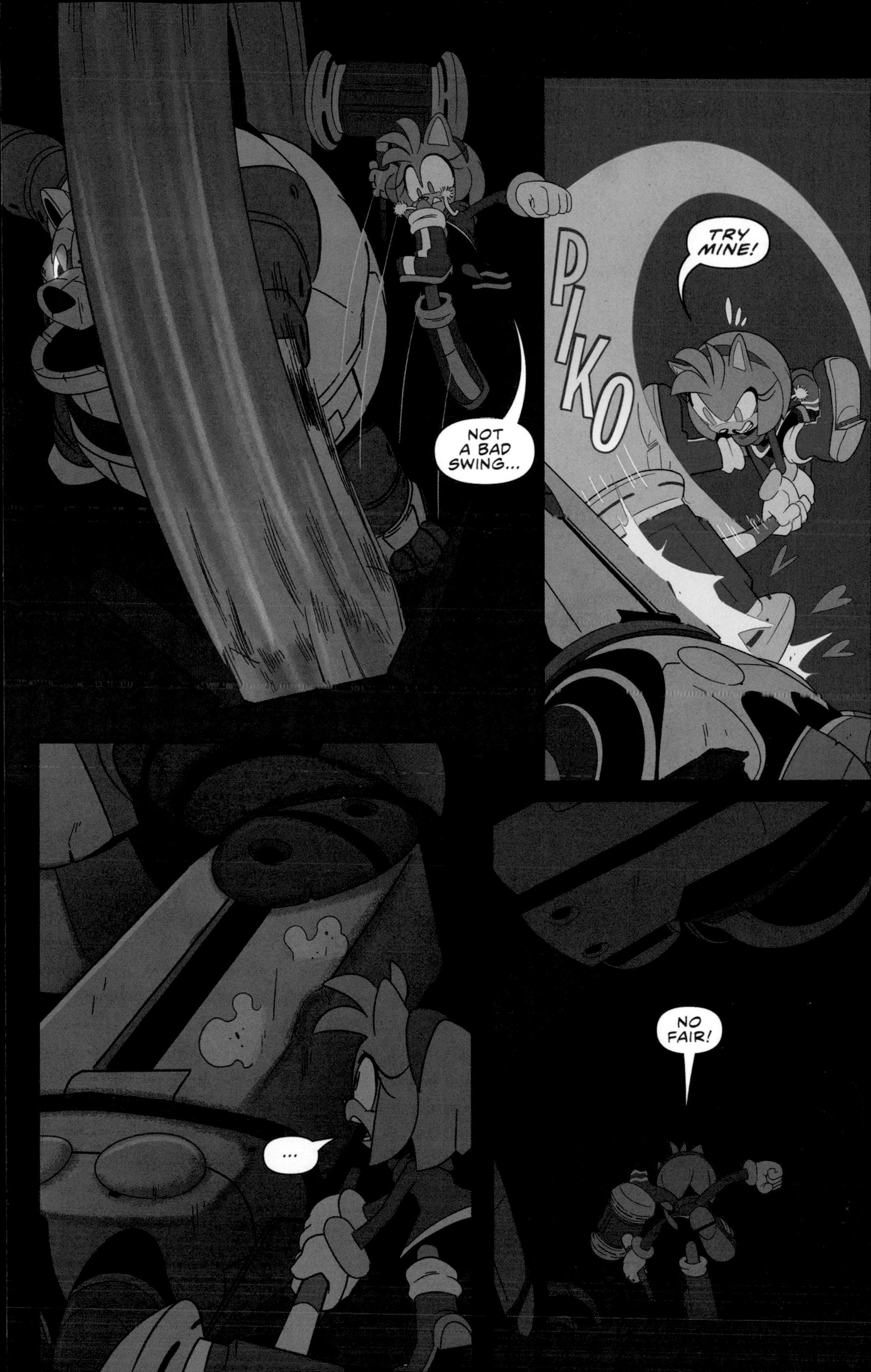
NOT A BAD SWING...
PIKO
TRY MINE!
...
NO FAIR!

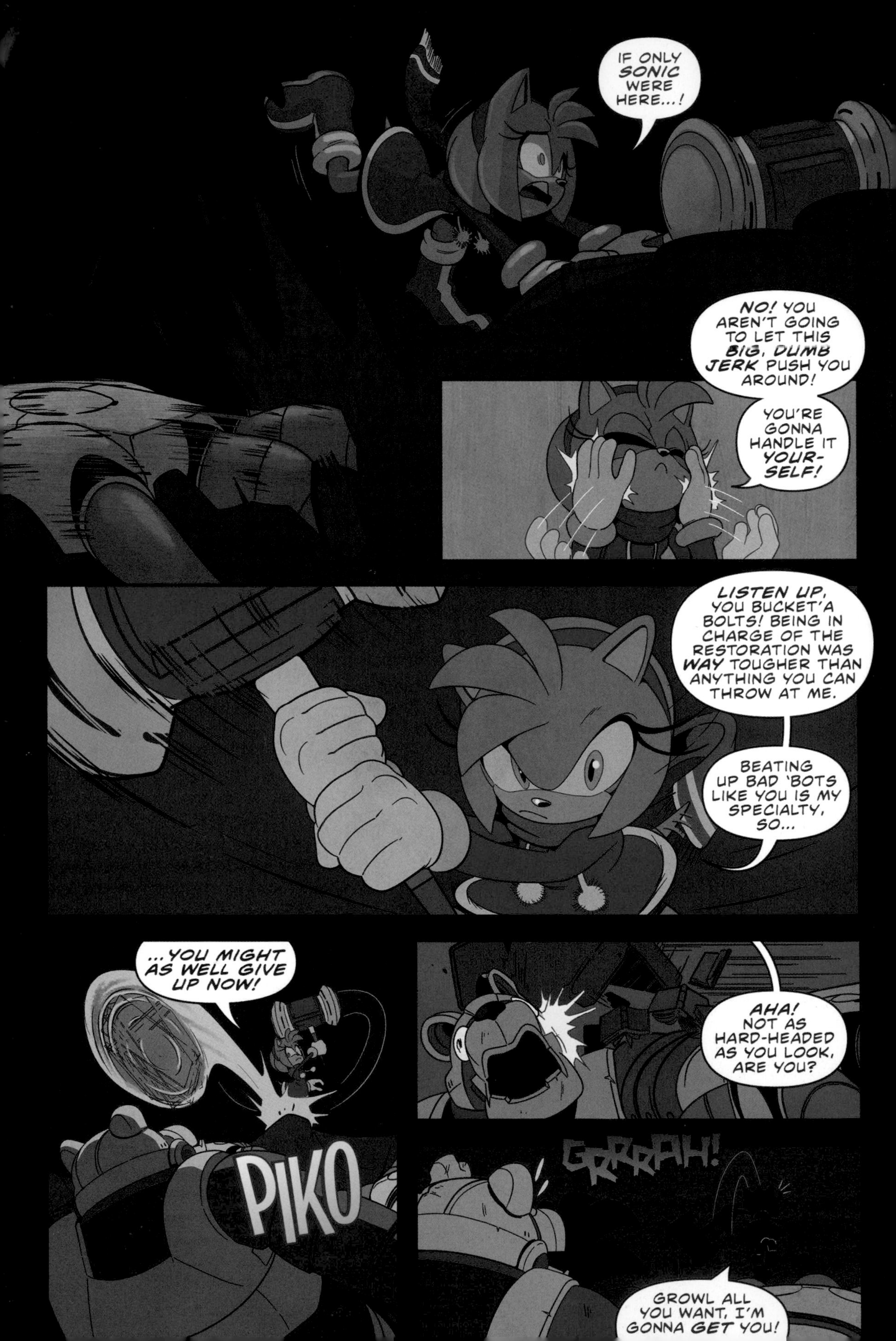
IF ONLY SONIC WERE HERE...!
NO! YOU AREN'T GOING TO LET THIS BIG, DUMB JERK PUSH YOU AROUND!
YOU'RE GONNA HANDLE IT YOURSELF!
LISTEN UP, YOU BUCKET'A BOLTS! BEING IN CHARGE OF THE RESTORATION WAS WAY TOUGHER THAN ANYTHING YOU CAN THROW AT ME.
BEATING UP BAD 'BOTS LIKE YOU IS MY SPECIALTY, SO...
...YOU MIGHT AS WELL GIVE UP NOW!
PIKO
AHA! NOT AS HARD-HEADED AS YOU LOOK, ARE YOU?
GRRRAH!
GROWL ALL YOU WANT, I'M GONNA GET YOU!

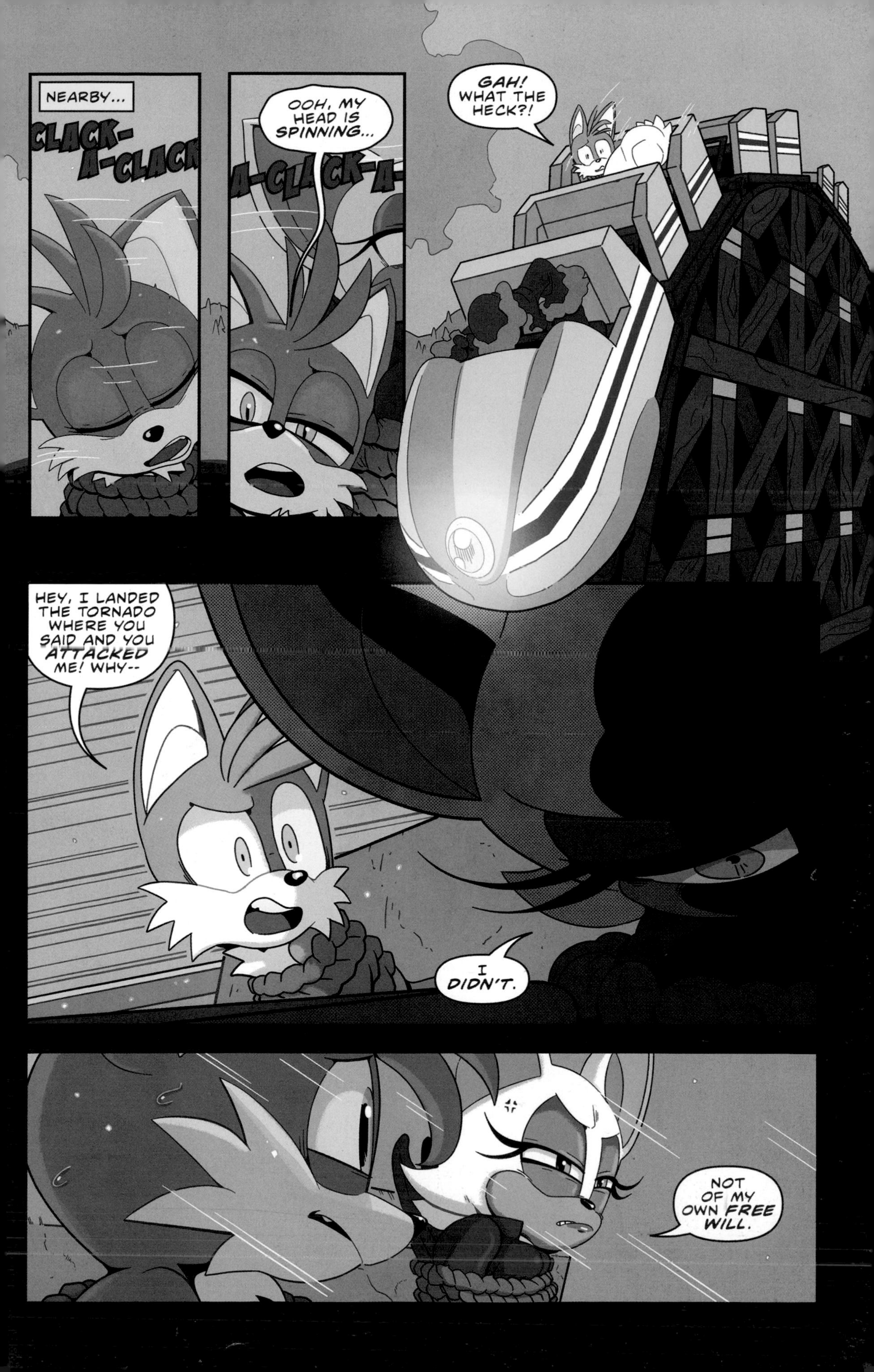
NEARBY...
CLACK-A-CLACK
OOH, MY HEAD IS SPINNING...
A-CLACK-A-
GAH! WHAT THE HECK?!
HEY, I LANDED THE TORNADO WHERE YOU SAID AND YOU ATTACKED ME! WHY--
I DIDN'T.
NOT OF MY OWN FREE WILL.

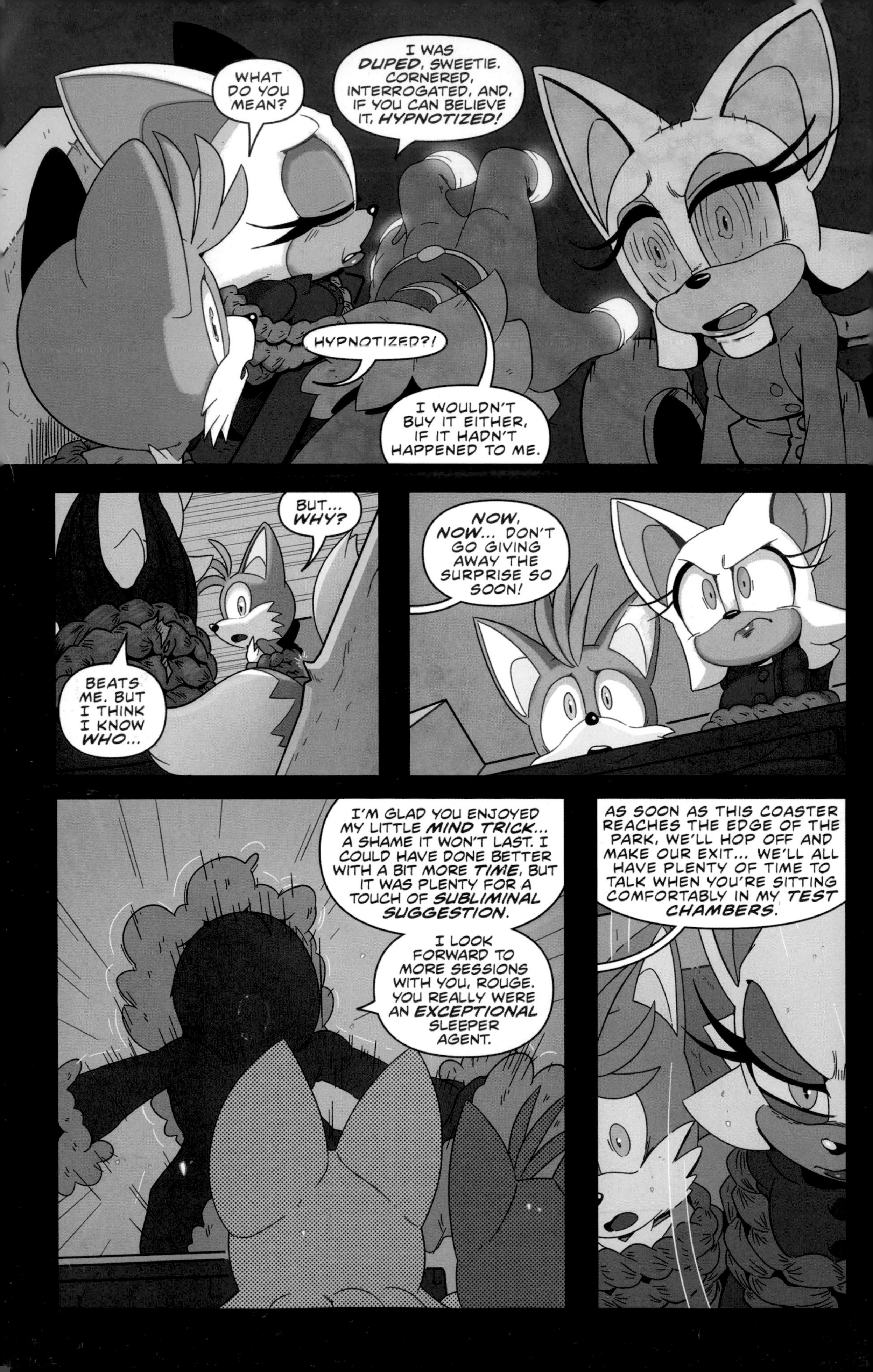
WHAT DO YOU MEAN?
I WAS DUPED, SWEETIE. CORNERED, INTERROGATED, AND, IF YOU CAN BELIEVE IT, HYPNOTIZED!
HYPNOTIZED?!
I WOULDN'T BUY IT EITHER, IF IT HADN'T HAPPENED TO ME.
BUT... WHY?
BEATS ME. BUT I THINK I KNOW WHO...
NOW, NOW... DON'T GO GIVING AWAY THE SURPRISE SO SOON!
I'M GLAD YOU ENJOYED MY LITTLE MIND TRICK... A SHAME IT WON'T LAST. I COULD HAVE DONE BETTER WITH A BIT MORE TIME, BUT IT WAS PLENTY FOR A TOUCH OF SUBLIMINAL SUGGESTION.
I LOOK FORWARD TO MORE SESSIONS WITH YOU, ROUGE. YOU REALLY WERE AN EXCEPTIONAL SLEEPER AGENT.
AS SOON AS THIS COASTER REACHES THE EDGE OF THE PARK, WE'LL HOP OFF AND MAKE OUR EXIT... WE'LL ALL HAVE PLENTY OF TIME TO TALK WHEN YOU'RE SITTING COMFORTABLY IN MY TEST CHAMBERS.

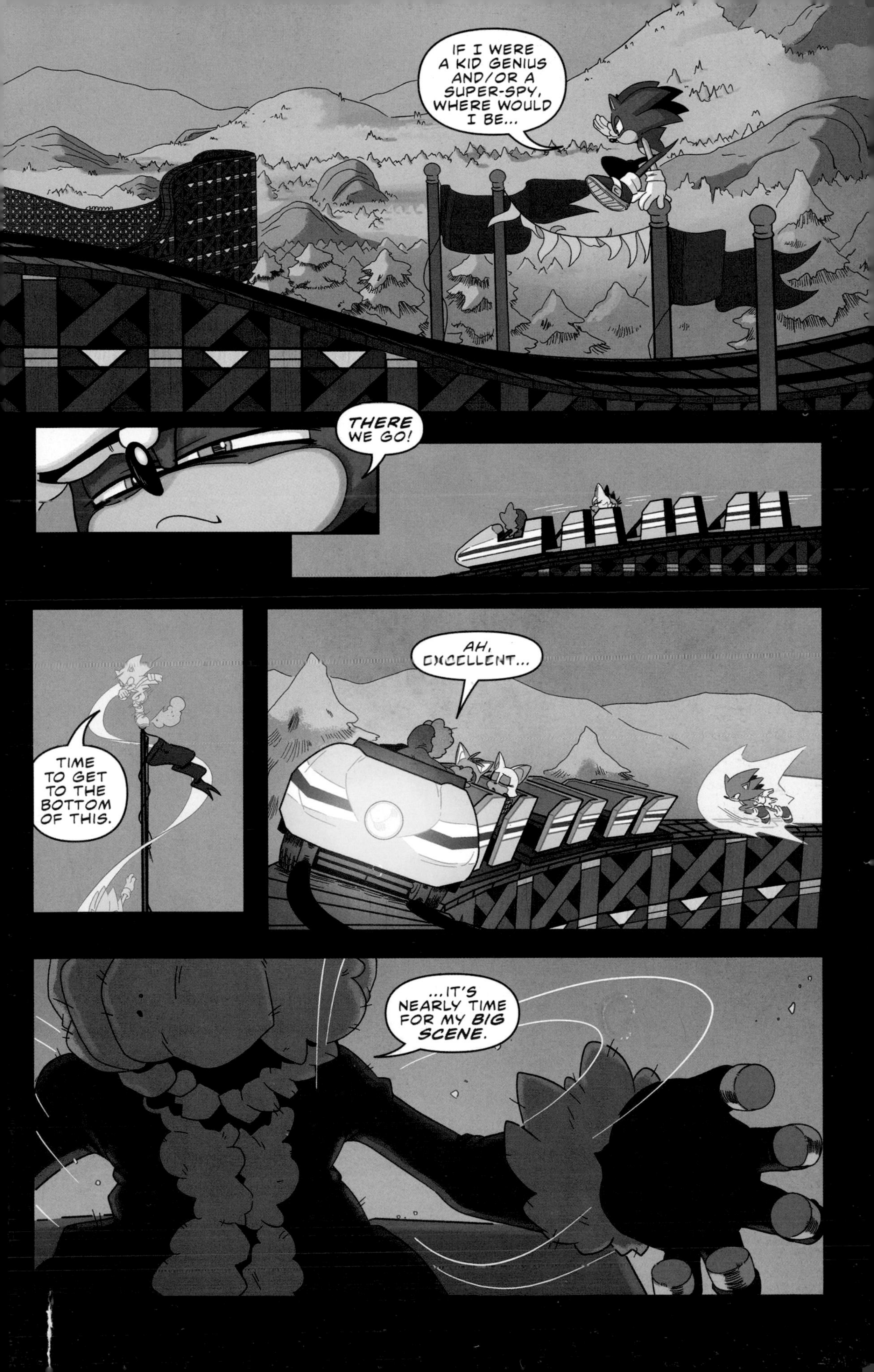
IF I WERE A KID GENIUS AND/OR A SUPER-SPY, WHERE WOULD I BE...
THERE WE GO!
TIME TO GET TO THE BOTTOM OF THIS.
AH, EXCELLENT...
...IT'S NEARLY TIME FOR MY BIG SCENE.

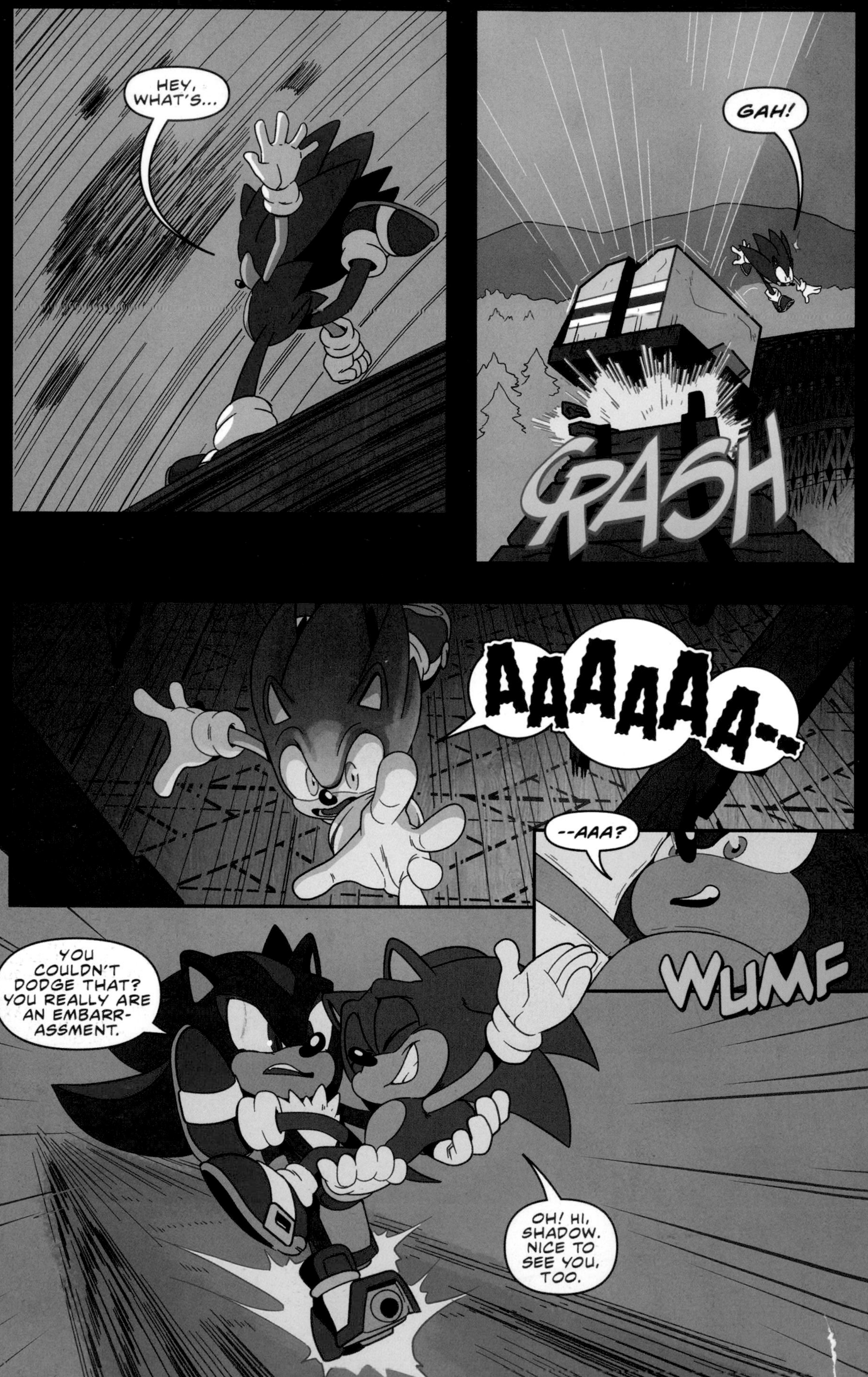
HEY, WHAT'S...
GAH!
CRASH
AAAAAA--
--AAA?
WUMF
YOU COULDN'T DODGE THAT? YOU REALLY ARE AN EMBARR-ASSMENT.
OH! HI, SHADOW. NICE TO SEE YOU, TOO.

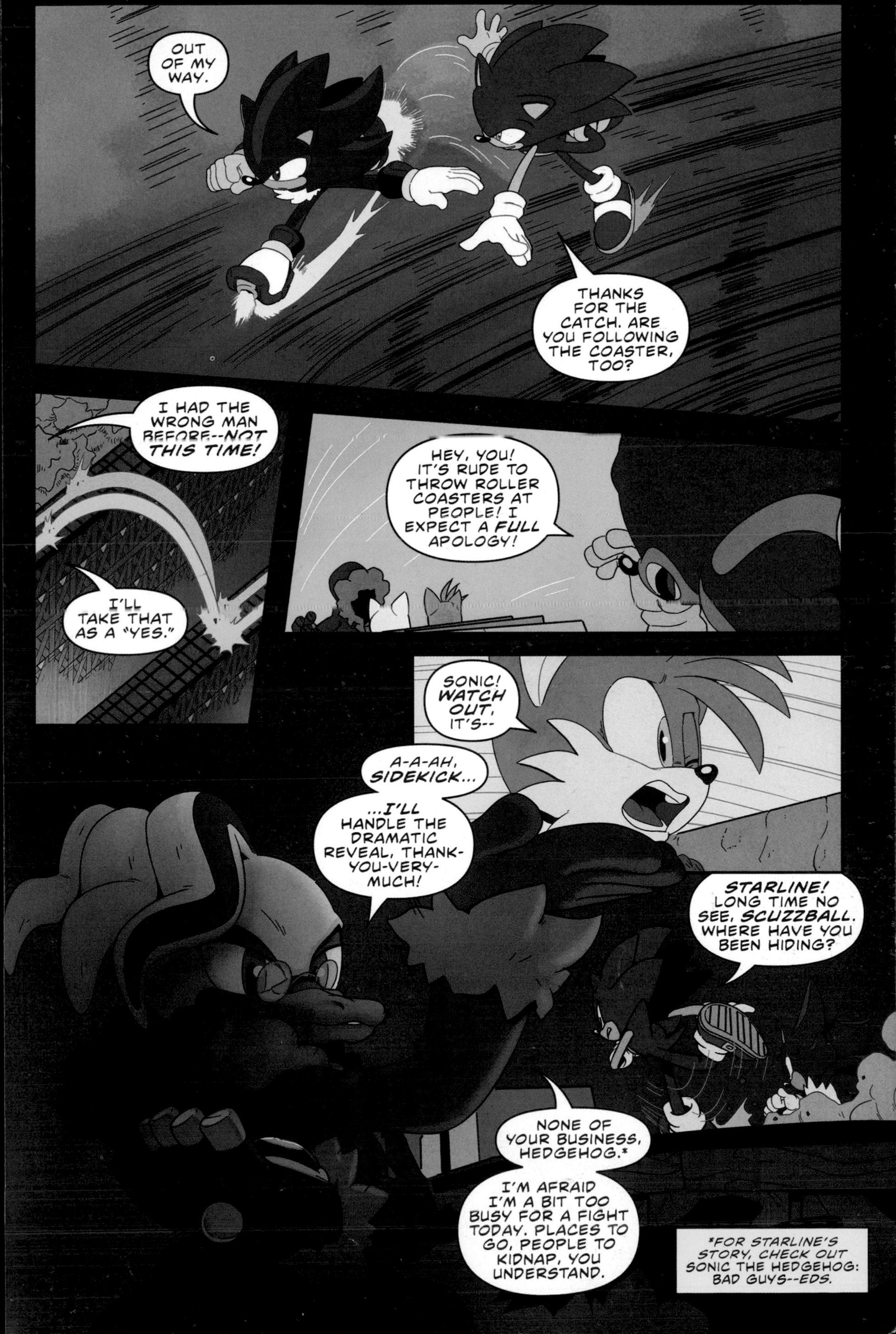
OUT OF MY WAY.
THANKS FOR THE CATCH. ARE YOU FOLLOWING THE COASTER, TOO?
I HAD THE WRONG MAN BEFORE--NOT THIS TIME!
I'LL TAKE THAT AS A "YES."
HEY, YOU! IT'S RUDE TO THROW ROLLER COASTERS AT PEOPLE! I EXPECT A FULL APOLOGY!
SONIC! WATCH OUT, IT'S--
A-A-AH, SIDEKICK...
...I'LL HANDLE THE DRAMATIC REVEAL, THANK-YOU-VERY-MUCH!
STARLINE! LONG TIME NO SEE, SCUZZBALL. WHERE HAVE YOU BEEN HIDING?
NONE OF YOUR BUSINESS, HEDGEHOG.*
I'M AFRAID I'M A BIT TOO BUSY FOR A FIGHT TODAY. PLACES TO GO, PEOPLE TO KIDNAP, YOU UNDERSTAND.
*FOR STARLINE'S STORY, CHECK OUT SONIC THE HEDGEHOG: BAD GUYS--EDS.

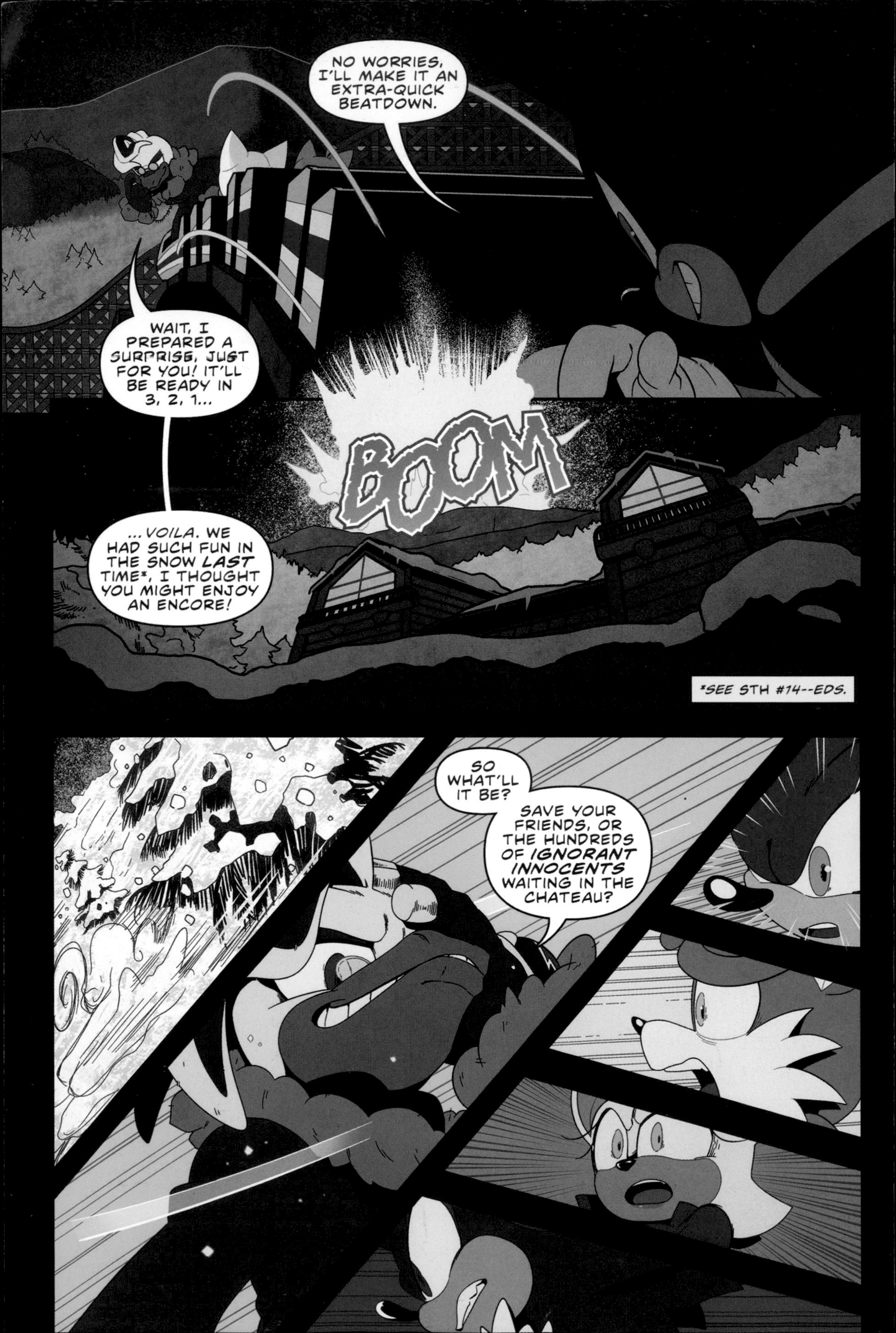
NO WORRIES, I'LL MAKE IT AN EXTRA-QUICK BEATDOWN.
WAIT, I PREPARED A SURPRISE, JUST FOR YOU! IT'LL BE READY IN 3, 2, 1...
BOOM
...VOILA. WE HAD SUCH FUN IN THE SNOW LAST TIME*, I THOUGHT YOU MIGHT ENJOY AN ENCORE!
*SEE STH #14--EDS.
SO WHAT'LL IT BE?
SAVE YOUR FRIENDS, OR THE HUNDREDS OF IGNORANT INNOCENTS WAITING IN THE CHATEAU?

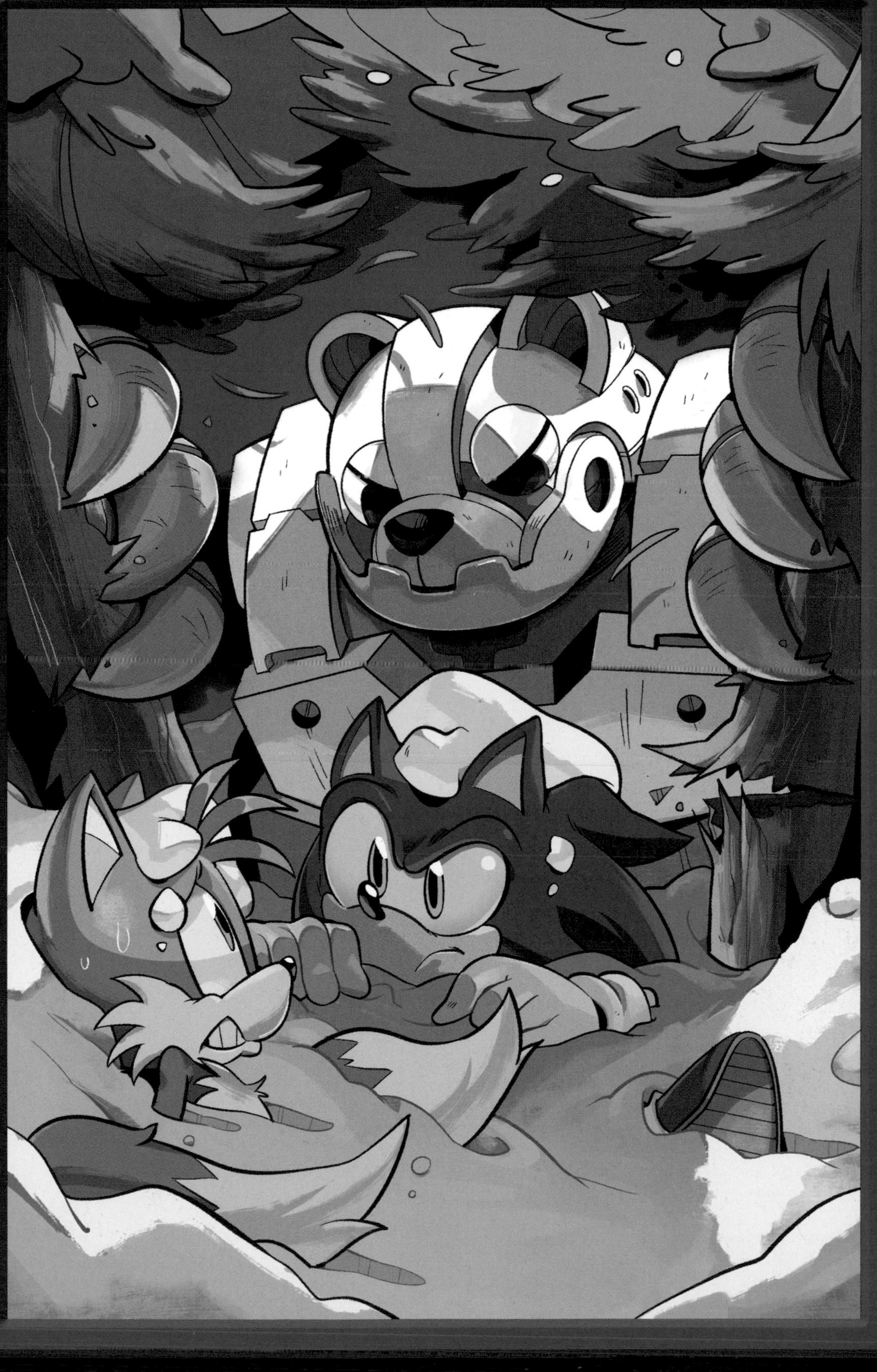

ART BY **THOMAS ROTHLISBERGER** COLORS BY **BRACARDI CURRY**

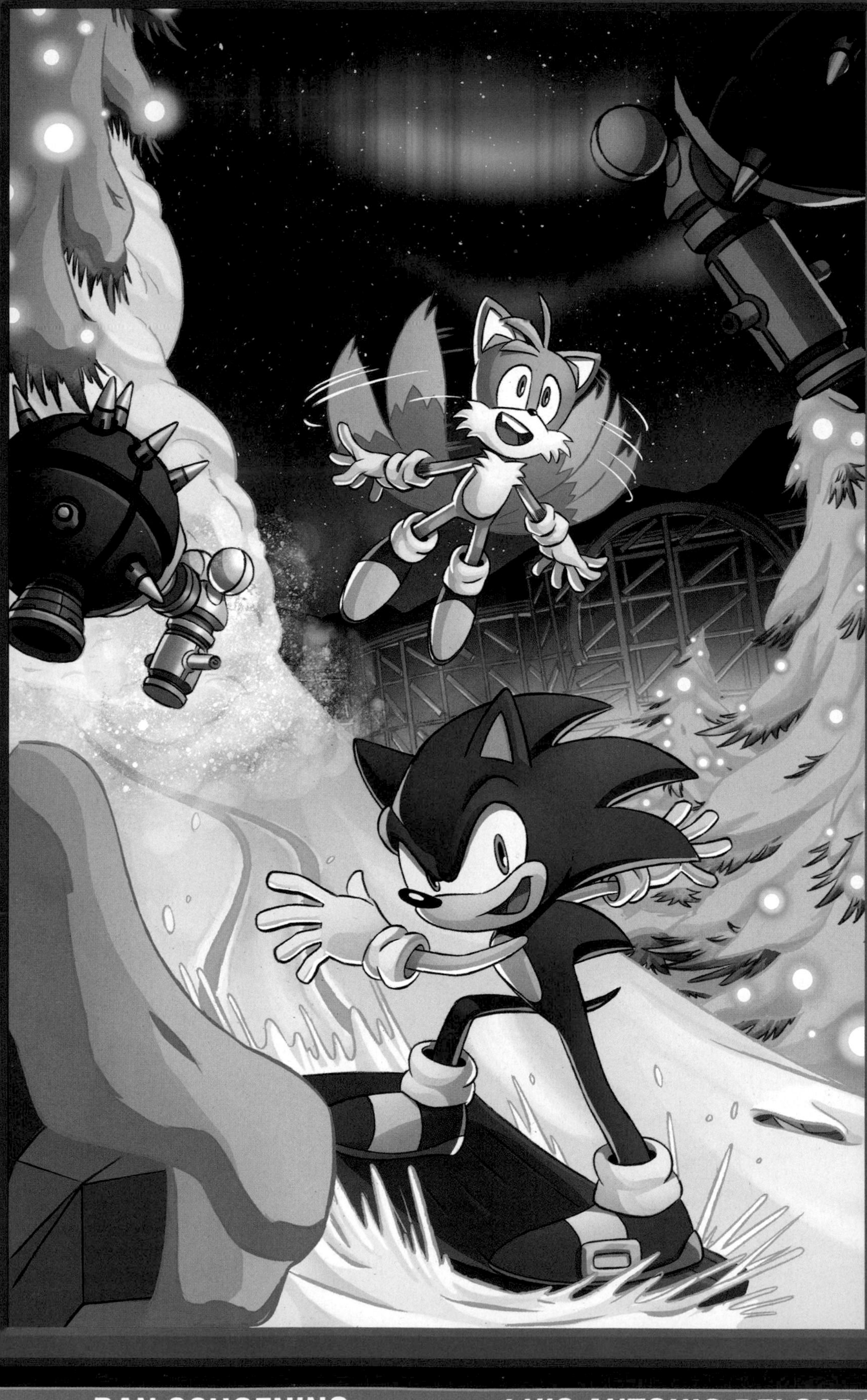

ART BY **DAN SCHOENING** COLORS BY **LUIS ANTONIO DELGADO**

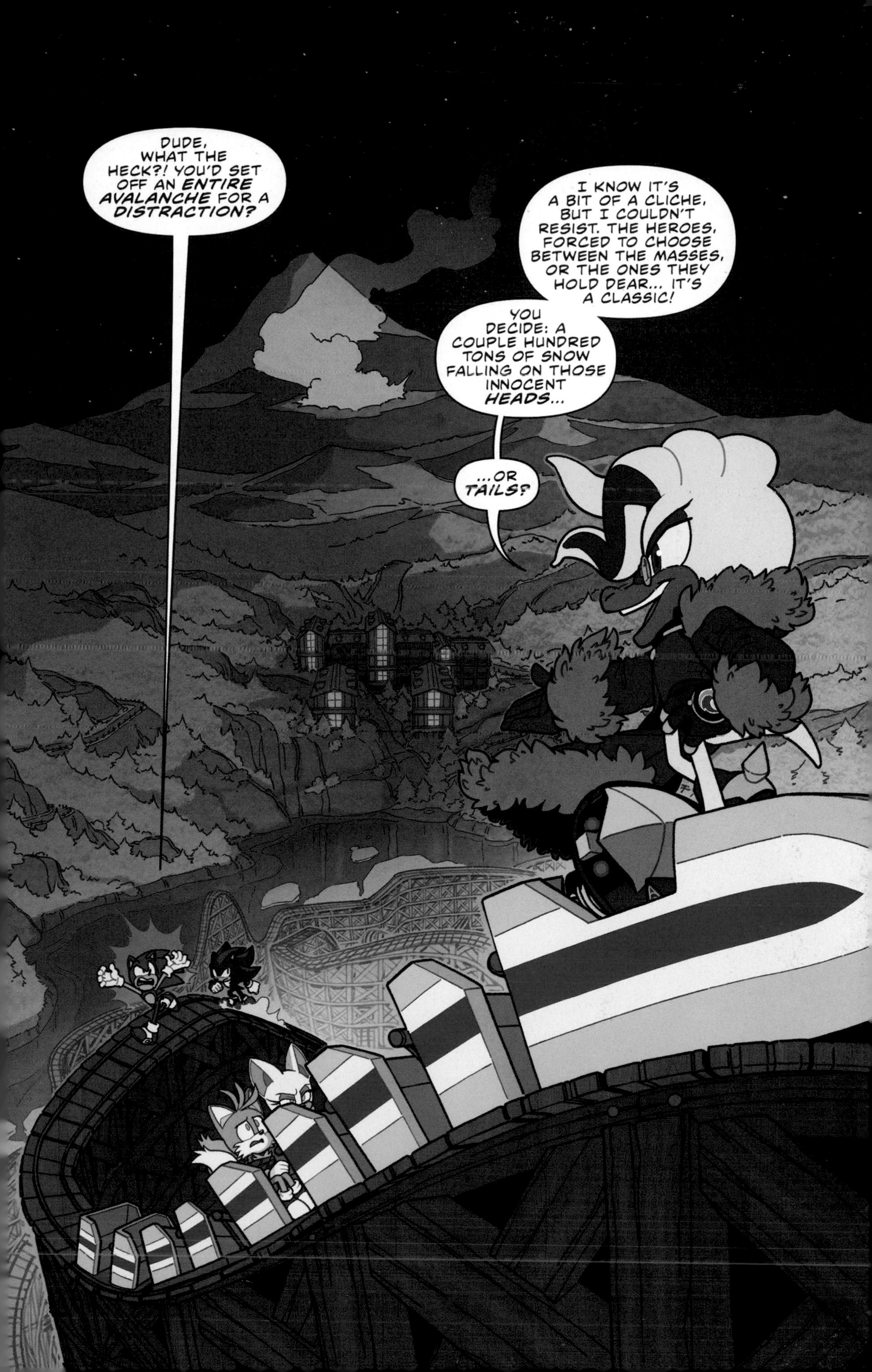
DUDE, WHAT THE HECK?! YOU'D SET OFF AN ENTIRE AVALANCHE FOR A DISTRACTION?
I KNOW IT'S A BIT OF A CLICHE, BUT I COULDN'T RESIST. THE HEROES, FORCED TO CHOOSE BETWEEN THE MASSES, OR THE ONES THEY HOLD DEAR... IT'S A CLASSIC!
YOU DECIDE: A COUPLE HUNDRED TONS OF SNOW FALLING ON THOSE INNOCENT HEADS...
...OR TAILS?

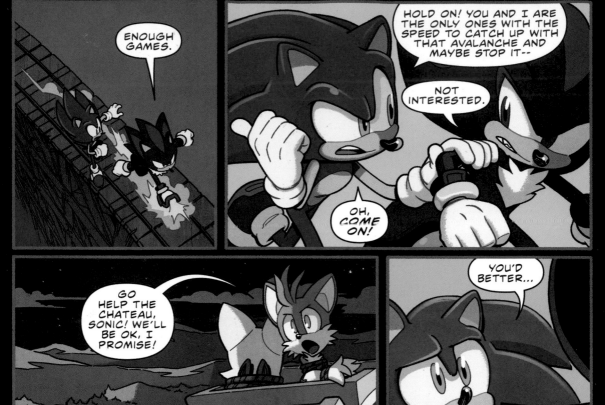

ENOUGH GAMES.

HOLD ON! YOU AND I ARE THE ONLY ONES WITH THE SPEED TO CATCH UP WITH THAT AVALANCHE AND MAYBE STOP IT--

NOT INTERESTED.

OH, COME ON!

GO HELP THE CHATEAU, SONIC! WE'LL BE OK, I PROMISE!

YOU'D BETTER...

BOOM

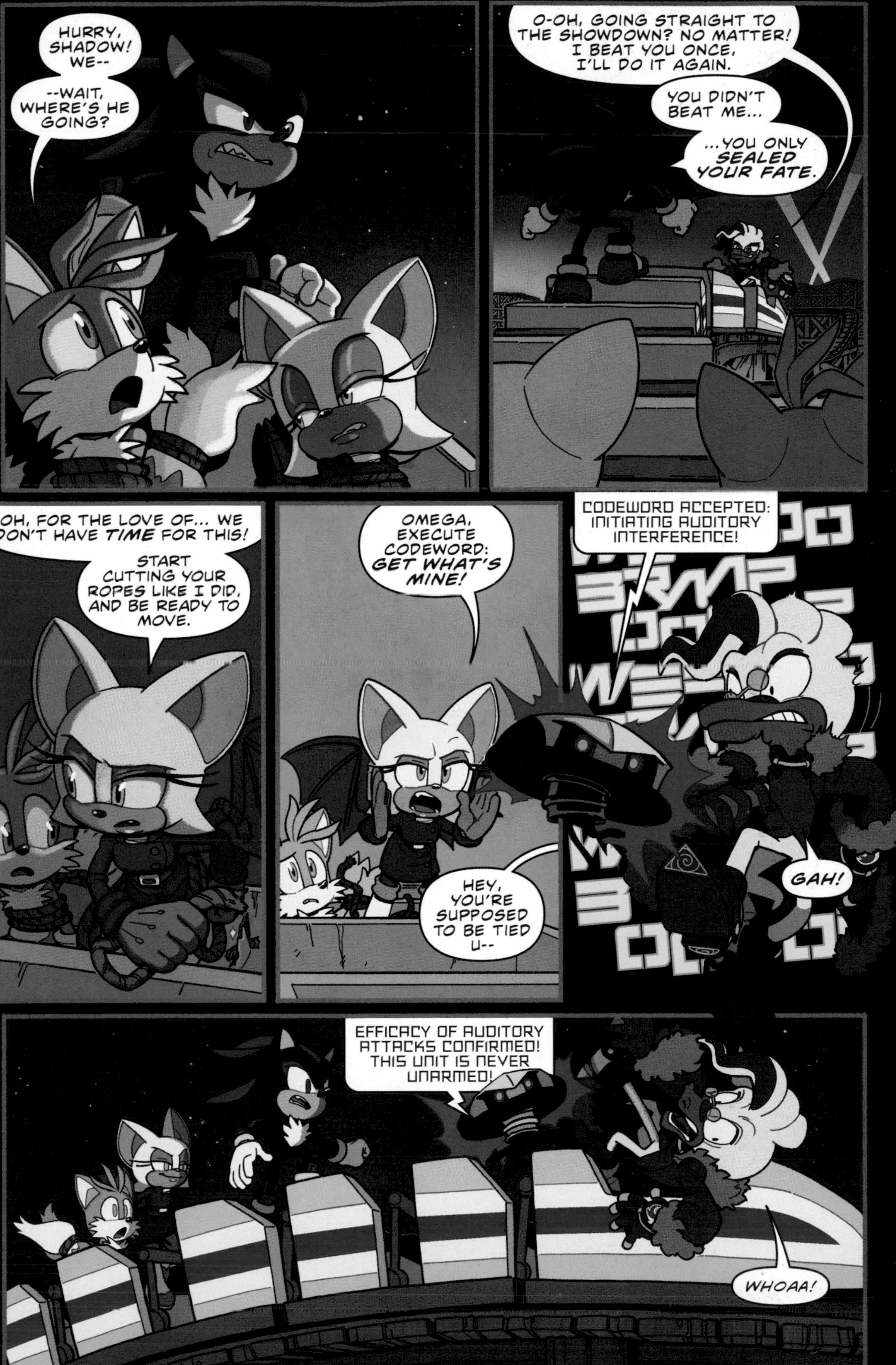
HURRY, SHADOW! WE--
--WAIT, WHERE'S HE GOING?
O-OH, GOING STRAIGHT TO THE SHOWDOWN? NO MATTER! I BEAT YOU ONCE, I'LL DO IT AGAIN.
YOU DIDN'T BEAT ME...
...YOU ONLY SEALED YOUR FATE.
OH, FOR THE LOVE OF... WE DON'T HAVE TIME FOR THIS!
START CUTTING YOUR ROPES LIKE I DID, AND BE READY TO MOVE.
OMEGA, EXECUTE CODEWORD: GET WHAT'S MINE!
HEY, YOU'RE SUPPOSED TO BE TIED U--
CODEWORD ACCEPTED: INITIATING AUDITORY INTERFERENCE!
GAH!
EFFICACY OF AUDITORY ATTACKS CONFIRMED! THIS UNIT IS NEVER UNARMED!
WHOAA!

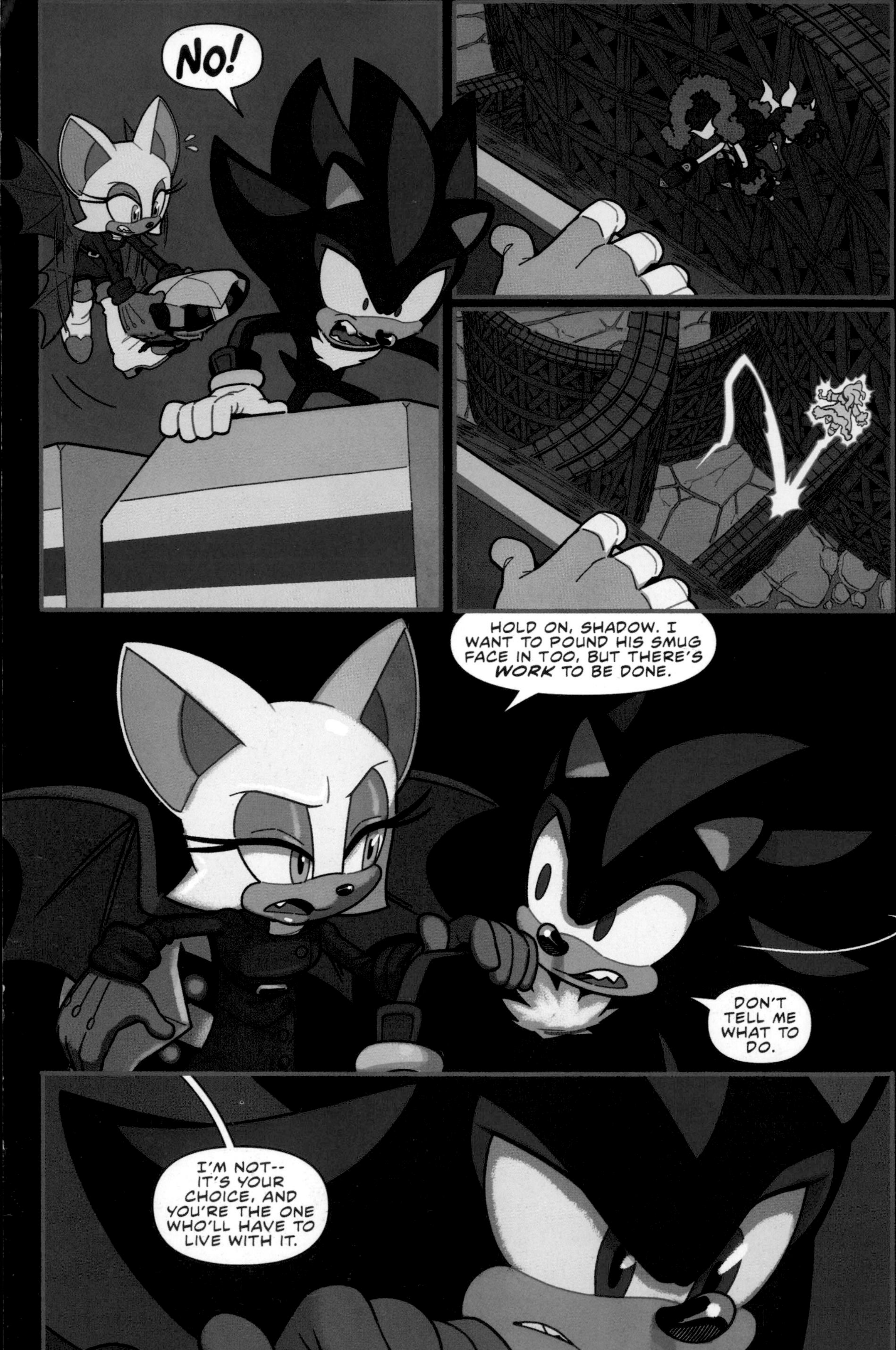
NO!
HOLD ON, SHADOW. I WANT TO POUND HIS SMUG FACE IN TOO, BUT THERE'S WORK TO BE DONE.
DON'T TELL ME WHAT TO DO.
I'M NOT-- IT'S YOUR CHOICE, AND YOU'RE THE ONE WHO'LL HAVE TO LIVE WITH IT.

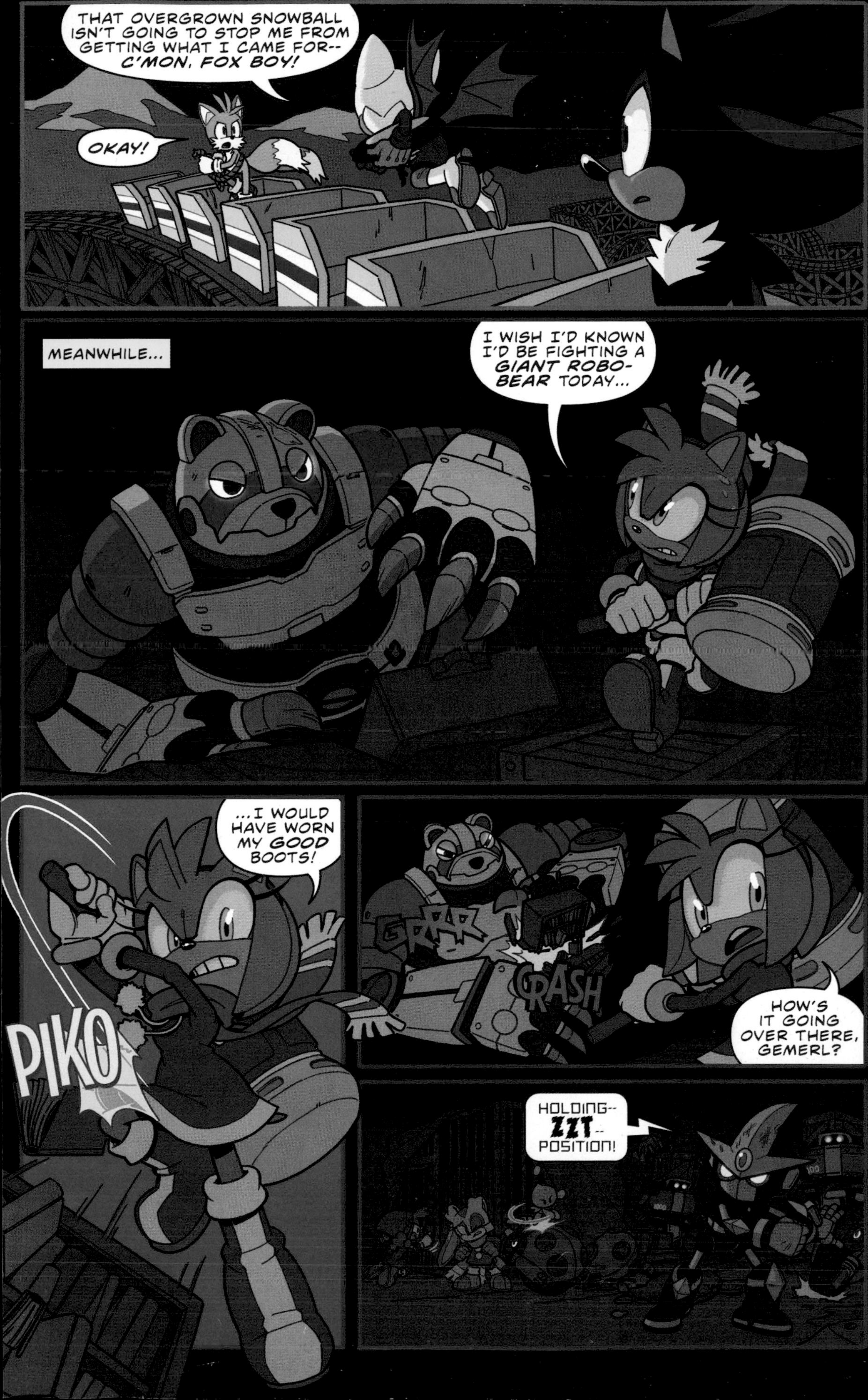
THAT OVERGROWN SNOWBALL ISN'T GOING TO STOP ME FROM GETTING WHAT I CAME FOR-- C'MON, FOX BOY!
OKAY!
MEANWHILE...
I WISH I'D KNOWN I'D BE FIGHTING A GIANT ROBO-BEAR TODAY...
...I WOULD HAVE WORN MY GOOD BOOTS!
PIKO
GRRR
CRASH
HOW'S IT GOING OVER THERE, GEMERL?
HOLDING-- ZZT-- POSITION!

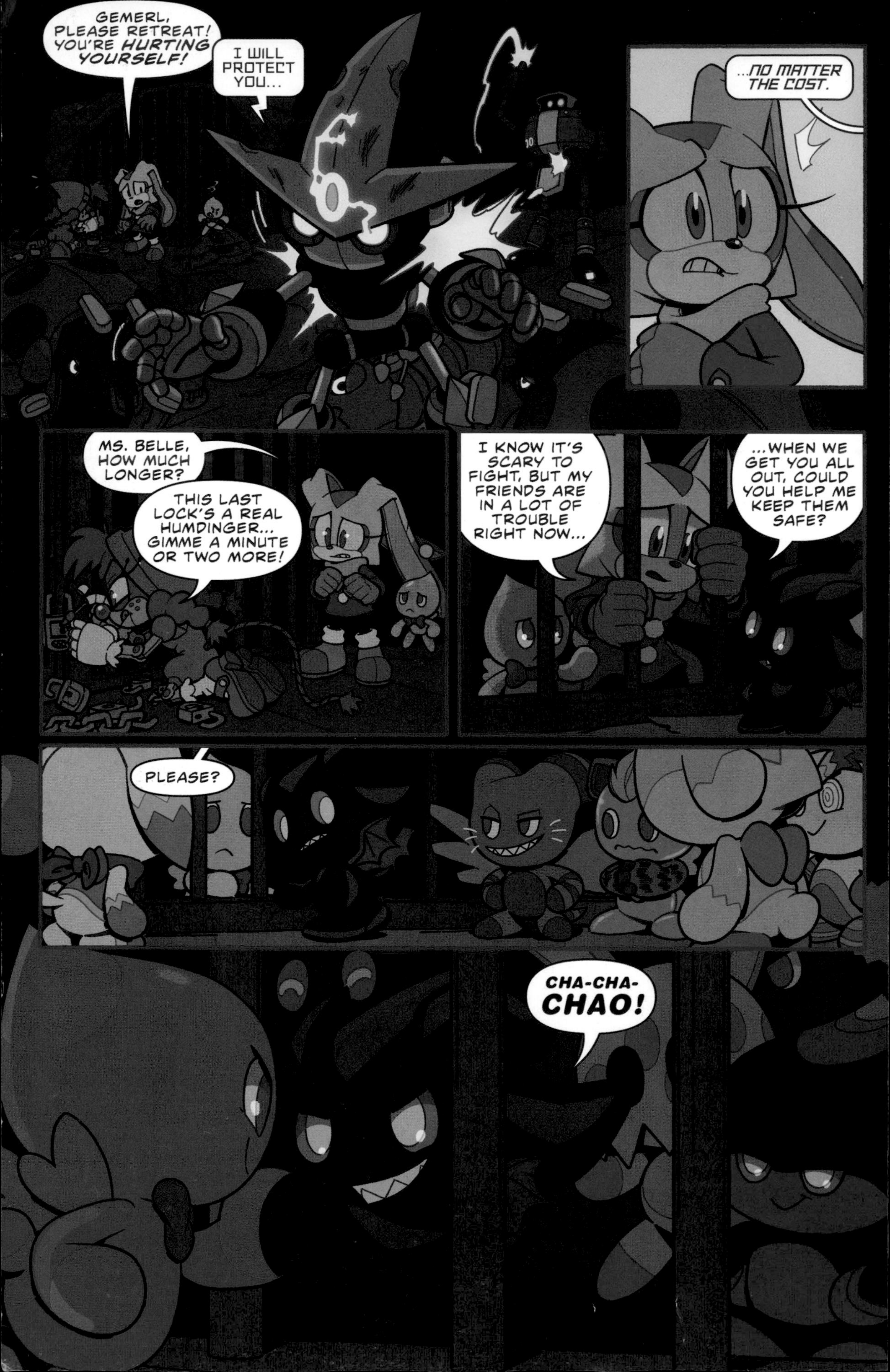
GEMERL, PLEASE RETREAT! YOU'RE *HURTING YOURSELF!*
I WILL PROTECT YOU...
...*NO MATTER THE COST.*
MS. BELLE, HOW MUCH LONGER?
THIS LAST LOCK'S A REAL HUMDINGER... GIMME A MINUTE OR TWO MORE!
I KNOW IT'S SCARY TO FIGHT, BUT MY FRIENDS ARE IN A LOT OF TROUBLE RIGHT NOW...
...WHEN WE GET YOU ALL OUT, COULD YOU HELP ME KEEP THEM SAFE?
PLEASE?
CHA-CHA-CHAO!

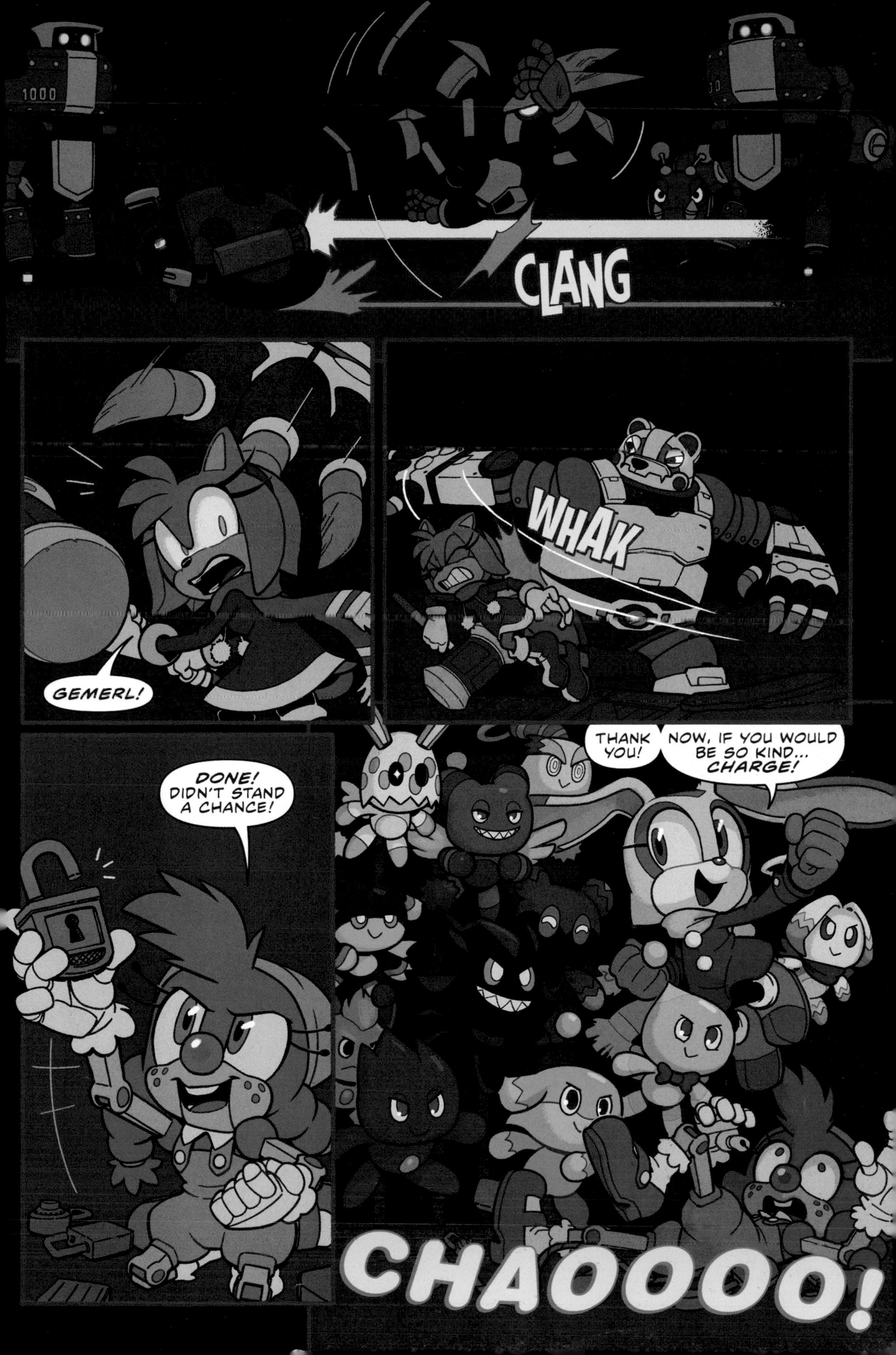
CLANG
GEMERL!
WHAK
DONE! DIDN'T STAND A CHANCE!
THANK YOU!
NOW, IF YOU WOULD BE SO KIND... CHARGE!
CHAOOOO!

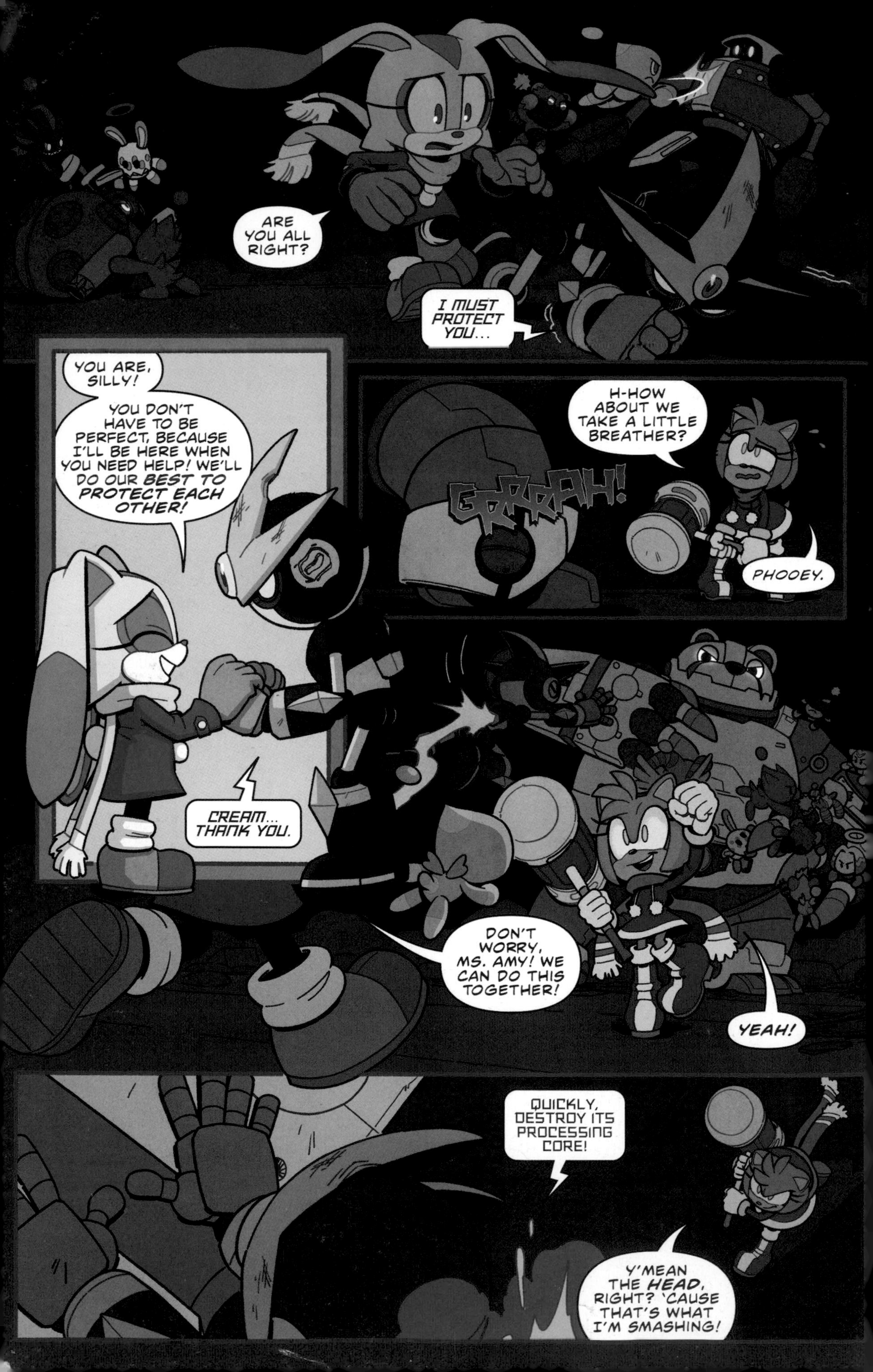
ARE YOU ALL RIGHT?
I MUST PROTECT YOU...
YOU ARE, SILLY!
YOU DON'T HAVE TO BE PERFECT, BECAUSE I'LL BE HERE WHEN YOU NEED HELP! WE'LL DO OUR BEST TO PROTECT EACH OTHER!
CREAM... THANK YOU.
H-HOW ABOUT WE TAKE A LITTLE BREATHER?
GRRRAH!
PHOOEY.
DON'T WORRY, MS. AMY! WE CAN DO THIS TOGETHER!
YEAH!
QUICKLY, DESTROY ITS PROCESSING CORE!
Y'MEAN THE HEAD, RIGHT? 'CAUSE THAT'S WHAT I'M SMASHING!

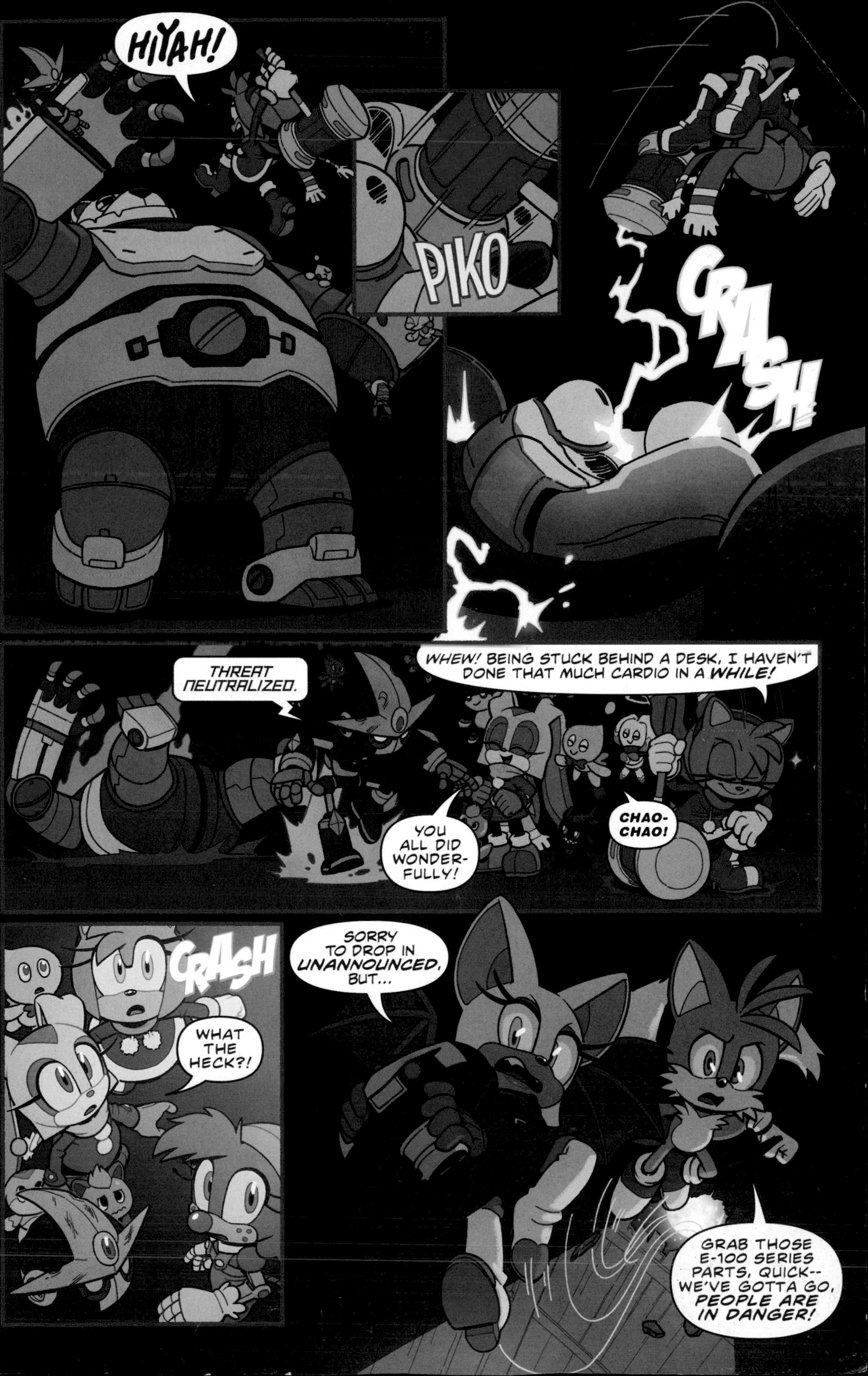
HIYAH!
PIKO
CRASH
THREAT NEUTRALIZED.
WHEW! BEING STUCK BEHIND A DESK, I HAVEN'T DONE THAT MUCH CARDIO IN A WHILE!
YOU ALL DID WONDER-FULLY!
CHAO-CHAO!
CRASH
WHAT THE HECK?!
SORRY TO DROP IN UNANNOUNCED, BUT...
GRAB THOSE E-100 SERIES PARTS, QUICK-- WE'VE GOTTA GO, PEOPLE ARE IN DANGER!

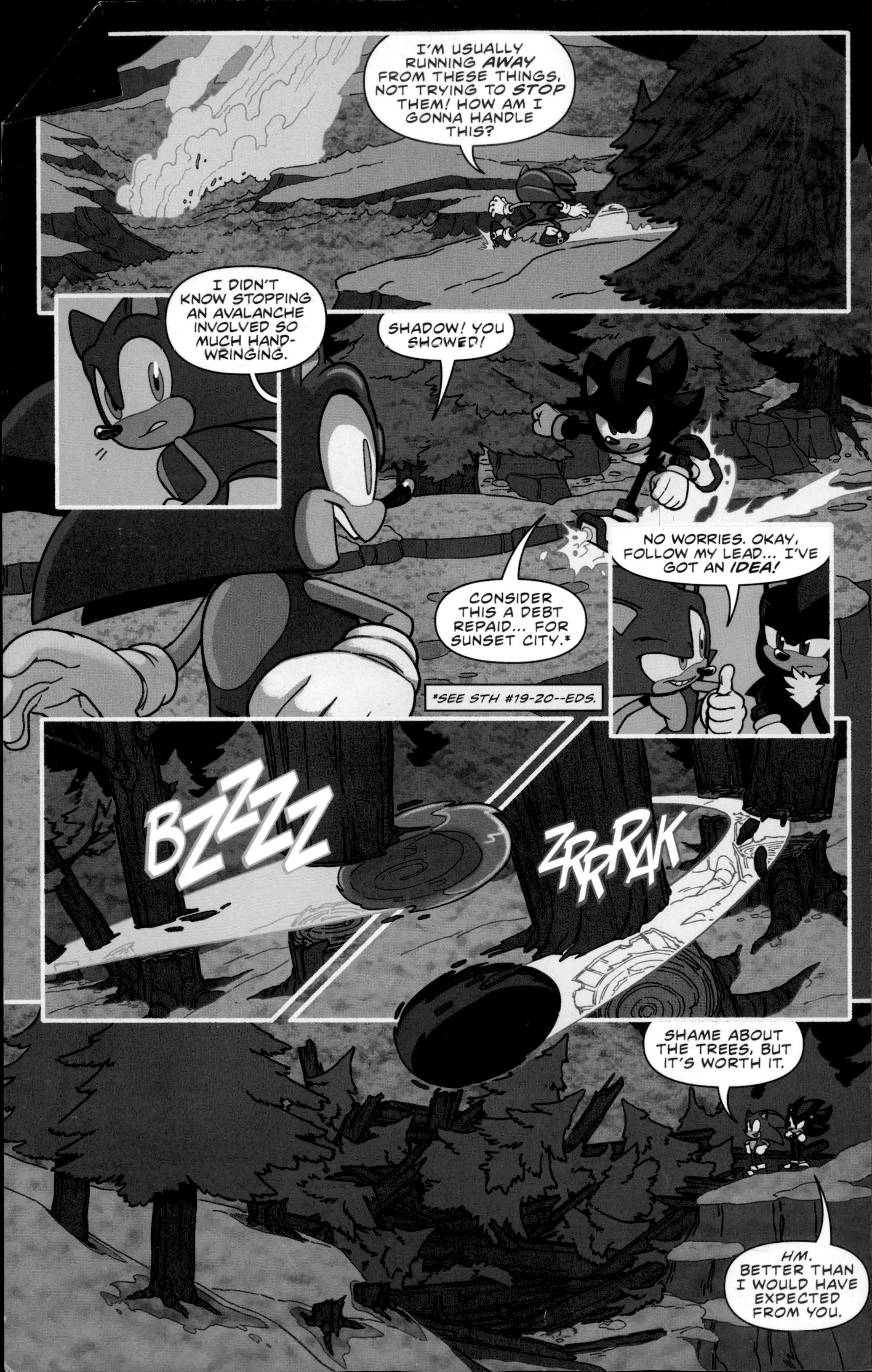
I'M USUALLY RUNNING AWAY FROM THESE THINGS, NOT TRYING TO STOP THEM! HOW AM I GONNA HANDLE THIS?
I DIDN'T KNOW STOPPING AN AVALANCHE INVOLVED SO MUCH HAND-WRINGING.
SHADOW! YOU SHOWED!
CONSIDER THIS A DEBT REPAID... FOR SUNSET CITY.*
*SEE STH #19-20--EDS.
NO WORRIES. OKAY, FOLLOW MY LEAD... I'VE GOT AN IDEA!
BZZZZZ
ZRRRRAK
SHAME ABOUT THE TREES, BUT IT'S WORTH IT.
HM. BETTER THAN I WOULD HAVE EXPECTED FROM YOU.

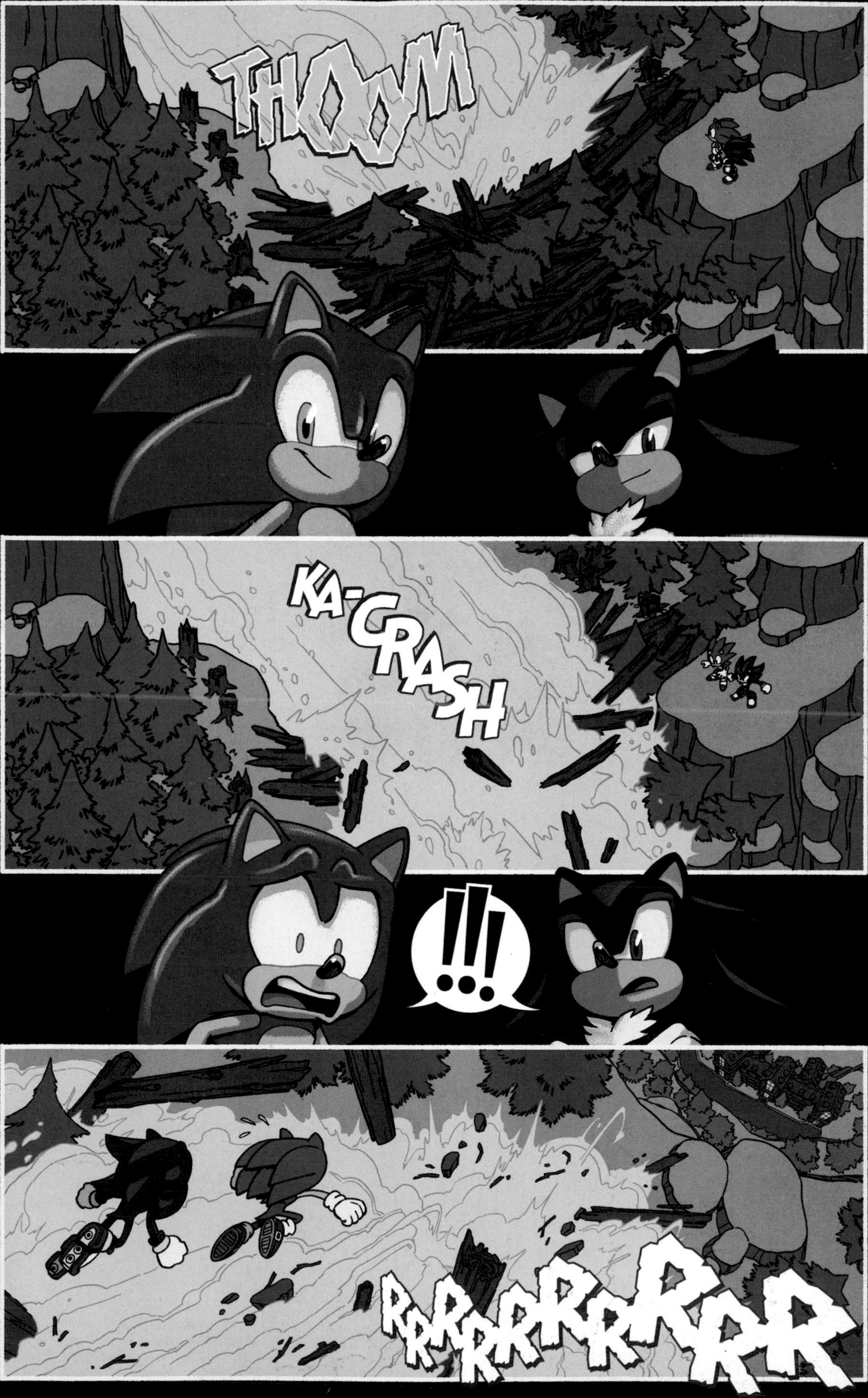
THOOM
KA-CRASH
!!!...
RRRRRRRRRRR

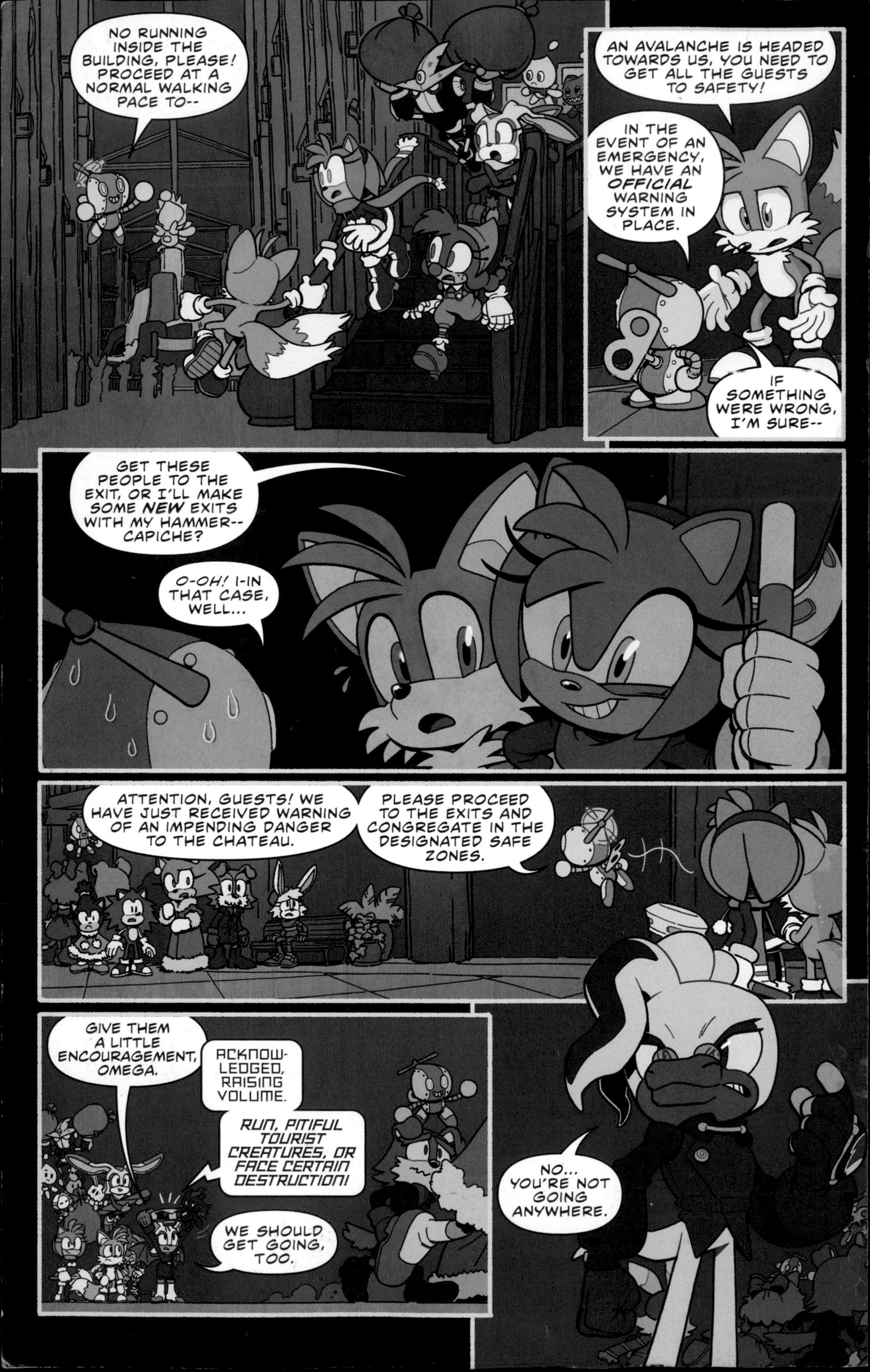
NO RUNNING INSIDE THE BUILDING, PLEASE! PROCEED AT A NORMAL WALKING PACE TO--
AN AVALANCHE IS HEADED TOWARDS US, YOU NEED TO GET ALL THE GUESTS TO SAFETY!
IN THE EVENT OF AN EMERGENCY, WE HAVE AN OFFICIAL WARNING SYSTEM IN PLACE.
IF SOMETHING WERE WRONG, I'M SURE--
GET THESE PEOPLE TO THE EXIT, OR I'LL MAKE SOME NEW EXITS WITH MY HAMMER-- CAPICHE?
O-OH! I-IN THAT CASE, WELL...
ATTENTION, GUESTS! WE HAVE JUST RECEIVED WARNING OF AN IMPENDING DANGER TO THE CHATEAU.
PLEASE PROCEED TO THE EXITS AND CONGREGATE IN THE DESIGNATED SAFE ZONES.
GIVE THEM A LITTLE ENCOURAGEMENT, OMEGA.
ACKNOW-LEDGED, RAISING VOLUME.
RUN, PITIFUL TOURIST CREATURES, OR FACE CERTAIN DESTRUCTION!
WE SHOULD GET GOING, TOO.
NO... YOU'RE NOT GOING ANYWHERE.

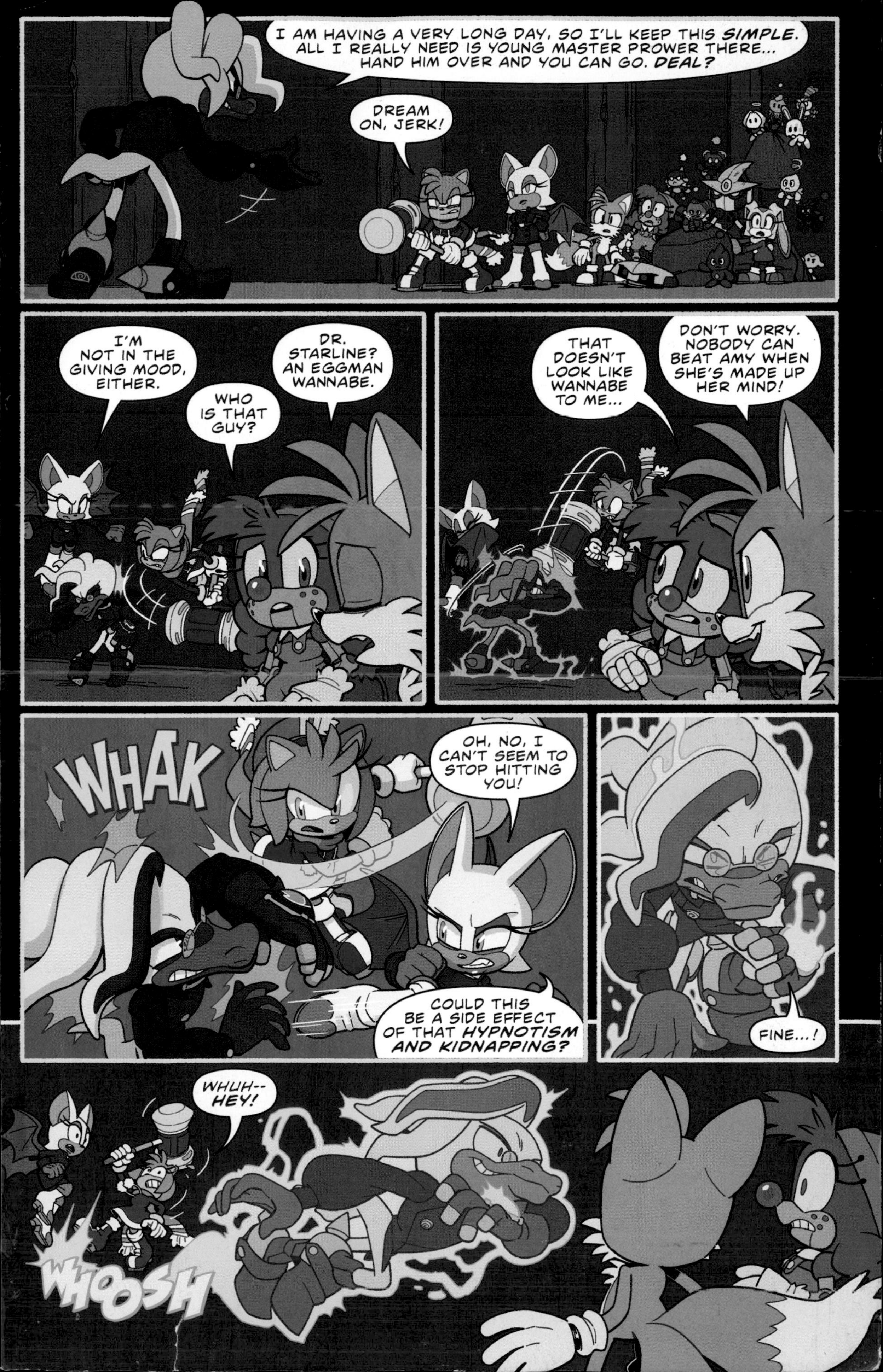

I AM HAVING A VERY LONG DAY, SO I'LL KEEP THIS SIMPLE. ALL I REALLY NEED IS YOUNG MASTER PROWER THERE... HAND HIM OVER AND YOU CAN GO. DEAL?
DREAM ON, JERK!
I'M NOT IN THE GIVING MOOD, EITHER.
WHO IS THAT GUY?
DR. STARLINE? AN EGGMAN WANNABE.
THAT DOESN'T LOOK LIKE WANNABE TO ME...
DON'T WORRY. NOBODY CAN BEAT AMY WHEN SHE'S MADE UP HER MIND!
WHAK
OH, NO, I CAN'T SEEM TO STOP HITTING YOU!
COULD THIS BE A SIDE EFFECT OF THAT HYPNOTISM AND KIDNAPPING?
FINE...!
WHUH-- HEY!
WHOOSH

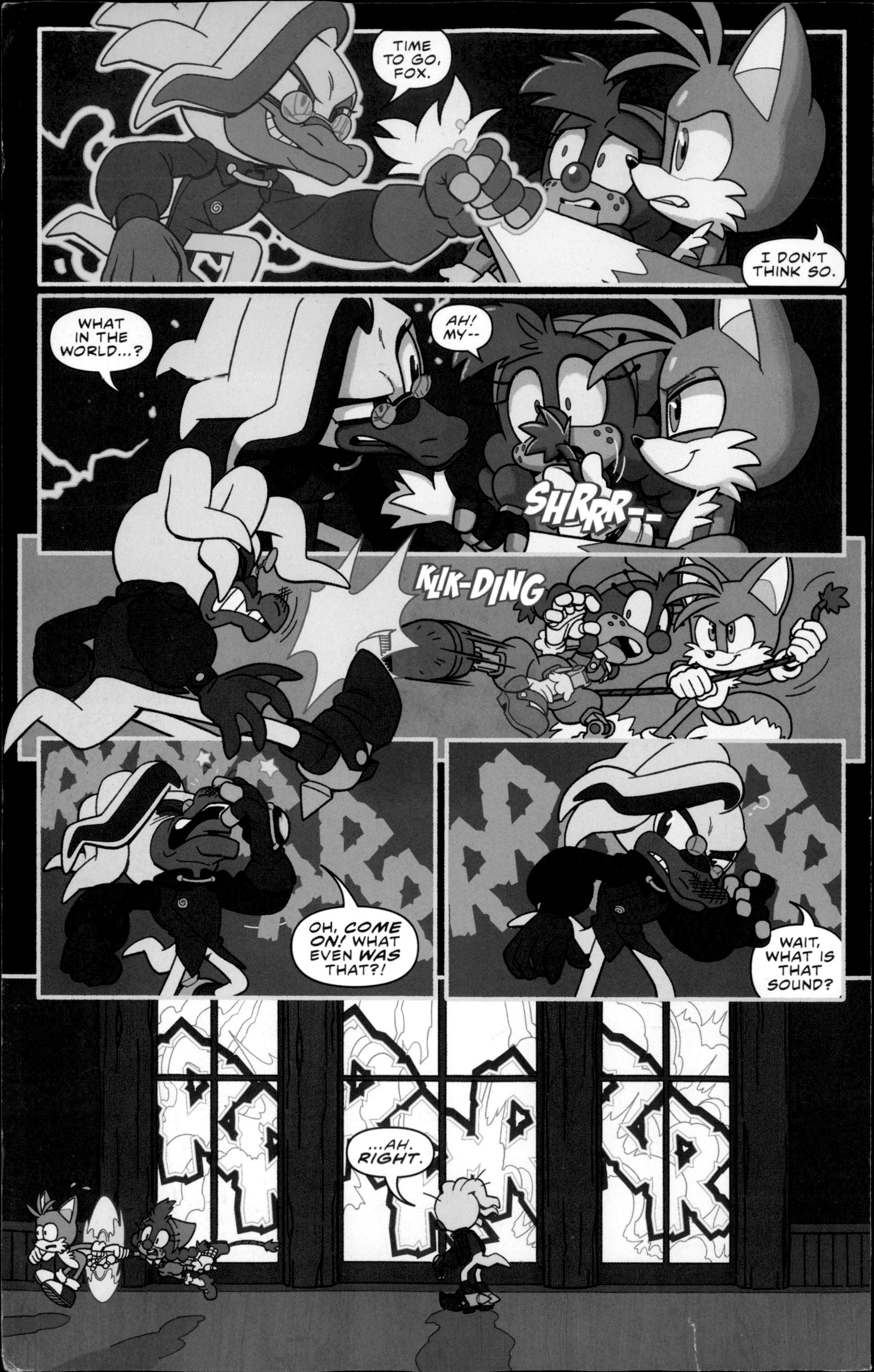
TIME TO GO, FOX.
I DON'T THINK SO.
WHAT IN THE WORLD...?
AH! MY--
SHRRR--
KLIK-DING
OH, COME ON! WHAT EVEN WAS THAT?!
WAIT, WHAT IS THAT SOUND?
...AH. RIGHT.

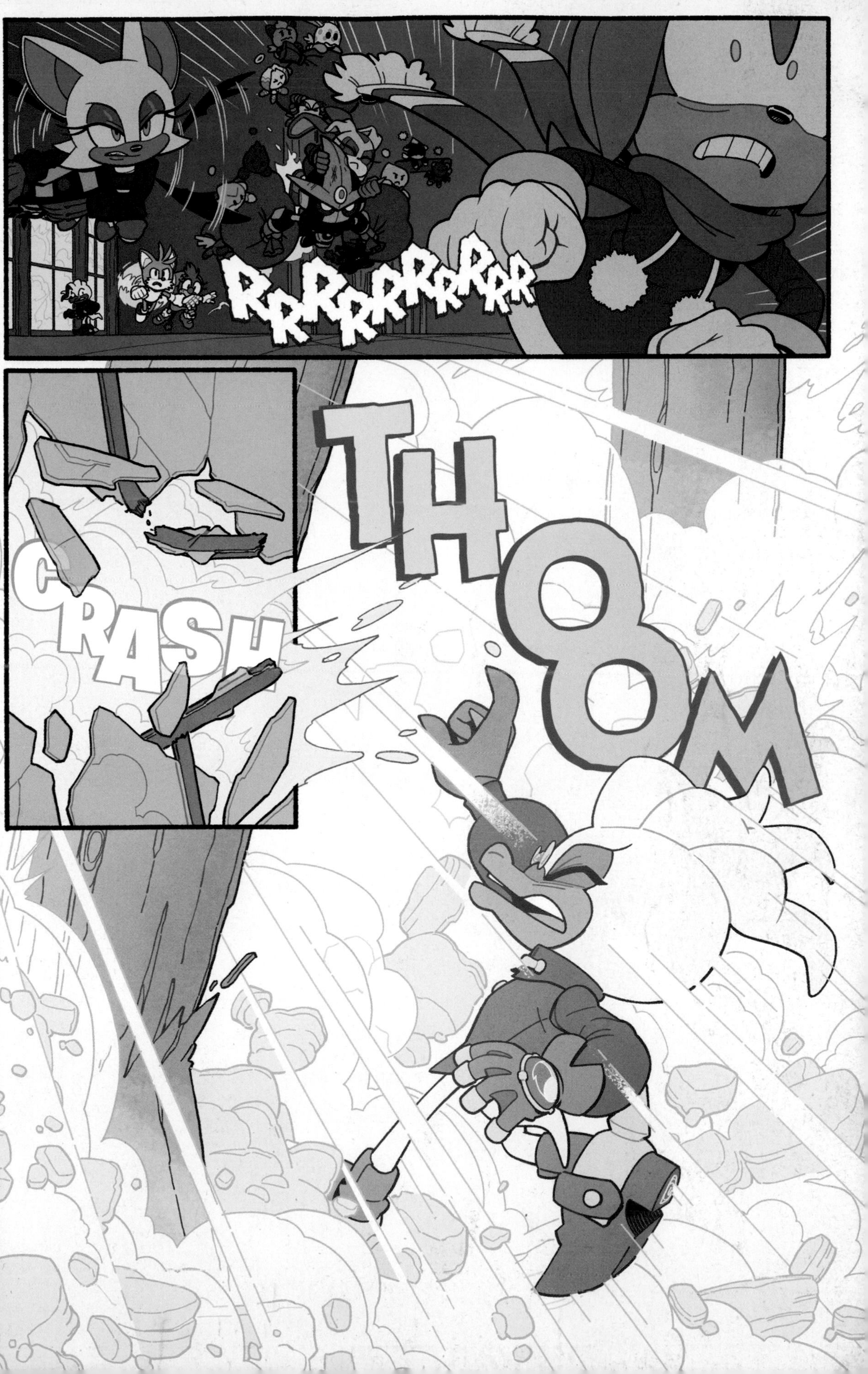
RRRRRRRRRRR
CRASH
TH8OM

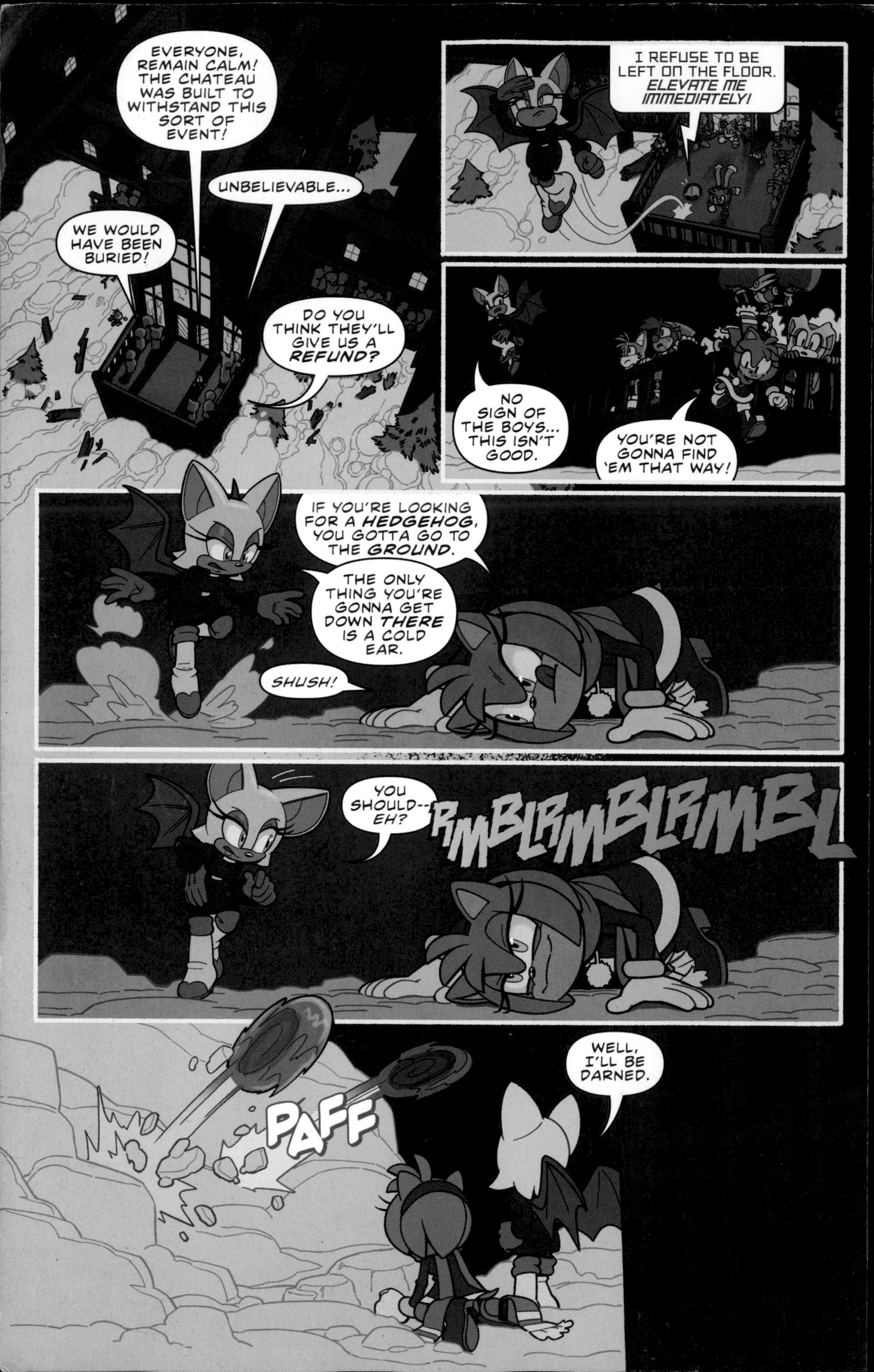
EVERYONE, REMAIN CALM! THE CHATEAU WAS BUILT TO WITHSTAND THIS SORT OF EVENT!
UNBELIEVABLE...
WE WOULD HAVE BEEN BURIED!
DO YOU THINK THEY'LL GIVE US A REFUND?
I REFUSE TO BE LEFT ON THE FLOOR. ELEVATE ME IMMEDIATELY!
NO SIGN OF THE BOYS... THIS ISN'T GOOD.
YOU'RE NOT GONNA FIND 'EM THAT WAY!
IF YOU'RE LOOKING FOR A HEDGEHOG, YOU GOTTA GO TO THE GROUND.
THE ONLY THING YOU'RE GONNA GET DOWN THERE IS A COLD EAR.
SHUSH!
YOU SHOULD-- EH?
RMBLRMBLRMBL
PAFF
WELL, I'LL BE DARNED.

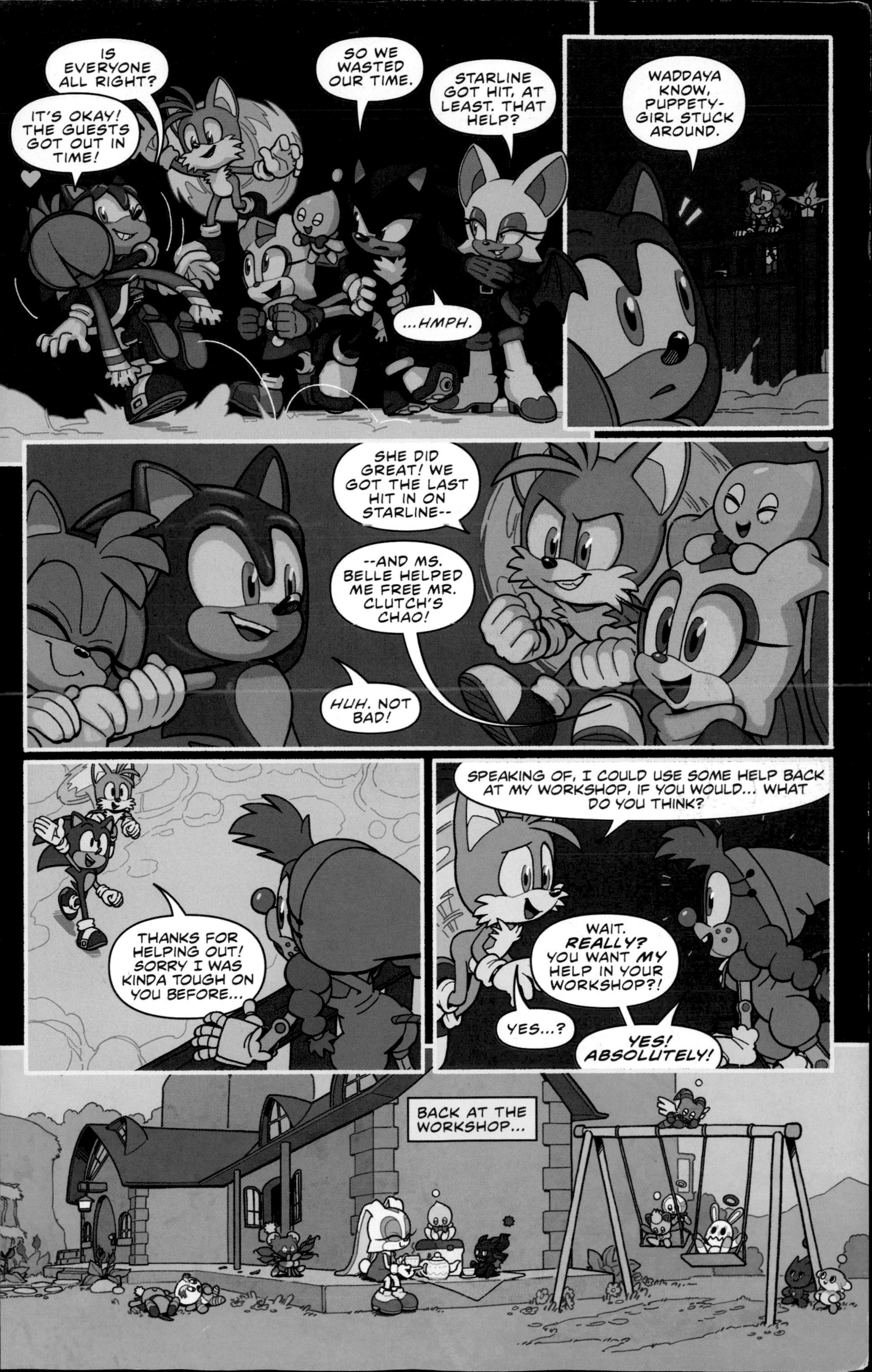
IS EVERYONE ALL RIGHT?
IT'S OKAY! THE GUESTS GOT OUT IN TIME!
SO WE WASTED OUR TIME.
STARLINE GOT HIT, AT LEAST. THAT HELP?
...HMPH.
WADDAYA KNOW, PUPPETY-GIRL STUCK AROUND.
SHE DID GREAT! WE GOT THE LAST HIT IN ON STARLINE--
--AND MS. BELLE HELPED ME FREE MR. CLUTCH'S CHAO!
HUH. NOT BAD!
THANKS FOR HELPING OUT! SORRY I WAS KINDA TOUGH ON YOU BEFORE...
SPEAKING OF, I COULD USE SOME HELP BACK AT MY WORKSHOP, IF YOU WOULD... WHAT DO YOU THINK?
WAIT. REALLY? YOU WANT MY HELP IN YOUR WORKSHOP?!
YES...?
YES! ABSOLUTELY!
BACK AT THE WORKSHOP...

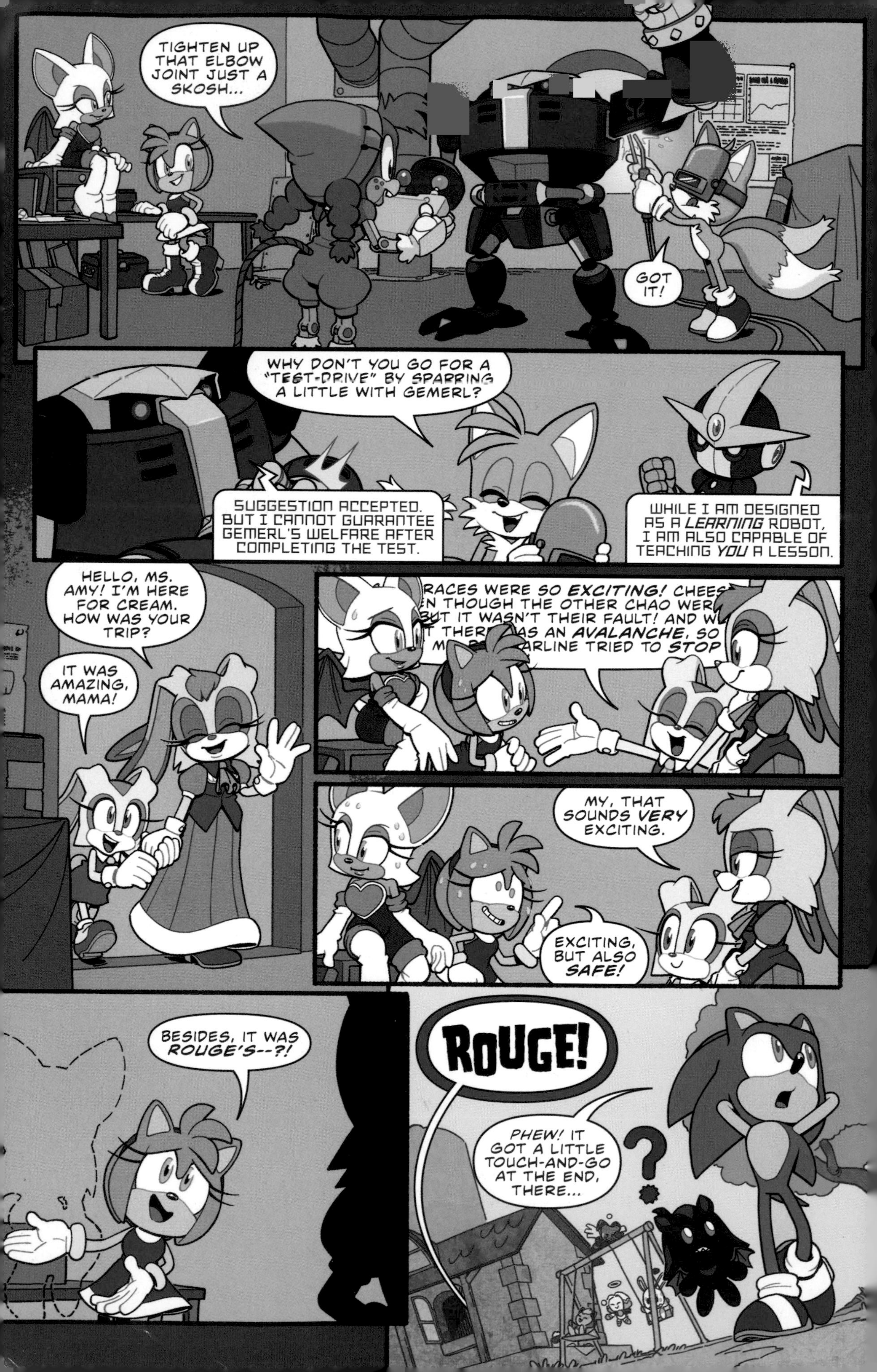

TIGHTEN UP THAT ELBOW JOINT JUST A SKOSH...
GOT IT!
WHY DON'T YOU GO FOR A "TEST-DRIVE" BY SPARRING A LITTLE WITH GEMERL?
SUGGESTION ACCEPTED. BUT I CANNOT GUARANTEE GEMERL'S WELFARE AFTER COMPLETING THE TEST.
WHILE I AM DESIGNED AS A *LEARNING* ROBOT, I AM ALSO CAPABLE OF TEACHING *YOU* A LESSON.
HELLO, MS. AMY! I'M HERE FOR CREAM. HOW WAS YOUR TRIP?
IT WAS AMAZING, MAMA!
RACES WERE SO *EXCITING!* CHEES
N THOUGH THE OTHER CHAO WER
BUT IT WASN'T THEIR FAULT! AND W
T THER AS AN *AVALANCHE*, SO
ARLINE TRIED TO *STOP*
MY, THAT SOUNDS *VERY* EXCITING.
EXCITING, BUT ALSO *SAFE!*
BESIDES, IT WAS *ROUGE'S--?!*
ROUGE!
PHEW! IT GOT A LITTLE TOUCH-AND-GO AT THE END, THERE...
?

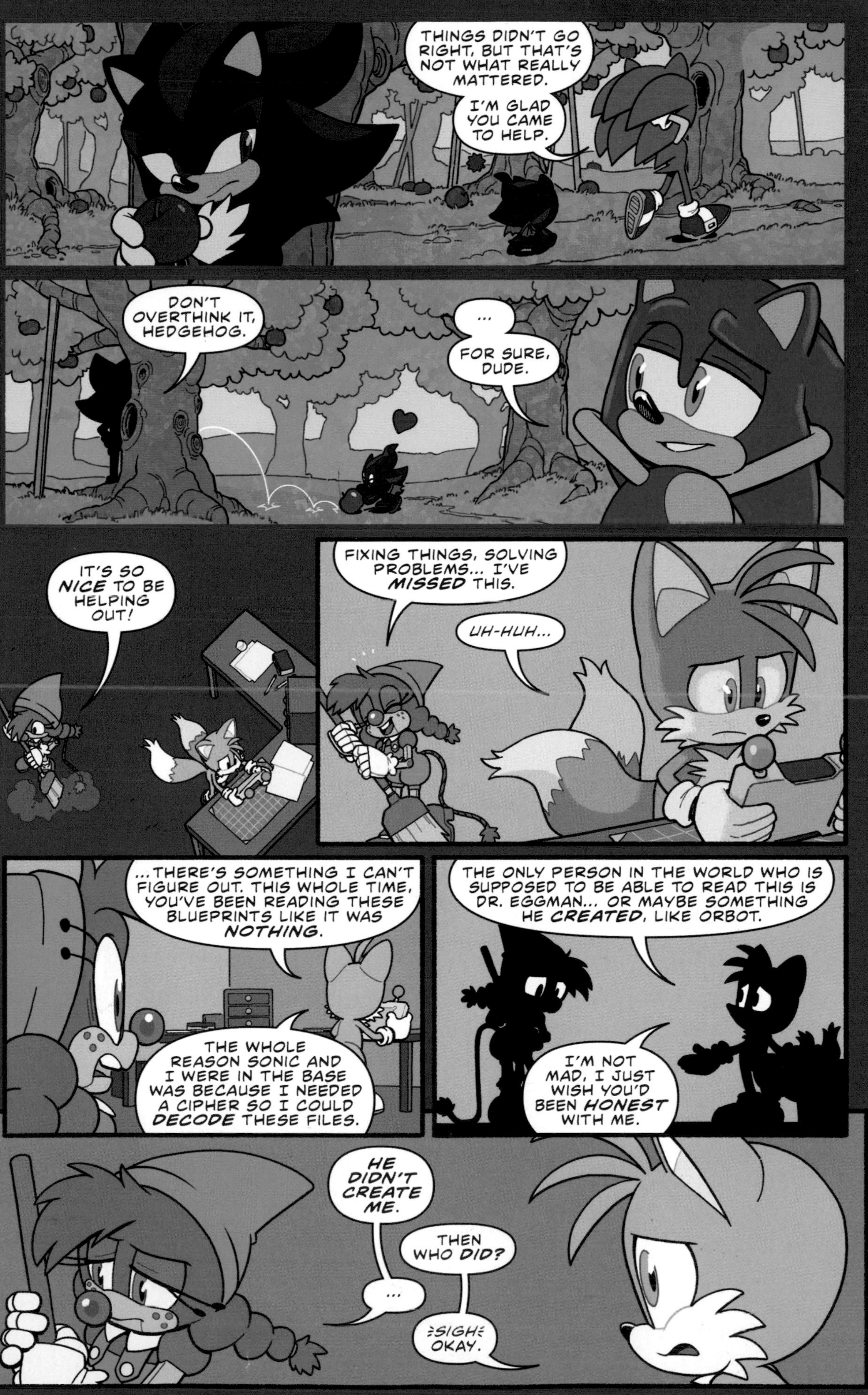
THINGS DIDN'T GO RIGHT, BUT THAT'S NOT WHAT REALLY MATTERED.
I'M GLAD YOU CAME TO HELP.
DON'T OVERTHINK IT, HEDGEHOG.
...
FOR SURE, DUDE.
IT'S SO NICE TO BE HELPING OUT!
FIXING THINGS, SOLVING PROBLEMS... I'VE MISSED THIS.
UH-HUH...
...THERE'S SOMETHING I CAN'T FIGURE OUT. THIS WHOLE TIME, YOU'VE BEEN READING THESE BLUEPRINTS LIKE IT WAS NOTHING.
THE WHOLE REASON SONIC AND I WERE IN THE BASE WAS BECAUSE I NEEDED A CIPHER SO I COULD DECODE THESE FILES.
THE ONLY PERSON IN THE WORLD WHO IS SUPPOSED TO BE ABLE TO READ THIS IS DR. EGGMAN... OR MAYBE SOMETHING HE CREATED, LIKE ORBOT.
I'M NOT MAD, I JUST WISH YOU'D BEEN HONEST WITH ME.
HE DIDN'T CREATE ME.
THEN WHO DID?
...
SIGH OKAY.

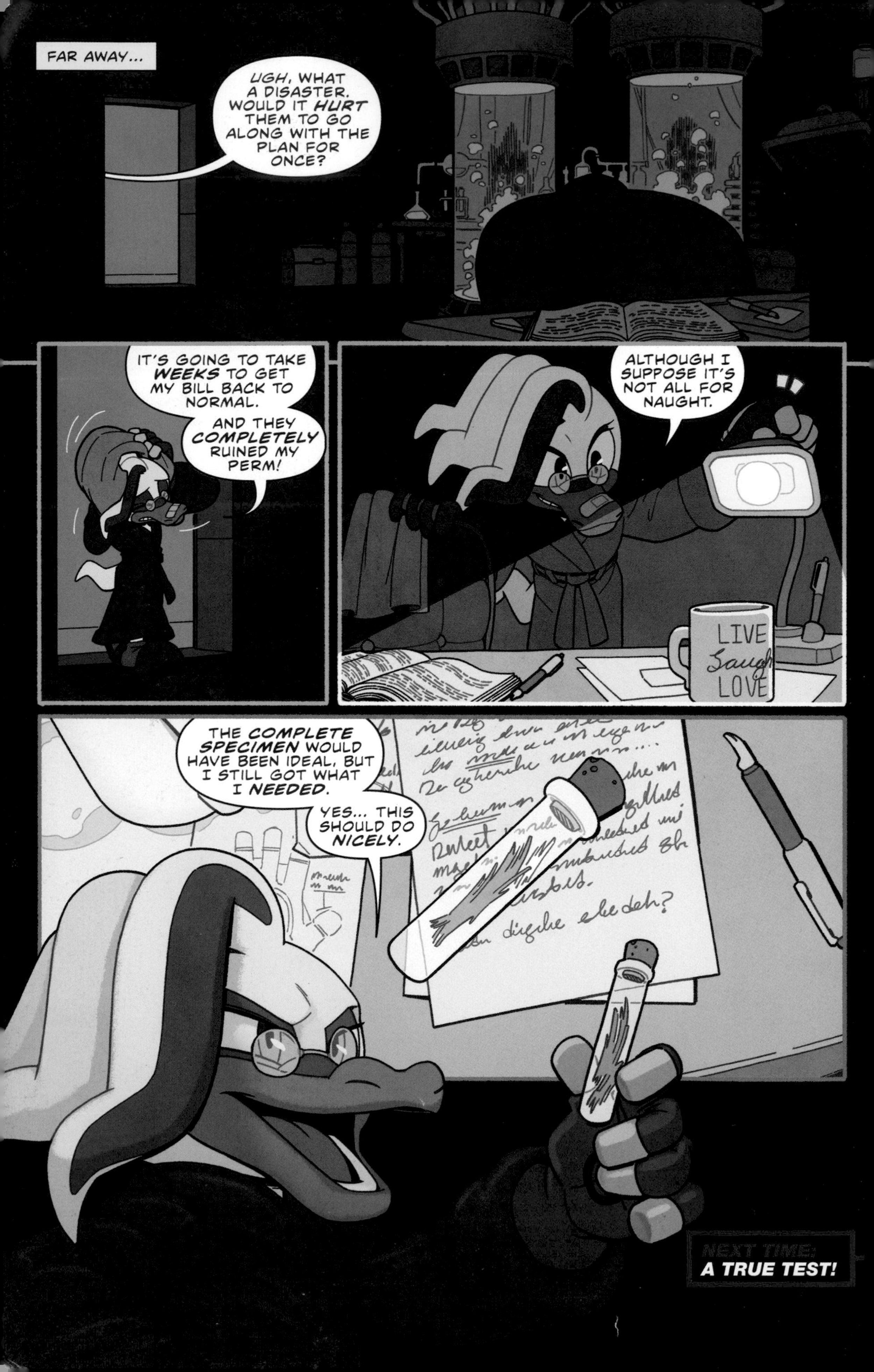
FAR AWAY...
UGH, WHAT A DISASTER. WOULD IT HURT THEM TO GO ALONG WITH THE PLAN FOR ONCE?
IT'S GOING TO TAKE WEEKS TO GET MY BILL BACK TO NORMAL.
AND THEY COMPLETELY RUINED MY PERM!
ALTHOUGH I SUPPOSE IT'S NOT ALL FOR NAUGHT.
LIVE Laugh LOVE
THE COMPLETE SPECIMEN WOULD HAVE BEEN IDEAL, BUT I STILL GOT WHAT I NEEDED.
YES... THIS SHOULD DO NICELY.
NEXT TIME:
A TRUE TEST!

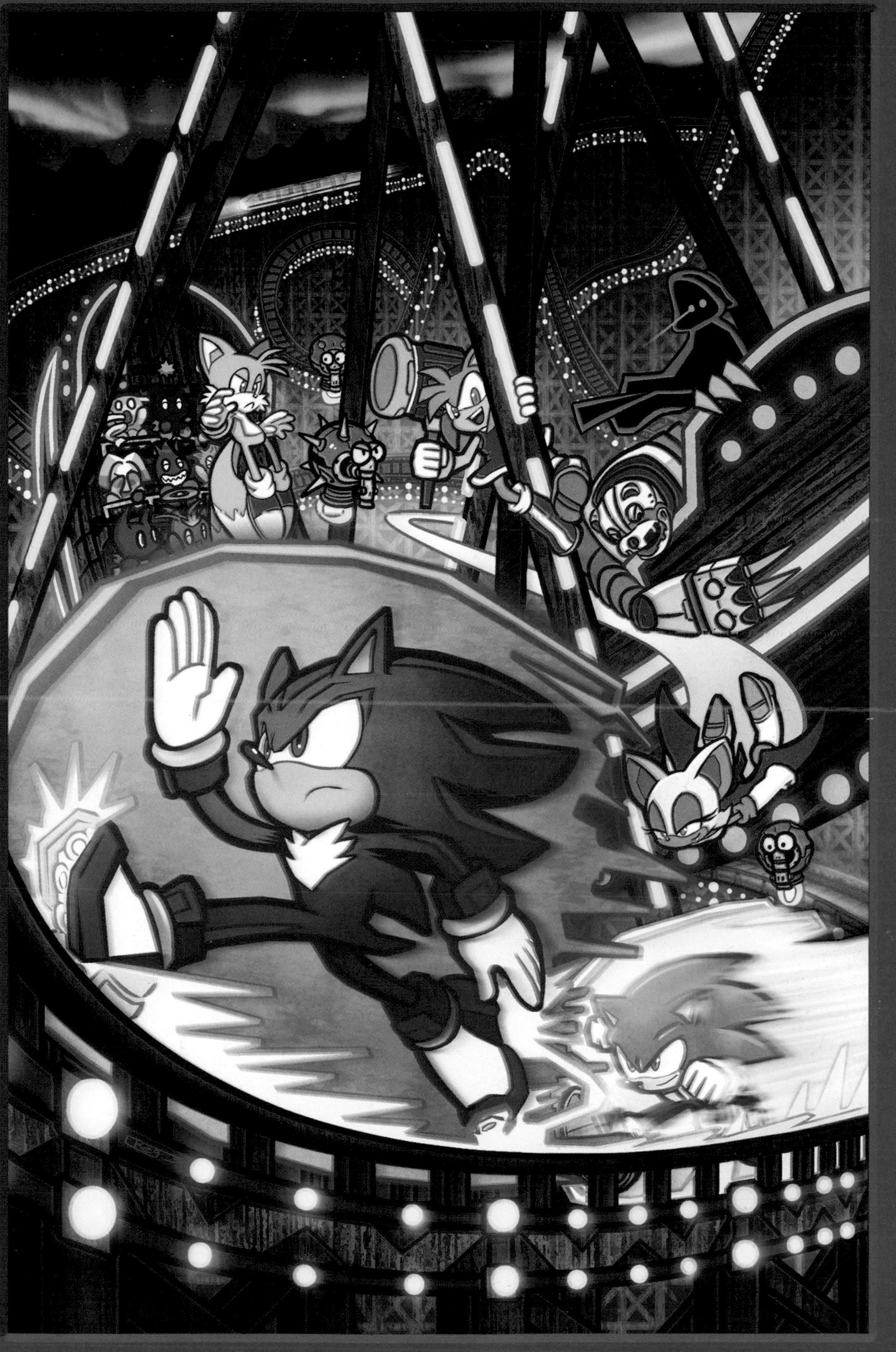

ART BY **REGGIE GRAHAM**

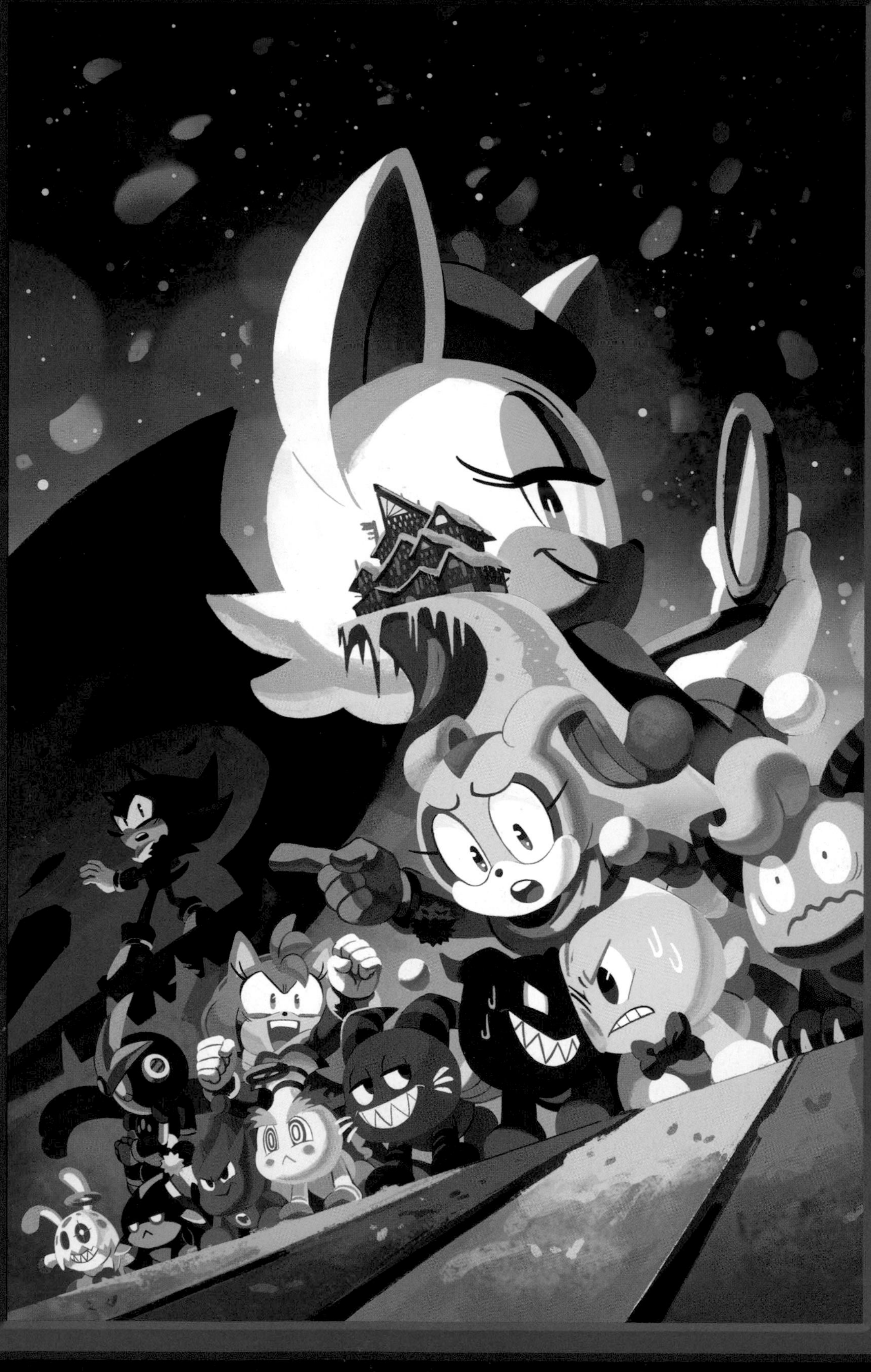

ART BY NATHALIE FOURDRAINE

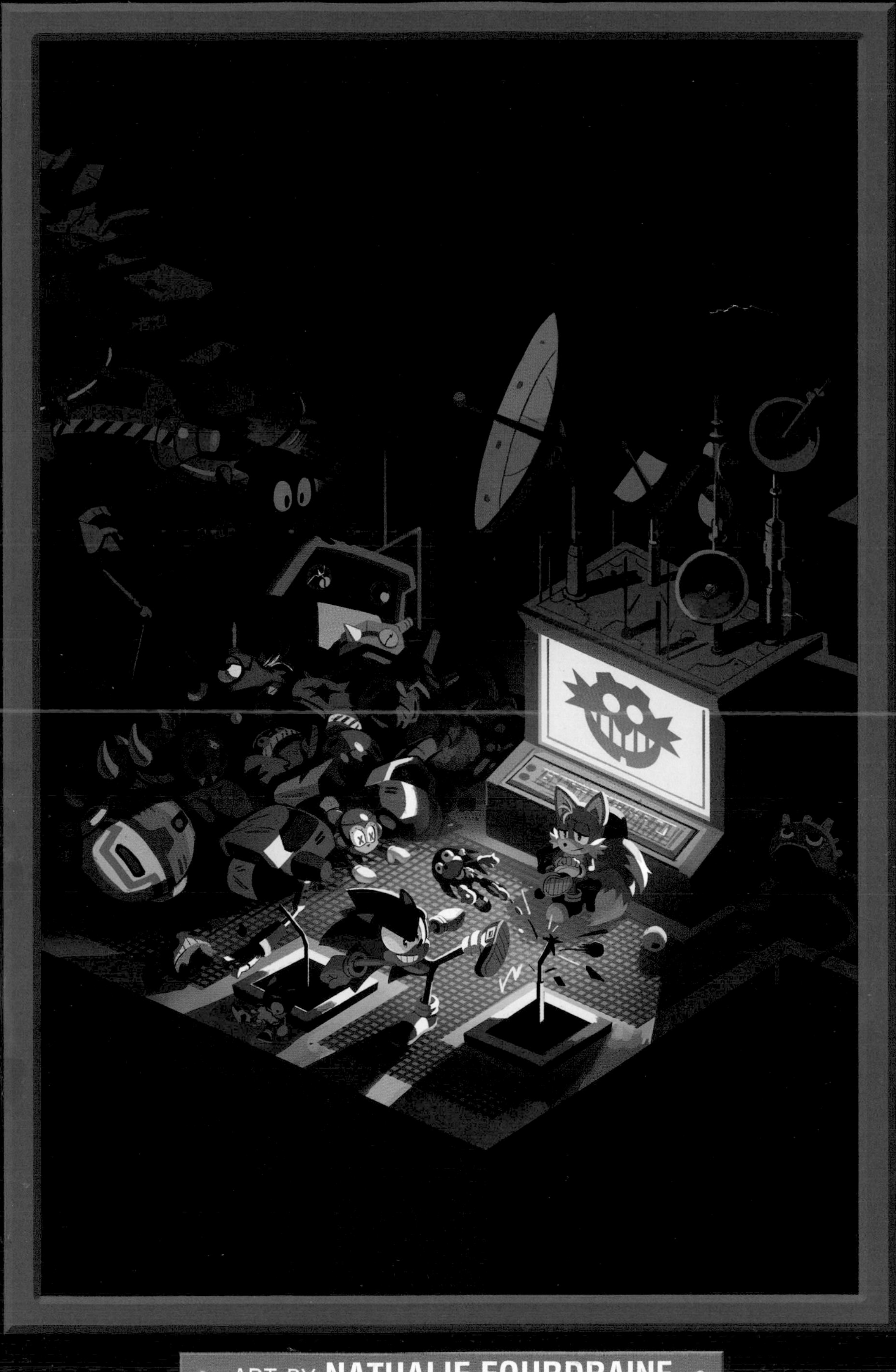

ART BY **NATHALIE FOURDRAINE**

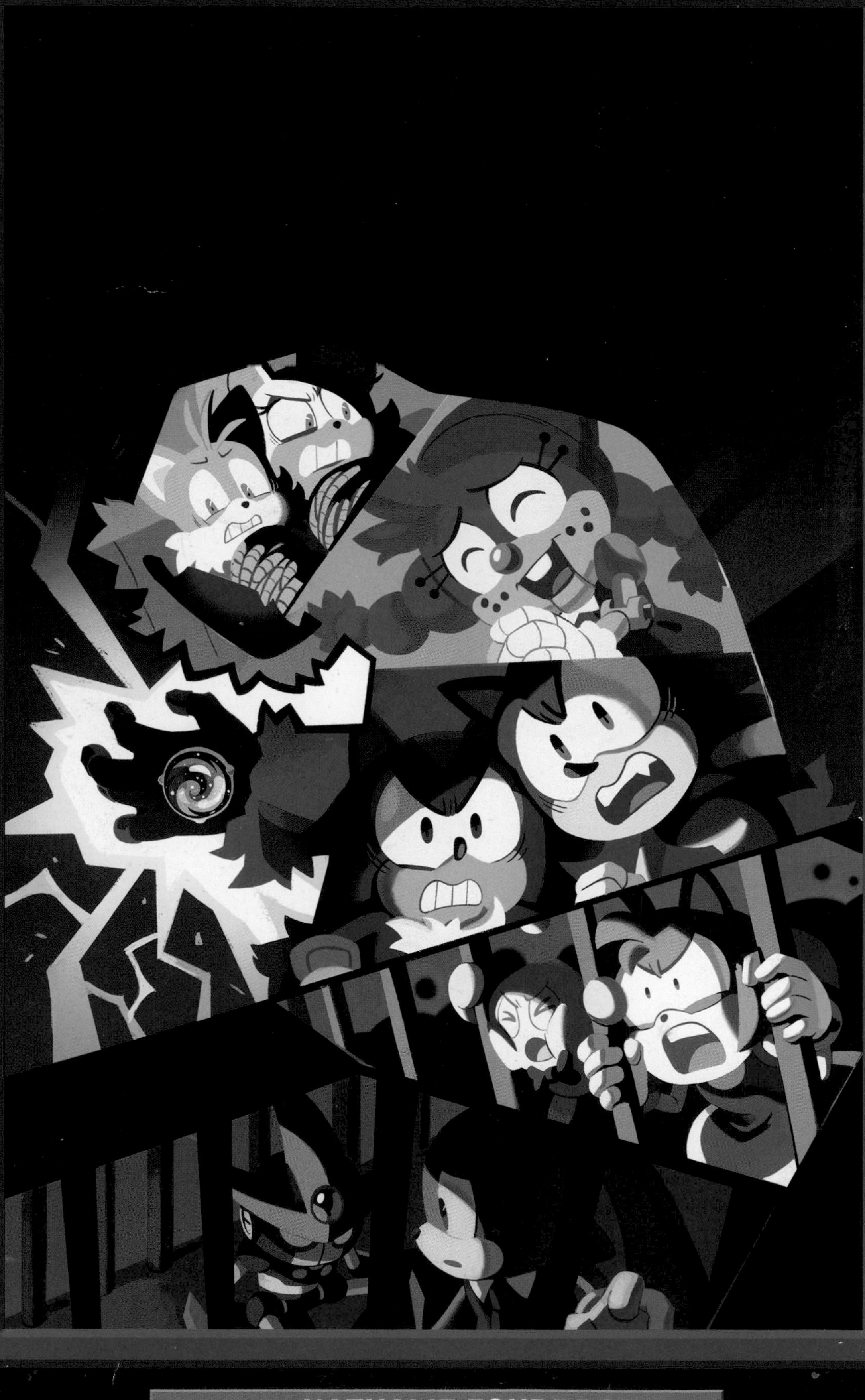

ART BY **NATHALIE FOURDRAINE**

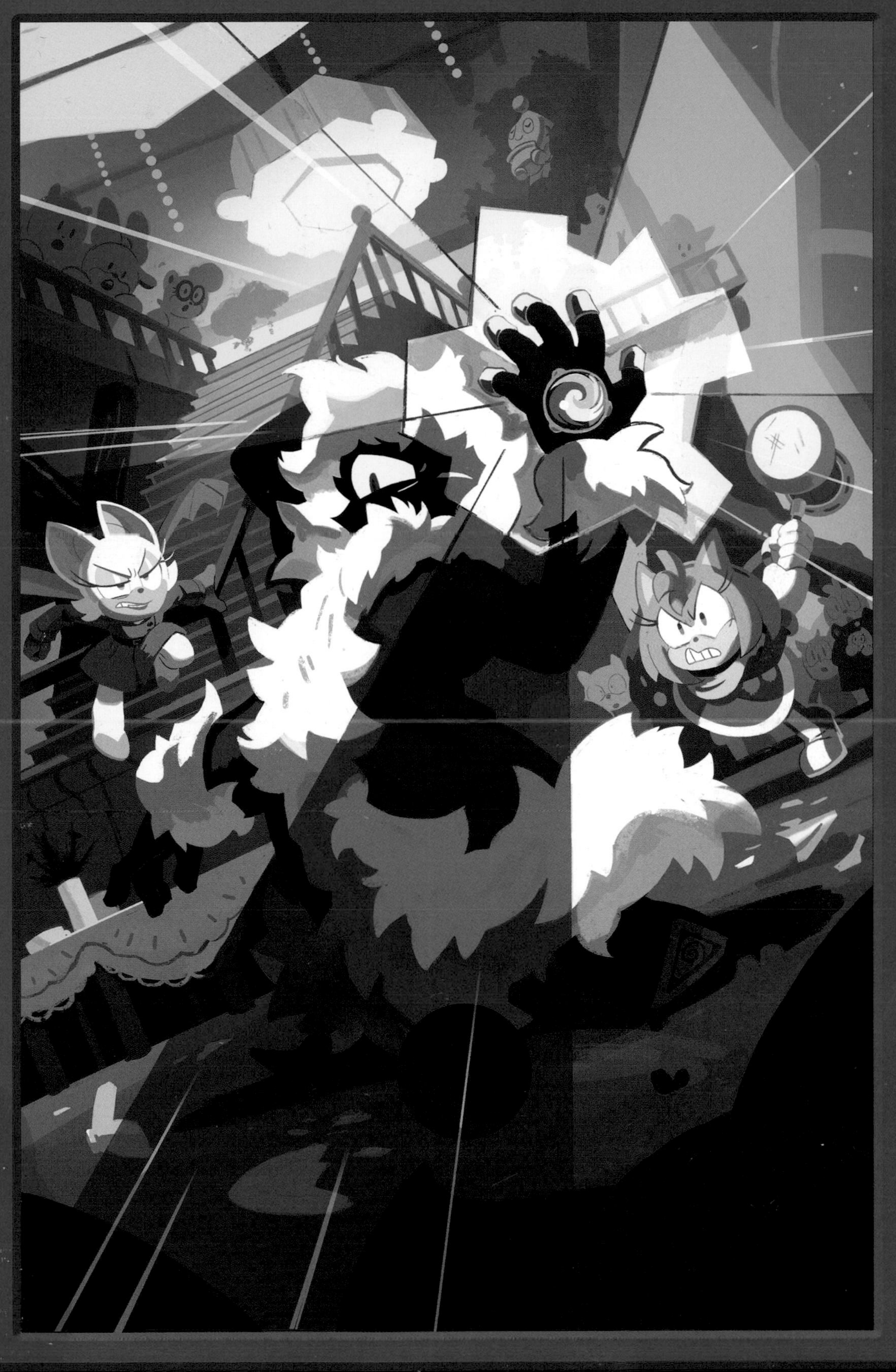

ART BY **NATHALIE FOURDRAINE**

ART BY **EVAN STANLEY**